DRAGON

PREY

S.A. HUNTER

Other books by S.A. Hunter:

Unicorn Bait

The Scary Mary Series
Scary Mary
Stalking Shadows
Broken Spirits

Cover design by Karri Klawiter
artbykarri.com

ISBN: 1503080854
ISBN-13: 978-1503080850

DEDICATION

To everyone who read Unicorn Bait and wanted to know more. You are the inspiration for this book.

CHAPTER ONE

Unicorns are fierce creatures and have been
known to best dragons.
*— From **Unicorn Bait***

Naomi was happy to see that she'd started her period. Of course, it meant she was in for a day of cramps and crabbiness, but hey, it also meant she was most definitely not pregnant. And that could not be repeated enough. She was not pregnant. She was NOT pregnant. She hummed a little tune to herself as she carefully tucked the clean rags into her sanitary harness.

It wasn't that Naomi didn't want kids. She'd always figured that she'd have them one day when she was married with a place of her own. She hadn't thought to stipulate on the nearby medical facilities. That was what was keeping her from going gung ho over the baby making. Naomi had known she was giving up a lot by leaving Earth to move permanently to Terratu. She'd done it to reunite with Tavik and to save him from the mad god Errilol. She did not regret it. She loved her husband, and he loved her. They were happy together. It was surprising how happy they were, except now everyone expected them to take the next step on their happy path, which was to have a baby, and Naomi's feet were frozen. She didn't want to move forward.

Having a baby was a life goal. She did want to become a mother. One day. And she was nervous about how her pregnancy would go. With no nearby hospitals ready to dispense lovely pain medicine, no ob-gyn to perform the sonogram, and no prenatal multivitamins, Naomi didn't like the odds of her pregnancy going smoothly. She knew the mortality rate for childbirth in undeveloped countries was high, and considering she hadn't been raised in an undeveloped country, she doubted she'd take very well to natural childbirth, but her worries about her own health felt somewhat disingenuous. If she were being truthful, even if a state-of-the-art hospital were next door, she'd still be overjoyed by the arrival of her period. Actually, she'd probably have a prescription for birth control from said hospital. She didn't want to get pregnant yet. It was as simple as that.

"Something wrong?" Tavik asked from the other side of the privacy screen.

He was becoming quite good at judging exactly how long she needed behind the screen in the mornings. He was on period watch too, but he was hoping for it not to come. Everyone was on the other side of the watch from Naomi. Yula and Agatha had the timing down, and she could expect inquiries from them, and if she tried to play coy, Mr. Squibbles would just tell them whether she was bleeding. The talking mouse could smell when she was menstruating, which was a little fact Naomi could have happily lived without knowing. And even the mouse was invested in the watch. He'd informed Naomi that he wanted the baby to call him Uncle Squibbles. When she had a baby, the child would have a loving family, that was assured, but Naomi just wasn't ready.

Naomi cinched the belt of her robe and stepped out from behind the screen. Tavik was already dressed and ready to leave to patrol the road to Ravant. There'd been reports of a bandit encampment. He and a group of men were going to rout them out. Their goal was to capture, not kill. This concession was for Naomi's benefit. If the trip was successful, they would bring the bandits back for a trial. If they were found guilty, they would be sent to the fields to work. Tavik expected to be gone for five days. Naomi was worried that he would get hurt, but so far, he'd always come back triumphant from similar tasks.

She put a cheerful lilt to her voice when she answered, which was not that difficult considering her quiet relief at her period, "Nothing's wrong." She smiled and went to give him a kiss on the cheek.

Tavik saw through her immediately. His shoulders slumped, and he took her into his arms. "We've only been trying for four months," he said as he rubbed her back. "Yula said it was nearly a year before she conceived her first son."

Naomi nodded and tried not to feel guilty about her secret happiness at not being pregnant. "I know. I'm sure we'll be blessed soon enough." *But not too soon*, she silently added. Was she a bad wife? She knew all good marriages were based on trust, and honesty was the cornerstone of trust, but Tavik's eagerness for a child was so sweet. She'd seen him play with the stable boys in the early evening. Roughhousing and laughing with them, he was primed to be an excellent father. The thought of dashing that joy and eager anticipation from his face made her want to cry. She squeezed him tight. She'd spare him that. She'd get pregnant eventually. He never had to know how she relished the protracted time it took.

With a kiss to her forehead, Tavik let her go. "Are you off to Agatha's today?"

Naomi nodded while trying to keep her swirling feelings off her face. "Yep, as usual."

There was a tap at the door, and Tavik opened it for Yula, who'd brought them their breakfast. Being the head housekeeper now, Yula could have delegated this task to a maid, but she insisted on personally bringing their breakfast up every morning. Naomi worried that Yula took on too much for herself, but the housekeeper always waved off Naomi's concerns, saying she had everything well in hand. As the castle ran smoothly without any input from Naomi, Naomi did not argue with her. The responsibility and trust instilled on her seemed to make Yula happy, and Naomi wouldn't dream of impinging on that.

"Good morning, Yula. How goes the day?" Tavik said as he dug into his meal.

Yula was already busy setting out Naomi's clothing. "We've aired out the north tower and taken the hall rugs out for a good beating. We should have all the linens washed by noontime."

Naomi shook her head. "Listening to you makes me feel like I've already wasted half the day."

"You have more important things to concern yourself with, milady," Yula said with a heavy glance at Naomi's tummy.

Tavik coughed and shook his head discreetly. Yula's cheerful smile wilted a touch at this silent communiqué. Naomi wished she could hide her stomach. She pecked at her food and dreaded the third reiteration of this conversation with Agatha. The witch had been pushing fertility aids for the last month. Naomi had been rejecting them, but she thought she saw Tavik drink something suspicious last week. She feared Agatha would begin secretly slipping her stuff. She no longer drank anything the witch brewed for her.

Once Tavik had departed, Naomi got up from the table and went over to the clothes Yula had set out. She began getting dressed without another word. She was trying not to get frustrated with everyone's eagerness for her to get knocked up, but it was becoming difficult not to get snippy.

Why did she need to have a baby right now, any-way? She and Tavik had been getting along really well. Couldn't they enjoy themselves for a little bit? Naomi scowled at herself, frustrated with the underlying guilt these thoughts invoked. Having a child was a serious thing. She should be allowed to want to wait. It wasn't her duty. She was more than just a baby-making machine, and while no one had suggested that, years of latent misogyny on her own world had led her to feel that was what everyone silently thought.

Naomi went down to the stables to get Stomper. Geoff gave her a strange look. Was he on baby watch, too? The whole castle probably was. She wondered if there was a betting pool. The stable master, though, didn't say anything beyond a few casual pleasantries. He saddled and bridled Stomper for her and helped her on. She pointed the horse toward the woods and let the steed find the way. He'd taken her to Agatha's cottage five times a week since she returned to stay and had worn the path that they now fol-lowed.

She'd begun going to Agatha's regularly after she came back. Naomi was unofficially the witch's apprentice. At least that was how she thought of herself. Agatha claimed not to want to train her in anything, but Naomi's wily strategy was just to hang around enough that she'd learn by watch-ing. And Mr. Squibbles could usually tell her a few things, especially if she offered some wine and cheese.

She arrived at the cottage and tethered Stomper to a tree with plenty of grass around it to munch on. She approached the open door and was about to call out a greeting when a large cauldron came flying out at her. Naomi dropped to the ground to avoid being clobbered, but as the cauldron flew over her, she got streaked by some sort of strange yellow pudding that smelled like bananas and old socks.

Naomi straightened with disgust, shivering as she felt the goop run down her back. "Agatha! What have you just contaminated me with?"

"You better wash that off quickly if you don't want to grow feathers," Mr. Squibbles said.

"Please tell me you're joking," Naomi said as she began furiously wiping the yellow goop off.

"That side effect only occurs with red-haired boys named George," Agatha said as she came out wearing a heavy leather apron and gloves. It was her usual attire when potion making.

"So what are the side effects for brunette women named Naomi?"

"It depends. Are you pregnant?"

Naomi growled and marched off toward the nearby stream. Had that whole incident been a setup for the pregnancy question? She shook her hands out to try and remove some of the goop. She took off her kerchief and began wiping off the mess. She hoped it didn't stain. The laundress always took special care of her clothes and apologized profusely when she couldn't get a dress back to pristine condition. She hated giving the woman impossible tasks.

Is all well, Mistress? Naomi looked up from her scrubbing at the unicorn that now stood on the other side of the stream. He dipped his horn and touched the water. It shimmered, and all traces of the yellow goop were gone. She at least didn't have to worry about poisoning any villages downstream.

"I'm not pregnant," she told Snowflake. That wasn't the unicorn's actual name. Unicorns didn't have names. It had something to do with mind-to-mind communication making names obsolete and all unicorns being the same and different, thus making names redundant. It had made sense when Snowflake had thought it directly into her head, but when she'd tried to express the concept aloud, she'd found herself tongue-tied and confused. She'd named the unicorn to help her feeble mind cope, and unfortunately Snowflake had been all she could come up with. She'd considered other names, but Alabaster had been too much of a mouthful, and Ivory had just seemed wrong. And she couldn't think of a name that didn't involve some reference to his white coat. She'd wracked her brain for something better, but Snowflake eventually stuck, and the unicorn hadn't offered any suggestions. He didn't seem to care.

You do not wish to be pregnant. Why is your

tone sour?

"Because everyone else wants me to be preggers, and they're disappointed that I'm not yet, and I feel like I need to keep apologizing to everyone, and you're right. I am happy not to be pregnant. I'm scared that if I get pregnant, the baby won't be healthy, and I might die, and why can't I do stuff before getting saddled with a baby anyway?"

Snowflake just stared at her. No thoughts beamed into her head. She went back to scrubbing the yellow goop off. Snowflake was sort of her unicorn. Or maybe she was Snowflake's human. That was probably more accurate. Anyway, Snowflake checked in on her regularly. He didn't seem to want to help her so much as make sure she wasn't doing anything to end the world or something.

She sometimes wondered if he'd done something to piss off the other unicorns, and they stuck him with her as punishment.

"She didn't mean to goop you."

Naomi looked over her shoulder and had to peer a few minutes before picking out the mouse from the underbrush. She bent down and offered Mr. Squibbles her palm to climb up on. He swiftly raced up her arm to her shoulder. It made goose bumps form on her flesh. She looked back across the stream, but Snowflake was already gone. He usually only showed himself to her and exited stage right when anyone else showed up.

Naomi sighed and went back to cleaning her dress. "What was she trying to do?"

"She was trying out this potion that a wizard had written to her about, but she should know better than to trust anything he sends her. He always leaves something out or jinxes it somehow."

"If he always sends her bad info, why does she attempt the spells?"

"She thinks she can figure out the mistakes. She does occasionally, and she's even improved them to do better than he claimed, but this time, I think he just sent random ingredients."

"So I'm not going to grow feathers?"

"No, but she does want you to lay an egg."

Naomi groaned. "You know a watched woman never preggers."

She gave up on the dress. Most of the goop was gone, and her skin wasn't burning. She turned and headed back to the cottage. She wondered if Agatha would let her do anything that day. Getting nearly brained by a cauldron had to get her something.

"What was that potion supposed to do?" Naomi asked. When Mr. Squibbles didn't answer, she jostled her shoulder. "What was it supposed to do?" she repeated.

The mouse sighed. "You know that question Agatha asked you?"

Naomi could feel her stomach dropping. "Yes," she said, her jaw tightening.

"That was what the spell was supposed to do."

"She launched a baby-making potion at me?"

"Well, no, like I said, she didn't mean to hit you with the stuff, but it was supposed to be for you. It didn't come out right, and in frustration, she hurled it."

"And what was it supposed to do? Make me insta-pregnant?" Naomi asked.

"Well..."

"Oh my God. What type of baby was the potion supposed to give me?"

Mr. Squibbles's whiskers twitched. "A curly-haired blond girl was what the wizard promised."

"Wait, she asked him for this potion?" Her voice rose an octave as she asked the question.

"No, she asked for a brunette boy."

Naomi rocked back on her heels. She needed to have that talk with Agatha right now, though if the witch had resorted to baby-making potions, maybe it would be no use. When they arrived back at the cottage, Naomi approached the door warily, watching for any more large flying household items. She peeked into the cottage and found Agatha at the worktable grinding something with her large pestle. "Is it safe to come in?" Naomi asked.

Agatha glanced at her and nodded her head. "Yes, it's fine. Bring me over a slip of yarrow."

Naomi reached up and carefully snapped off a stem of yarrow from the bunch hanging from the wall. She brought it over to the witch. "Whatcha making?" she asked.

Agatha added the yarrow to the mortar and started grinding again. "Tea. You could probably use something for the cramps."

Naomi looked away but nodded. "Yeah," she said quietly.

"Sorry about the cauldron," the witch said.

"Mr. Squibbles told me what you were trying to make."

"I was going to offer it to you, not douse you with it when you weren't looking."

Naomi stared at the tabletop and built up her resolve. She had to tell Agatha what she wanted. Everyone assumed she wanted a baby immediately, and that just wasn't the case. "I'm fine waiting a while."

"What?"

"I just think that having a baby right now may be too much. Tavik and I just settled down. We're still getting used to each other. I'm still getting used to Terratu. A baby would be too much on top of that."

"You say that now, but once you have it, you'll love it, and you'll have plenty of help."

Naomi sighed. "I know that's true, and I do want a baby but down the road."

Agatha harrumphed to herself. Naomi didn't know if she'd accepted what Naomi had said or was now plotting ways to douse her with baby-making potions when she wasn't looking.

"Is there anything you need me to do?"

The witch nodded. "You can go out and gather some plants for me. Take Mr. Squibbles. He can help you identify them. I've left a list in the basket."

Naomi took the large basket off its hook and unfolded the small piece of paper inside. "All right, I'll go get these. Don't take what I said the wrong way. I do want a baby, but I want to wait a little while."

Agatha nodded without looking up. Naomi let herself out of the cottage. She felt better for saying her piece but wished Agatha had acknowledged her more.

She walked through the woods, keeping an eye out for the plants on her list. This was a common chore for her at Agatha's, and she was beginning to recognize some of the plants.

"How upset do you think she is?" Naomi asked the mouse.

"Don't worry about it. She'll be fine."

She tried to take his words to heart but still felt uneasy. "Why doesn't she want to train me in witchcraft anyway?"

"She is training you."

"Not willingly. She seems so proud to be a witch. Why wouldn't she like an apprentice? Does she think I won't make a good witch?"

"There's no such thing as a good witch."

"What? Come on, Agatha's a good witch."

"She would like to be called a good woman by her friends, but there's no way to be a good witch.

A witch can't worry about morality. Magic is not good or bad, and a magic user can't pigeonhole it either. Every spell can be used for good or evil. And even if the witch's intentions are good, the spell can still do evil. If a witch worries about the moral outcome, she might as well not call herself a witch. The only way to be a good moral witch is not to do witchcraft at all."

Naomi sighed and tried to wrap her brain around what Mr. Squibbles had said. She could understand what he meant, but she still didn't think Agatha was bad. "So why perform witchcraft at all if you're not concerned with doing good?"

"Curiosity, a thirst for knowledge, a glee in doing something no one has done before."

"So, because it's fun?"

"Isn't that why any of us do anything?"

That seemed as good a reason as any other. Naomi spotted a plant from her list and began snipping off leaves. "Is she working on anything other than baby-making potions?"

"She was trying to figure out how to make four-legged chickens."

"She likes drumsticks that much?"

"Doesn't everybody?"

"Mr. Squibbles, you don't eat chicken, do you?"

"When it's nicely cooked, I will happily partake."

Naomi shook her head. "That's not right."

"Why not? You eat chicken."

"Yes, but I could conceivably kill a chicken if I needed to. A chicken could kill you."

"Yeah, so? When it's cooked, I'll eat it. I'll always win in that fight. You missed the silversaw," the mouse said. She stopped and scanned the area. She saw the plant and crouched down to snip it.

"Oh, this is too easy," said someone from behind Naomi.

Naomi didn't know who had spoken. She didn't know anything at all as stars erupted behind her eyes and everything went dark. She collapsed to the ground, squashing the silversaw.

CHAPTER TWO

Dragons are equally fierce creatures and have been known to kill unicorns.

Naomi's head hurt as consciousness came back to her. As she woke back up, she became aware of Mr. Squibbles quietly telling her, "Naomi, wake up. I think you should really open your eyes. You probably won't agree with me once you see the situation you're in, but you should really wake up to find out how bad things are."

She cautiously opened her eyes and looked around. Everything looked normal. She wasn't seeing double, and the light didn't seem to be hurting her head, so she didn't have a concussion. That was a small relief. She was on her side on the ground. All she could do was look around because her hands were tied behind her back and her feet were tied together. She appeared to be in a small encampment. There were saddlebags, a few small tents, and a cold cook fire, but no campers. She could hear horses behind her, and when she strained to look, she could see a fancy carriage.

"Who hit me?" she whispered.

Mr. Squibbles snorted. "Harold, the builder who secretly wants to be a dancer; he's a follower of Rhylim, married with two children, and likes inordinate amounts of cabbage. How the hell should I know? He was a big guy with a club."

"Was he alone?" She thought she remembered hearing a woman's voice right before she was knocked out.

"There were two other men and a woman. They didn't strike me as bandits, but what do I know about human criminals?"

"Where'd they go?"

"Don't know."

Naomi tested her restraints. They cut into her skin as she moved. She had no hope of wiggling out of them. "Can you untie me?"

"If I had a week, maybe. Do you think we have that sort of time?"

Naomi sighed and tried to inch her way across the ground to the saddlebags. Maybe they had something she could use. "Thanks for staying with me, but shouldn't you go alert Agatha?"

"I would, but there's an owl who keeps trying to eat me."

"An owl? But it's daytime."

"I tried to explain that to the feather duster with talons, but he didn't seem to care for my well-reasoned zoological argument."

"Stupid bird."

"Exactly."

Naomi was halfway to the saddlebags. She

knew she was getting dirt and grass stains on her dress with her caterpillar crawl. She'd have to burn this dress as to save the laundress from abject despair.

"Stop moving. They're coming back."

Naomi debated pretending to be still unconscious but decided that since she saw no way to get out of her bindings, and she'd moved from her previous spot, she'd rather get a good look at her captors and get a few questions answered.

Three men and a woman came into the camp. The three men were wearing blue and gold livery, and the woman had on a pale pink gown that had delicate beadwork and flowery embroidery across the bodice. These individuals were clearly not a ragtag band of bandits. Unless banditry paid really well. "It's about time you woke up," the woman said, coming to stand over her. Naomi didn't recognize the woman or the men. The emblem the men wore on their chests was also unknown to her. It looked like an angry rooster.

"Who are you?" Naomi asked.

"Why, isn't it obvious? I'm you."

"Come again?"

The woman turned to the men. "Who am I?" she asked.

The three men got down on bended knees and in unison, said, "The Lady Naomi of Harold's Pass, the most beautiful woman in Terratu."

"What?" Naomi said.

The other woman gave her a withering look.

"Dear Calax, how could such a simple slattern have deceived the Great Lord Tavik?"

Naomi didn't feel like enlightening this woman that the "Great" Lord Tavik—and who called him that?—had known full well that she wasn't the real Lady Naomi when he'd branded her. "Aren't you supposed to be hiding somewhere in safety?"

The other woman looked up at the sky and shrugged. "That was what everyone expected me to do, and I went along with the cowards. Had I known more about Lord Tavik, I would have stayed in the castle and welcomed him with open arms."

"What? You know he was a bloodthirsty warmonger, right?"

The other woman leveled a shrewd look at her. "Everyone keeps saying that, but he marries me and hasn't pillaged another town since. Doesn't sound very bloodthirsty to me."

Naomi was getting uncomfortable with how the other Naomi kept referring to everything she had done in the first person, but her discomfort could also be attributed to her bindings. "Yeah, he mellowed, but you don't know what I had to do for that."

"I'm sure it was very courageous. I'll get a bard to create a song. I love being sung about." There she went again, talking about things Naomi had done as if they'd been her actions. It was starting to piss her off.

"Why have you kidnapped me?" Naomi

demanded.

"But I haven't kidnapped you. I've caught an imposter, who must be properly punished. I'm sure Lord Tavik's dungeon will do very nicely."

Naomi couldn't hold her tongue any longer. "Think again. I'm Tavik's wife. He knows I'm not you, and he's perfectly happy with that. We're in love."

"Oh, I wouldn't be so sure; after all, I am a proper lady, whose beauty is unparalleled. He will take one look at me and cast you quickly aside."

Okay, she was obviously delusional. Naomi could admit the lady was pretty, but she was no Helen of Troy. Maybe she should just play along. It sounded like she planned to take Naomi to Tavik, and once they were in the castle, everything would be straightened out.

"You're right. Let's go and tell Tavik everything. Once he sees us side by side, he'll make the right decision, and everyone will be happy."

The other woman nodded. Naomi couldn't bring herself to call her Naomi, even in her own mind. She'd actually never met another Naomi. She'd always felt sorry for the Jennifers and Sarahs she'd gone to school with because it was so difficult to refer to one without confusion. And the fact that her name had been what had married her to Tavik... It was just too weird to call that woman Naomi, especially as in a sense she was the "real" Naomi. She quickly tried to think of a nickname for her. All she could come up with was Lady Crazy. Naomi really sucked at naming stuff.

Lady Crazy turned to her men. "Pack up everything. I want to reach the castle before nightfall."

Naomi silently groaned to herself as she remembered that Tavik wouldn't actually be back that evening. He would be out hunting for bandits. The castle wouldn't pitch her into the dungeon on this woman's word alone, though. Yula would make sure of that.

The men began breaking camp while Lady Crazy supervised. When they were ready, they picked Naomi up, none too gently, and set her in the carriage. Lady Crazy got inside, too. They started going, and Naomi wondered if anyone knew anything was amiss yet.

She wanted to talk to Mr. Squibbles, but she didn't want Lady Crazy to find out about the small familiar. The mouse was currently hiding in her pocket. She thought he was probably just as miserable as she was.

Lady Crazy was content to look out the carriage window as they traveled, but eventually her eyes turned to Naomi and didn't leave. Naomi tried not to stare back.

"I hope you haven't displeased my husband very much while I was unavailable."

Naomi rolled her eyes. "He is quite pleased. More than pleased. You really should reconsider this. He knows that I'm not you, and he's okay with it. If you come in and say you're going to take my place, he isn't going to be okay, and stuff could happen that would be bad for you."

"Really, if any man had to choose, do you think he'd choose you over me?"

Naomi really didn't get this woman's extreme confidence in herself. She talked like she was the most beautiful woman in the world, but really, she was only rather pretty. She had long black hair, Cupid's-bow lips, and green eyes. Yes, she could be a Disney princess without much dressing up, but that meant she was cute, not lay-down-your-life beautiful. Naomi tried to think of someone that beautiful. The only person who she thought came close was Princess Diana, and she wasn't sure, but the fact that the royal had been tragically killed could be skewing her judgment.

"I hope you haven't done anything irreversible to my castle. I'm sure it will need a complete renovation, but it would be nice if it wasn't too arduous."

"I haven't done anything to the castle," Naomi said. She remembered Tavik offering to give her free rein to redecorate the castle when they'd first traveled to it. She hadn't taken the suggestion seriously at the time and hadn't taken him up on the offer since. The castle had seemed fine to her, and Yula seemed to have a much surer sense of possession of the place than Naomi. She wondered what the housekeeper's reaction would be to this Lady Naomi.

"What about the staff? How big is it?"

Was Lady Crazy really trying to pump her for information about the home she was trying to take her from?

"I don't know. I let Yula manage all of that."

"Yula?"

"The housekeeper. She takes care of everything."

"Then she obviously needs to go," Lady Crazy murmured.

Naomi shook her head. She wouldn't let herself get upset by Lady Crazy's pronouncements. Lady Crazy wasn't going to take her place. Naomi may have taken her place, but she'd made it her own. The castle knew her. Tavik loved her. Wait. Wasn't Lady Crazy still married?

"Hey! What about your husband? I remember Agatha saying she got you and him safely out before the raid."

"Oh, you know Agatha? Tavik hasn't killed her, has he? A capable witch is so hard to find. Anyway, my first husband, Lord Gerald the Spineless, is still alive, but he wouldn't dare challenge Lord Tavik for me. He's probably at this moment boo-hooing into some lace handkerchief his mother made him. He is such a simpering twit."

"If you hate him so much, why'd you marry him?" Naomi asked. The husband did sound awful, but that wasn't any reason to steal hers.

"Because he was the only lord available! I thought his wealth and power would make up for his lack of manliness but no such luck."

"I guess that's too bad, but I'm not going to give you my husband."

Lady Crazy's eyes narrowed, and she leaned toward Naomi. "He's not yours to give. I was supposed to marry him. Oh, if only I hadn't run away! I'm trying to be fair. You stole the man I should have married. I should have my men kill you. But I'm feeling magnanimous. I'll let Lord Tavik decide. If you've been as good as you say, I'm sure he'll only banish you."

Naomi decided there really was no reasoning with Lady Crazy. She embodied her name too well. Naomi sat back and looked out the window again and hoped they arrived at the castle soon.

When they finally pulled into the courtyard, stable boys came to take care of the horses, and Lady Crazy's men hauled Naomi out of the carriage. Yula and Geoff, who'd come to greet the new arrivals, grew visibly alarmed when they saw Naomi tied up. Geoff quickly disappeared into the castle.

"Where is the Lord Tavik?" Lady Crazy asked in a loud, imperious tone. Naomi could never remember speaking like that. Maybe she wasn't a real lady, especially if it meant she had to be a bitch.

Yula took a few tentative steps toward Naomi, but Lady Crazy's men stepped in to block her. They didn't have their weapons drawn, but they looked formidable enough without them. Geoff came rushing back with Boris on his heels and several guards. They ranged out in the courtyard around the carriage.

"What is the meaning of this?" Boris demanded.

Naomi and Boris had gotten more comfortable with each other since her return. When it became apparent that she wouldn't mess with the way the steward did Lord Tavik's business, he grew much easier around her. She'd even met his family. His wife was a weaver named Gilga, and he had a six-year-old boy called Pip and a three-year-old girl named Rose. They were a nice family. She and Tavik had dinner regularly with them.

Lady Crazy looked askance at Boris. He was a large man with a solid gut and was about fifteen years older than Tavik. "Are you Lord Tavik?" Lady Crazy asked.

Boris shook his head. "I am his steward, Boris. Why do you have the Lady Naomi restrained?"

"She isn't Lady Naomi. I am," Lady Crazy announced.

Boris looked toward Naomi with a frown. Naomi didn't know if Tavik had ever told Boris her true origins. Besides Yula, Agatha, and Mr. Squibbles, Naomi wasn't sure who knew the truth. Boris frowned at Lady Crazy. "Please accept my apologies, milady, but Lord Tavik is not in residence. He left this morning to attend to business in the eastern fields."

Lady Crazy cast a derisive look at Naomi. "You could've told me that he wasn't here," she said.

Naomi refrained from rolling her eyes directly at her. "My apologies. Being kidnapped addles me, I'm afraid. Would you please untie me? You're upsetting the servants."

Lady Crazy sighed and shrugged her shoulders. "You may cut her loose," she told her men. They untied her bindings and stepped back. Naomi rubbed her wrists to soothe them.

"Please prepare some refreshments for our guests. Let's go into the hall to speak," Naomi said.

Yula looked quite put out by this request, as did Boris and Geoff. Everyone was looking at her like she should be the one called Lady Crazy, but they all filed into the hall. Naomi motioned Yula and Boris over to her. They huddled together as Lady Crazy looked around the hall with a critical eye.

"Naomi, are you all right?" Yula asked.

"I've got a knot on the back of my head and rope burns on my wrists."

"Who are these people, and why aren't we throwing them out of the castle?" Boris asked.

"I'm open to throwing them out," Naomi said.

Yula had taken Naomi's hands to examine her wrists. As she examined the damage, she cast a dark look over at Lady Crazy. "I'm so glad we ended up with you." Her words touched Naomi. She squeezed her hands in thanks.

"So that woman is the real Lady Naomi?" Boris asked.

Yula and Naomi shared a quick look. Naomi wasn't sure how Boris would take the news that Naomi wasn't the capital L Lady Naomi, but then again, she couldn't keep lying. "She's the Lady Naomi of Harold's Pass."

"Then who are you?" Boris asked.

"I'm the Naomi of Atlanta, Georgia. Tavik knows all of this."

"That's fine. I just wanted to know what's going on. I'm going to have our guests escorted out now."

"Don't hurt them. But yeah, get them out of here," Naomi said.

Boris nodded. He turned and motioned to a couple of guards, and with swords drawn but with tips down, they circled the three men and Lady Crazy.

Lady Crazy instantly got upset. "Don't you know who I am?"

"I do, and I don't care, milady. We already have a Lady Naomi. Don't need another."

Lady Crazy turned and looked at Naomi. "You won't get away with this!"

"It was nice meeting you. I hope you have a safe journey home. Give my regards to your husband," Naomi said.

Lady Crazy sneered. Her men moved in tight around her to protect her as Boris and his men herded them out of the hall.

"I need to get word to Agatha about what happened, and Stomper is still at her cottage," Naomi said.

"We'll send a couple of stable boys to take care of it. You're not leaving this castle again until Tavik returns. We should send a message to him as well," Yula said.

"I guess you're right. I don't think it's that big of a deal, though. She's crazy, but not psychotic."

"She kidnapped you!" Yula said.

Naomi shrugged. "Stuff like that seems to happen a lot around here. I've done it myself, remember?" It was how Tavik and she fell in love.

"It wasn't the same," Yula grumbled. She turned and began dispatching servants.

"I think Yula's right. You shouldn't take that Lady Naomi lightly. She could cause a lot of trouble," Mr. Squibbles said. He'd finally ventured out of her pocket and up onto her shoulder.

"What sort of trouble?" Naomi asked.

"Not everyone is happy to be under Tavik's rule, especially the newly acquired Harold's Pass. If they found out that Lord Tavik hasn't married their Lady Naomi, they could use that as serious cause to revolt and overthrow him as their lord."

"Why are the people so unhappy?"

"Higher taxes. The wealthier merchants aren't happy that Tavik requires more taxes from them than Lord Gerald did. They have a lot of money and could hire a lot of soldiers to go against Tavik's army."

Naomi nodded and wondered if there was anything she could do to make things better. She hadn't gotten involved in Tavik's governance of the various cities and towns he controlled. She'd already changed his religion. She wasn't sure she should get into his politics as well. He'd stopped his quest to conquer the world. That had to count for something, and the rich always grumbled about taxes.

"Well, what should I do now?" Naomi wondered.

One of the reasons she'd begun going to Agatha's cottage daily was because otherwise, she didn't have anything to do. The castle ran itself. She had no craft or hobby to take up her time. Gardening held no special interest for her, and neither did cooking, plus they had gardeners and cooks.

The guards reported that Lady Crazy and her men had left the area. Boris stationed guards to make sure they didn't come back. Later in the day, the stable boys returned from Agatha's with Stomper. Agatha sent along a message with them to tell Naomi not to come to the cottage the next day either. Naomi was put out by the witch's decree, but she also knew that if she insisted on going, guards would be sent with her, and she couldn't justify taking several men just to see someone who would get mad and tell her to turn around and go home.

The next day, she was in the garden admiring the flowers. She was still under house arrest. She'd thought about sneaking out that morning, but when she left her bed chamber, she found a guard waiting, and he'd escorted her everywhere she went. Boris was obviously not taking any chances with her. She appreciated his concern, but she didn't like feeling like a prisoner in her own home. She sighed to herself and wondered what else she could do. From the castle, a maid came looking for her.

"Milady, Lord Tavik's group was spotted returning."

Naomi sighed in relief. Tavik would know what to do about the crazy woman. "Thank you, Tilda. How long until they arrive?"

"I think he'll be here within the hour, milady."

"Then I'll freshen up. I'm sure Yula is already preparing refreshments. You may return to your regular tasks." The maid dropped a curtsy and followed her back into the castle.

Naomi went to her room and washed her face. She brushed her hair and dabbed herself with rose water. She hoped Tavik's trip had gone well, and she wondered what he would say about the appearance of the "real" Lady Naomi. If Lady Crazy could cause trouble, she wanted to do whatever possible to mitigate it.

She joined the servants on the front steps to welcome back Tavik. Yula came to stand beside her.

"It'll be good to have the Lord back. I've been nervous since that woman appeared."

"It'll be good to have him back, period," Naomi said.

Yula smiled at her, and they all turned when they could clearly hear horses on the road. They came in at a trot. All the men were present and appeared fine. The castle folk began calling cheerful greetings to them, but none of the returning men raised their arms or expressed happiness to be home. Naomi began to worry.

Yula took her hand and squeezed it. Naomi squeezed it back. The horses came into the courtyard, and a familiar carriage followed them.

"What's she doing with them?" Yula asked.

Naomi went down the steps toward the returning men. Tavik was easy to pick out on Victor, his large black charger. He looked right at her but didn't acknowledge her. She thought maybe he hadn't seen her. She raised her arm and waved. He turned his head away.

"Tavik!"

He brought Victor to a stop and got down. He must be distracted, Naomi thought as she went to him.

"Tavik, welcome home!" She went to give him a hug, but he put up a hand and held her back.

"What's wrong?" she asked.

He dropped his hand and turned to everyone else on the steps. "Gather everyone in the hall. I have an announcement!" he shouted.

Naomi stepped closer. "Tavik, what's going on?"

He still refused to look at her. It was beginning to really irritate her. She grabbed his arm and turned him toward her. "Talk to me, dammit!"

He finally looked at her with empty eyes. "We made a mistake."

"What mistake? Tavik, what's wrong?"

There was a loud cough from the carriage. Tavik immediately went to it and opened the door. He reached in and helped Lady Crazy down.

"What is she doing here, Tavik?" Naomi asked, struggling to keep her voice calm.

"I'm supposed to be here," Lady Crazy said.

Tavik's eyes were firmly set on Lady Crazy, and the look in them made Naomi's stomach turn. He looked besotted. There was a smile tugging at his mouth, and his eyes were wide and bright. He put his arm around Lady Crazy's waist and pulled her in close to his side. Naomi would have screeched in anger at the sight, but she was still too shocked to find her voice. Together the couple turned away from her and began going up the stairs.

Finally finding her voice, Naomi shouted, "TAVIK!"

He didn't even glance back at her.

As she watched them disappear into the castle, Lady Crazy's men flanked her and took her by the arms. She was too stunned to put up a struggle.

CHAPTER THREE

Dragons know when you're lying.

"You let her go right now!" Yula said as Lady Crazy's men restrained Naomi.

"We don't take orders from you," they said.

"Milady, would you like these men to let you go?" Boris asked.

"Yes, please," she answered.

Boris and three of the castle's guards moved in closer. Lady Crazy's men tightened their hold on her.

"You don't want to do that. There's about to be some big changes around here," one of Lady Crazy's guards said.

"Well, they haven't happened yet, and the lady you're holding is the one we take orders from," Boris replied.

"Not for long," Lady Crazy's guard countered.

"I don't care. She's our lady, and I won't let you manhandle her," Boris said.

"Your lord doesn't seem to care."

And Naomi would like to know why Tavik didn't care. She looked around at all of the serv-

ants still gathered on the steps. None had followed Tavik and Lady Crazy into the hall. They all
stood silently, waiting for her.

"Let me go. I don't know what is going on, but
Tavik wants everyone in the hall," she said.

"No," the lead guard said.

Boris and the castle guards stepped in closer
with their swords drawn and raised. "I'm losing
patience with you. If you don't take your hands
off her, you will lose them."

Lady Crazy's men finally released her, but they
didn't retreat. Naomi quickly stepped away from
them and into the clump of castle guards. "Thank
you, Boris. Let's go inside like Tavik wants."

"Very well, Lady Naomi, but stay close to me
and my men. Don't let them grab you again."

"Oh, I definitely won't *let* them do that again."

Boris threw her a wry grin. Yula quickly re-
joined her and clasped her hand. "What is wrong
with Lord Tavik?"

"I'm scared to find out," Naomi replied as their
group entered the hall.

Tavik and Lady Crazy were waiting for them.
They stood on the main staircase hand in hand.
The rest of the castle's household streamed into
the hall. Once they were all gathered, Tavik
raised his arm for silence.

"I have an important announcement to make.
The person everyone knows as the Lady Naomi is
a fake. She is not even from Harold's Pass. She
was an imposter planted by the witch Agatha to

trick me. I realized the deception early on, but it was too late to expose her. I brought her back as my wife, but our marriage is a sham. Luckily, the real Lady Naomi has found me and desires to be my wife. As she is who I intended to marry from the beginning, I am delighted to present her to you today."

Naomi couldn't believe this rewriting of history. Why was Tavik telling these half-truths and outright lies? "You were prepared to kill the Lady Naomi. It was all the same to you," Naomi protested.

"No, I was prepared to kill you. It was all the same to me," he said, leveling a cold, hard look down at her.

"Tavik, what's going on? We love each other. We're trying to have a baby."

Lady Crazy looked alarmed and whispered something into Tavik's ear. Watching her easy intimacy with her husband made Naomi shake with rage. Tavik shook his head at whatever Lady Crazy had asked and announced to the crowd, "The imposter is not pregnant. Thankfully, I think she's barren."

Everyone gasped. Naomi's jaw dropped. "Tavik!"

"Address me as Lord Tavik, wench."

"No, I'm gonna call you Lord Dumb Ass until you say something that explains this insanity!" Her colorful language elicited some twitters from the staff.

"Guards, restrain her," Lady Crazy ordered.

Her guards tried to move in and take her, but Boris and the castle guards closed in tighter to shield her.

"My lord, what is the meaning of this?" Boris asked.

"I believe I've been perfectly clear. That woman is not my wife. She's to be taken to the dungeon to await punishment."

Naomi could only stare at Tavik. This couldn't be happening. Had Lady Crazy blackmailed him in some way? Being the "real" Lady Naomi couldn't be enough for him to totally abandon her. What the hell was going on?

"Do I need to repeat myself?" Tavik asked.

Boris clenched his jaw but turned and took one of Naomi's arms. She let him. Another castle guard took her other arm. "Milady, please come with us," the steward murmured.

She nodded her head and allowed them to escort her out of the hall. Lady Crazy's men followed them. "We don't need any assistance," Boris said to them.

"Oh, I'm sure, but we need to know how to get to the dungeon. Might as well follow you to learn the way."

Boris clenched his jaw. Naomi sighed and said, "Let them follow us. It doesn't matter."

"Milady, they don't need to escort us."

She shook her head and whispered, "I don't want to leave yet. I have to know what Tavik's thinking. Tell him I'd like to see him and send a message to Agatha."

"One of the guards has already been dispatched to the witch's cottage."

She smiled. "Thank you, Boris. You're an excellent steward."

He nodded, and they continued toward the dungeon. Naomi had been to the dungeon once. She'd felt like she had to see it. In relief, she'd found no one in residence when she'd made her trip. It had prompted her to issue one of her rare orders, and she'd been strict about it. The dungeon was to be regularly swept, kept free of vermin, and in general good repair, though no one had been imprisoned since she'd been back with Tavik. She'd asked him who except Agatha had ever been put down there. He'd said he hadn't had much use for it, implying he never took prisoners. She hadn't questioned him further on the matter.

She was happy to see that her orders had been honored since she'd given them several months earlier. A fresh pallet of hay and clean linens were already in the cell when the door was locked behind her. Boris stood on the other side of the bars. "Is there anything milady desires?"

Naomi shook her head. "And you should probably stop calling me that before it upsets Tavik."

Boris's face grew grim. "A servant will be down with food and water. I'll leave two guards with you at all times. Tell them if you need anything, and they'll get it for you."

Naomi nodded. "Thank you, Boris. I'm sure Lord Tavik needs to speak to you."

Boris nodded and turned to Lady Crazy's guards. "Well, you now know the way to the dungeon. Allow me to show you the way out."

One of Lady Crazy's guards smirked. "We'd be happy to take guard duty. I'm sure you and your men have much more important things to do."

Boris gave them a snide smile. "And here I thought you'd want to get back to your mistress, seeing as she's all alone in a big castle."

"Is that a threat, steward?"

"No, just a helpful warning. Something tragically accidental could happen to your lady. The castle is old, and who knows what might happen. Our Lady Naomi is perfectly safe here."

Lady Crazy's guards exchanged glances. Boris held the dungeon door for them as they left. He gave Naomi one last nod before closing the metal door behind him.

Naomi sat down on her pallet and wondered how long she'd have to wait before Tavik came to explain himself. His words in front of everyone had been incredibly hurtful. Did he really think she might be barren? They'd only been trying for a handful of months. Sure, they'd been going at it like rabbits, but four months wasn't very long. She lay down and stared at the ceiling. When she'd insisted on the dungeon being kept neat and tidy, she hadn't imagined she'd be the one partaking of its dubious hospitality.

When she heard the dungeon door open, she got up and went to the bars. The person, who came through them though, was Yula, carrying a large covered tray. It reminded her of her first meeting with the woman. She'd been carrying a tray that time as well. In that first meeting, the servant had informed her that she was a prisoner and just to accept her plight. Naomi hoped she wasn't in for a repeat of that talk, though she was quite clearly a prisoner. But she had no intention of accepting her plight. She was going to figure this out and get rid of Lady Crazy.

The guards didn't hesitate to open the cell door to let Yula in. They didn't even ask about what was on the tray. Naomi suspected that if she asked, they'd open the jail door for her with a bow, but she wasn't ready to ask yet. She wanted Tavik to come talk to her.

"Milady, are you all right?" Yula asked.

Naomi nodded and helped her set the tray on the pallet. There wasn't a table in the cell. She made a mental note to have one installed. Yula lifted the lid of the tray, and from among the dishes, the only mouse allowed within the dungeon stood up and gave her a stern look.

"Naomi, this is a fine mess you've gotten us all into," Mr. Squibbles said.

Naomi rolled her eyes and popped a piece of cut fruit into her mouth. "What's going on upstairs?"

Yula took a deep breath and rubbed her arms. "They're making wedding arrangements."

Naomi's mouth quirked. "Are they heating up the good old branding iron? Can't say I feel much sympathy for the bride-to-be."

"It's to be a traditional marriage festival, not a war bride ceremony," Yula said.

"Oh." Naomi willed herself not to get upset. They'd been to a traditional Terratu wedding. It was between two farming families. A priest of Calax had officiated. There'd been flower boughs and dancing. The couple had exchanged loving vows while wearing wreaths of ivy. She'd found the entire ceremony very lovely. Tavik had held her hand throughout it. As they'd danced later, he'd asked if she'd like to remarry him in a ceremony like that. She'd smiled and nodded, but asked to wait until their one-year anniversary. She'd thought it would be a lovely way to celebrate their union. Now another Naomi was making plans to share that with him. Tavik had better appear soon to explain himself. He couldn't intend for a second to go through with this.

Yula threw her arms around Naomi. "Oh, milady, you're being so very brave! I don't know what Lord Tavik thinks he is doing. We all know he adores you and that he wants to make a family with you. You saved him from Errilol! Why he would go along with that woman is a mystery to everyone. None of us likes her. She's awful. She's already ordering for all these changes! None of us knows what to do. Lord Tavik says we're to do as she commands, but we know you won't like it."

Naomi pulled away from Yula with a shake of her head. "If Tavik ordered for you to do what she says, do it. I don't want anyone to join me down here. Has Agatha had a chance to speak to him?"

Mr. Squibbles sighed. "No, he's issued an order for her to be put down here if anyone in the castle sees her or any black cats for that matter, and the other Lady Naomi won't leave his side. Agatha's growing quite cross about the whole situation. The other Lady Naomi may be waking up to boils tomorrow."

Naomi couldn't help smiling. After the upheaval Lady Crazy had caused her life, she deserved boils. "Tell Agatha not to do anything drastic. Tavik still hasn't come down to tell me what's going on. I don't want any trouble to stop him." Mr. Squibbles and Yula exchanged troubled looks. "What? He must have a reason for going along with Lady Crazy's demands."

"Lady Crazy. I like it," the mouse said, "But, Naomi, Tavik's been acting very strangely since returning with her."

"That's because he's obviously acting," Naomi said.

"He's doing a damn convincing job," Mr. Squibbles said. Yula nodded unhappily.

"He must have his reasons. Have a little faith, guys. She's gotten him over some barrel, and he's going along for now. But he's not serious. Once we figure a way out of this, everything will go back to normal."

"Naomi, if he goes through with this wedding, it will supersede your marriage. You'll be effectively cast out, and you won't be able to win him back."

Naomi shook her head, refusing to take Mr. Squibbles's concerns seriously. "He won't go through with it. He's just biding his time. See if the servants can help him, make sure anything that has to be done for the wedding moves at a snail's pace. Don't refuse to do it, but come up with reasons for it to take longer."

Yula nodded and stood. "I'll tell all the servants. We would've done that anyway, but we'll make doubly sure to do everything we can."

Naomi rose too and hugged Yula. "Thank you for everything. I know you'll make it happen. You and Boris are the ones who really run this castle."

Yula smiled, and the guards let the housekeeper out. Mr. Squibbles stayed behind.

"Don't you need to get back to Agatha?" Naomi asked.

"Naomi, something isn't right with Tavik. You need to prepare yourself."

"What do you mean?"

Mr. Squibbles's whiskers twitched. "Agatha doesn't think he's acting."

Naomi shook her head and began to pace. "What do you mean he isn't acting? Of course he's acting!"

"Agatha thinks he's under a spell."

Naomi stopped and turned to the mouse. "Under a spell? Like a love spell?"

Mr. Squibbles nodded. "She thinks Lady Crazy slipped him a love potion."

"Can she undo it?"

"Yes, but she needs a special plant."

"What?"

"It's called fool-me-not."

Naomi had never heard of the plant. She was sure she'd never collected it for the witch. "Where does it grow?"

"Not too far away, but, Naomi, it may be for the best if you leave the castle. Agatha has moved the cottage closer. I can lead you to it. You can hide there until the spell is broken."

"You think Tavik would hurt me?"

"He's under a spell."

"Is she sure Tavik isn't acting?"

"From what we've seen, it can be the only explanation."

A cold lump formed in her stomach. "What have you seen?"

"You don't need to know, Naomi."

The guards tapped the door. "Lady Naomi, someone is coming."

Mr. Squibbles quickly hid under the pallet. The metal dungeon door opened, and Tavik entered. Naomi was relieved to see that he was alone. "Leave us," he ordered.

The guards quickly complied. They hesitated though before exiting the dungeon. "We'll be just outside. Shout if you need us," one guard said. He said this to Naomi. Mr. Squibbles's warning had obviously reached more than just her ears. The guard waited until she nodded before slipping out. She was finally alone with Tavik, except for Mr. Squibbles hiding under the pallet. Naomi faced Tavik but didn't move closer to him. He kept to the other side of the cell.

"Thank you for coming to see me," she said. He nodded but looked away. "I understand you're getting ready to be married."

"Yula keeps you well informed."

She took a tentative step closer. Tavik stepped back. "How did your brigand hunt go?"

"We chased them deep into the woods, but lost them. I would've stayed longer looking for them, but Lady Naomi found me, and I couldn't keep her out there."

Naomi couldn't help her small gasp at hearing Tavik call that other woman by her name. It was obviously both their names, but she was Tavik's Lady Naomi. She turned away and wondered what next to say to him.

Tavik spoke before she could come up with another question. "I'm not planning to punish you."

"But you said in the hall—"

"I spoke rashly. Lady Naomi doesn't know all the details of how you came to be my war bride. I

44

know you didn't want it and that I forced it on you."

"But we fell in love after," Naomi said quietly.

Tavik took a deep breath and paced away from her. "We grew comfortable with one another, and we went through some extraordinary ordeals together, so that made us feel closer, and you did something incredible for me that made me feel beholden to you, but it wasn't love between us."

"It is love," Naomi said. "Why would we go through all of that if it wasn't love?" She could feel the tears welling up in her eyes. "You defied Errilol because you loved me. I fought Errilol because I loved you. We've shared a bed the past four months. We were trying to have a baby."

Tavik's pacing stopped. His back was to her, and she could see how tense it was. She wanted to go over and touch him. She wanted to make him feel better, but his next words kept her on the other side of the cell. "Were we?"

"Were we what?"

"Trying to have a baby? Don't pretend, Naomi. I know you didn't want to have my child. You were always relieved when your monthly came. You're more interested in learning witchcraft from Agatha than being with me."

Naomi couldn't believe he'd known about her not wanting a child. He'd shown no indication. "I'm just not ready to have a child yet. Having a baby is a big deal, and I was scared about how safe having a baby would be. Even on my world where we have medicine that would seem like magic to you, infants and mothers still die."

"So you weren't willing to take the risk?" There was a deep-seated anger in his question, and it cut her to the core.

"Tavik, don't misunderstand. If I'd gotten pregnant, I would've been happy. I'm just not baby-desperate. It'll happen when it happens."

"Don't lie, Naomi. You don't want my child."

She couldn't stand this. How could he say that? She moved closer. He tried to keep his distance. She wouldn't let him. She ended up backing him into a corner.

"Is it a spell that's making you say this stuff? Tavik, listen to me. I love you. I want to have a family with you. I'd do anything for that. I just thought we had more time."

Tavik looked at her with lowered brows. "Well, time ran out."

He tried to move past her, but she threw her arms around him. "Tavik, wait! Please, don't go. Don't marry that woman. Give Agatha some time. She'll figure out a way to break the spell."

"There is no spell." He unwrapped her arms from around his neck and went through the cell door.

She followed him. "How can you say that? We love each other!"

Tavik stopped and turned back. "I never loved you."

She didn't hold back as her hand shot out and

slapped him across the face. "Dumb ass. If you keep talking like that, I might start believing you."

"You should." She'd hit him hard enough to split his lip. He touched the split and licked away the blood. He jerked open the metal door and ordered the guards to put her back in her cell. The guards shuffled back in with unhappy expressions. They held the cell door open for her and shut it gently behind her.

Her hand hurt from the slap. She cradled it against her chest and began to pace. She needed to go to Agatha's cottage. It was all that was left for her to do.

She tapped on the cell door. "I want to leave now."

The guards opened the door. They hadn't even relocked it. "If Lady Crazy's men see you, they'll raise an alarm," one of the men said. Her mouth quirked at their acquisition of her name for the other Lady Naomi. She wondered if the entire castle would start calling her that. The thought gave her a warm feeling in her chest.

"And if it appeared you helped me, you'll get into trouble. Like I said, I don't want anyone else put down here. I don't suppose there's a secret passage out?"

"We wouldn't know since it would be secret."

"Mr. Squibbles, do you know?"

"I'm afraid there isn't one," the mouse said. Naomi bent and picked him up as she thought about how to escape.

There was one avenue of help she could turn to. She closed her eyes and thought very hard. A warmth spread over her, and she opened her eyes to a pair of brilliant blue eyes in an equine face. The guards gasped and moved back. Snowflake barely fit inside the dungeon and did not look right in it at all.

Why have you called me, Naomi? The unicorn's question appeared in her mind, and she hoped she wasn't overstepping whatever bond she had with the magical beast. She'd never asked anything of him before, not even to take her home so she could visit her parents. There'd been like a silent mental block that had prevented her from requesting any special favors from the unicorn, similar to the mental block against pain that the unicorns had given her when she'd set out to defeat Errilol. She hadn't begrudged them the mental tampering. They didn't owe her anything. Even if she'd been able to ask, they could simply deny her. But her mind was in such turmoil, any blocks they may have placed in her mind were tumbling over now.

"Would you please transport me to Agatha's cottage?"

Why do you ask that? You are capable of traveling there on your own.

"Yes, but I'm kind of in a pickle right now. I've been put in this dungeon, and no one is supposed to help me escape. Tavik's under a spell that's turned him against me, and I have to help him."

The unicorn looked around the dungeon. She got the impression that he did not like the place one bit. She couldn't blame him.

I will help you this time, but you cannot rely upon my assistance.

She turned to the guards. "If asked, you tell them the truth. I summoned a unicorn to teleport me out of the dungeon. There was nothing you could do."

The guards nodded dumbly. Their amazed gazes never wavering from the unicorn. Snowflake paid no attention to them.

Naomi held out her hand. She pictured Agatha's cottage, and the unicorn dipped his horn to touch her finger. When she looked around her, she was outside the cottage. Snowflake wasn't there. She silently sent out a thought thanking him. She thought she felt a faint acknowledgment. There was light inside the cottage. She pushed on the door and went in. Yula turned from the fire and smiled.

"Thank goodness you've made it. We can start preparing to leave."

"Yula, what are you doing here? Where's Agatha?"

Mr. Squibbles was the one to answer. "Agatha is staying behind to do all she can to delay the wedding. Those boils I mentioned should give us a few days."

Yula nodded. "And it appeared that I was

about to be dismissed anyway, so I left."

"Dismissed, why?"

"Lady Crazy could see well enough that I was loyal to you. The servants overheard her asking Tavik if there wasn't a better person to run the household. I'm half-afraid he'll bring back Mrs. Boon."

"If he does, we'll just have to send her packing again. Where are we supposed to be going?"

"To the forest on the other side of the eastern fields. Within it there grows the fool-me-not that can neutralize any love spell," Mr. Squibbles said.

"Huh, shame Tavik didn't pick some up while he was there."

"The flower is rare. It won't be easy to find."

"Well, let's get going."

Under Mr. Squibbles's direction, they secured cupboards, put away loose items, and took down the ship wheel that hung from the ceiling. Yula manned the wheel. She had some experience with it, after all. Naomi lay down before the fire and wondered how difficult this quest was going to be.

She awoke the next morning to birdsong. She opened her eyes and found Yula had given her a pillow and blanket sometime during the night. She looked around for the older woman.

"She's gone to sleep. She flew the cottage all night, and she's exhausted," Mr. Squibbles said. Naomi scooped him up and carried him to the door. She opened it and looked out. They were on the edge of a dark, old forest.

"Tell me about this flower," Naomi said. She ducked back into the cottage and quietly looked around for breakfast. She set Mr. Squibbles on the table and went to work cutting some bread and cheese.

"Fool-me-not generally grows along a stream deep in the forest. It has small, flat yellow flowers with blue centers. It grows close to the ground and is usually hidden by taller plants. You'll need to pick a posy of the flowers and keep them well watered until we can present them to Tavik."

"Okay, what about the forest? Are there umbreks?"

Mr. Squibbles sighed and nodded. "Umbreks are known to hunt here occasionally. There are also poisonous snakes and possibly other things."

"Other things?"

"The forest is old and dark. A lot of things live in there."

"Wonderful," Naomi said. They finished eating their breakfast.

"Does Agatha have anything in here to help me in the forest?"

"Nothing that I know of offhand."

Naomi cast her eyes around the room. She didn't think poking around would be a good idea. Agatha had most likely booby-trapped certain things.

"Well, there's no time like the present," Naomi said as she began gathering items to take into the forest.

"There are lots of better times, like in an hour or tomorrow or next week," Mr. Squibbles argued.

"The longer I wait, the more time Lady Crazy has to dig her claws deeper into Tavik."

"Agatha's taking care of it."

"You said so yourself, she's buying us time, that's all. We need to get back as quickly as possible with this flower and release Tavik from the spell."

"This will be dangerous, Naomi. You should at least wait until Yula wakes."

Mr. Squibbles's suggestion was a good one. She should at least tell her friend that she was going out, but Yula would be adamant on going with her, and Naomi didn't want to put her in any danger. She settled on leaving a note, knowing she would get a full scolding when she returned.

She'd put on a cloak, packed a basket with more of the cheese and bread, a lantern, and a knife. Unable to think of anything else to take with her, she set out. As she closed the door quietly behind her, she felt like her cloak should be red rather than gray. She just hoped she didn't meet any cross-dressing wolves along the way. Mr. Squibbles rode in the basket. She warned him not to eat so much as to get sick. He'd told her that he'd leave her plenty.

She set off down a deer path. The forest canopy was very dense. The forest seemed to be in a perpetual twilight. She hadn't thought she'd need the lantern during the day. She lit the wick and held the lantern out before her.

"I don't think the lantern is a good idea," Mr. Squibbles said.

"If I don't have light, I might step on one of those poisonous snakes you were telling me about."

"I'm sure the snakes will appreciate your care for them, but now everything else can see you as well."

"Shit."

"Yeah, don't step in any of that either."

Naomi continued down the path. She debated blowing out the lantern, but if she did, she would be blind. She quickened her pace and hoped this stream that Mr. Squibbles had told her about wasn't too far away.

She was worried most about coming across umbreks. And with the speed they moved, she would have no warning before they were upon her, and into their pouches, she'd go. Well, parts of her at least. She shuddered at the imagined fate.

Mr. Squibbles picked up on her uneasiness. "We shouldn't be here," he said.

"I didn't force you to come with me."

"No, but someone has to be the voice of reason."

"Oh, so I'm Lady Crazy now?"

"If anything comes upon us, what are you going to do? All you have is a carving knife."

"And what will I have if I go back?"

"Yula and the cottage. Maybe we could fly it over the forest and find a place to set it down inside."

"Doubtful. You see how thick these trees are."

Mr. Squibbles didn't reply to that. She kept going, but the hairs on the back of her neck began to stand up. She looked around but couldn't see anything.

"Mr. Squibbles, do you hear or smell anything?"

"Can't do either from in here. Put me on your shoulder."

She stopped and set the basket down to reach in and pick up the mouse. When she straightened, an umbrek was standing in front of her.

"Hey, Naomi, I smell something really foul and hear a stomach growling, and it isn't yours or mine. I think it's hers."

CHAPTER FOUR

Dragons mark their prey so all others know that the kill is theirs.

Naomi dropped the basket and the lantern and dove off the path as the umbrek snarled and reached out with one of her stunted forepaws to swipe at her. "Where the hell did she come from?" Naomi asked as she peeked out from behind some bushes.

She was surprised to find the umbrek still on the path. She looked around for other umbreks but couldn't see or hear any. She looked back at the lone umbrek and watched her root around in her basket and pull out the bread and cheese. She chewed on a slice of bread as she stuffed the rest into her pouch.

Naomi edged further back into the forest, but she couldn't see the ground very well, and she snapped a branch. She froze as the umbrek's head swiveled to her direction, and the beast raised her nose to sniff the air.

Naomi froze and held her breath. She knew there was no way to outrun an umbrek, and unfortunately, her one weapon was in the basket at the umbrek's feet. She jumped when she felt something run down her arm. When she looked down, all she saw was the pale tail of Mr. Squibbles disappear into the brush.

"Yoo-hoo! Over here!"

The umbrek turned toward Mr. Squibbles's loud calling voice. Naomi watched as the beast began to follow his voice. "Come on, stinky breath, nice tasty morsel over here!"

The umbrek wasn't crashing into the brush after the mouse. "Hey, get over here, bloodthirsty. I know my bread and cheese couldn't have been enough for you. Don't you want more for your pouch?"

The umbrek seemed loath to leave the path. She edged along it and craned her neck out as if to better hear Mr. Squibbles. She'd moved several yards from Naomi's fallen basket at least. Naomi crept back to it and pulled out the knife.

"Hey, idiot, can't you find one loud-mouthed meal? What do you expect me to do, start a fire and put myself on a spit?"

Naomi held the knife close and edged back along the path. Running with the blade would be stupider than running with scissors, but she felt better with it. She kept retreating silently back along the path. Mr. Squibbles's voice grew fainter. Once the glow of the lantern was out of sight, she turned and began running back along the path. It had been clear earlier. She wasn't worried about tripping over a root. Any snakes would have to watch out for themselves.

She hurried back to the cottage and hoped Mr. Squibbles made it back safely on his own. He had more to fear from snakes than she did, poisonous or otherwise.

Her spirits lifted when she made out the back of the cottage through the trees. She let herself in and leaned against the back of the door in relief.

From somewhere in the room, a voice said, "Hello?"

Naomi jumped and dropped the knife. She looked around the sunny cottage in alarm.

"Naomi, are you there?"

It was Agatha, she realized. How had she gotten to the cottage? "Agatha, when did you get here? How's Tavik?"

"Over here, Naomi."

Naomi followed the sound of Agatha's voice, but she didn't find the witch. "Agatha? Where are you?"

"Over here. Lift the cloth from the mirror."

Naomi turned around and finally spotted on the wall a cloth hanging over something. She took the cloth down and found Agatha peering out at her from within a large ornate frame. "You have an enchanted mirror?"

"Of course. Now did you get to the Darkon Forest safely?"

"Yeah, we landed last night. I went into the forest, but an umbrek scared me out. Mr. Squibbles is still in there. Is there anything in the cottage we can use?"

"Naomi, who's that you're speaking to?"

Yula looked down from the loft with bleary eyes.

"It's Agatha. She's in the mirror."

Yula blinked sleepily at her and frowned. Her head disappeared back into the loft. Naomi turned back to the mirror. "How's Tavik? What's happening with the wedding?"

A truly evil smile spread across Agatha's face. Naomi was so glad the witch was on her side. "Lady Crazy has developed quite a deplorable case of diarrhea and can't be three feet from her chamber pot. Tavik has ordered me killed."

"What?"

"Oh, he's done this before, as you know. He never means it."

"But he's under a spell. He could think he means it."

"Well, the castle guards don't think he does. The only ones taking it seriously are that woman's guards, but seeing as they've all developed nasty rashes on their little boy bits, they're beginning to reconsider."

Naomi shook her head, chuckling. "You're marvelous."

"Yes, I know. Now, you need something to help you in the forest?"

"Why not use the shield? It was very useful before," Yula said, yawning as she came into the room.

"That's still in our bedroom in the castle."

"Why's it in your bedroom?" Yula wondered.

Naomi could feel her cheeks heating up. "Um, Tavik likes it."

"Yes, but why's it there and not in the armory?"

Naomi didn't know what to say. Agatha and Yula were both staring at her. "He likes me to reenact my showdown with Errilol."

"Reenact...But you were—" Yula gasped and quickly looked away.

"And you're still not pregnant?" Agatha asked dryly.

Naomi's cheeks burned. There was nothing like mentioning sex to your mother-in-law. "Do you have anything else in this cottage, preferably something that I don't have to use in my birthday suit?"

"I don't know. What do you think you could use?"

Remembering the danger of the lantern, she said, "Something that gives me night vision would be useful. I can't see in there without light, but if I take light, everything is going to see me."

Agatha nodded. "I have a spell for that. Do exactly what I say. Get the small copper cauldron. Take down the clay jar with the wax seal from the top shelf. Break the seal carefully. Inside is purified water. Fill the cauldron a quarter of the way with it. Next find my jar of ash bark. Crumble a pinch into it. Next take a bit of nightshade root and put that in. While stirring it clockwise repeat this chant: Eyes brighten as days darken; give me sight when there's no light. Once the pot begins to boil, tap the spoon on the side twelve times. With my cheesecloth strainer, pour the concoction into the eyecups. Put the cups over your eyes. You need to open and close your eyes twelve times while the cups are over them. And when you're done, you'll have night vision. Save what's left of the tincture and reuse as needed. It usually wears off after a day."

"So how high should the fire be for the cauldron?" Naomi asked.

"Fire? You don't put it on the fire. It bubbles when the spell's ready."

"Oh."

Agatha looked away from the mirror. "I need to go. I think something's happening. I'll report back if there are any developments. Be careful, you two."

"You too, Agatha. Thanks." Agatha's image faded from the mirror.

Yula and Naomi worked together to get the ingredients ready. Naomi was about to begin dropping the ash bark into the pot when there was a scratching at the door.

Both women froze and turned to each other.

"Who do you think that is?" Yula asked.

Naomi approached the door. "Hello?" she called.

"Naomi, can you open the door, please?"

Naomi felt a wave of relief. It was Mr. Squibbles. He'd come back safely. She opened the door ready to welcome the mouse home and found herself greeting the umbrek.

"I'm afraid she got me," Mr. Squibbles said.

Naomi slammed the door on them. "Naomi, wait!" Mr. Squibbles called.

"Mr. Squibbles, I'm very sorry you were eaten, but I'm not about to join you in her stomach."

"Naomi, it's not like that. I'm not in her stomach. I'm in the pouch. Use your head."

"Oh, even better! I'm not getting dismembered and joining you!"

She stepped aside to let Yula slide a large chest in front of the door.

"Are you barricading yourselves in? Oh, that's real hospitable."

"Mr. Squibbles, have you lost your little mouse mind? That umbrek will kill us, and you brought her here?" Yula cried.

"She won't kill you, especially if you set a place for her at the table."

"What?"

"Let us in. I think she's getting antsy."

"And that's supposed to encourage us?"

"She's blind!"

"What?"

"She's a young, blind umbrek. Didn't you notice how she seemed more interested in your bread and cheese than chasing you down and tearing you limb from limb? It's because she can't. She's been surviving on roots and berries since the mob kicked her out. They would've killed her, but she fell down a ravine, and they left her for dead. She's been on her own ever since."

"Oh, the poor thing," Yula murmured.

Naomi had to admit the story did pull at her heartstrings, but they were still talking about a vicious predator. "How do we know she won't kill us in our sleep?"

"Um, because she'll probably be asleep too?"

"What?"

"Umbreks sleep more than cats. If she eviscerates someone, I'll take full responsibility."

"Not comforting, mouse."

"Really, just let us in. You'll see. She's practically harmless."

Naomi looked to Yula for her opinion. She wasn't very reassured by the "practically harmless" comment, but Yula was biting her lip. "She hasn't killed Mr. Squibbles yet. She mustn't be that ruthless," she said.

"Fine, but if she eats me, I'm going to be really pissed off," Naomi said, and with Yula's help, they moved the chest away from the door. As a precaution, Naomi picked up a heavy metal pan, and Yula grabbed a broom. She opened the door and stepped back. The umbrek stood there a second, and it sounded like Mr. Squibbles said something in animal speak to her. She lowered to her front paws and tentatively entered the cottage. Her ears swiveled every which way, and her nose constantly twitched. Now that she wasn't staring at her in abject terror, Naomi noticed her murky blue eyes and her smaller frame. She was only six feet tall, where the other umbreks she had seen had been over eight feet. The umbrek bumped into the table and shied away from it. She seemed to be curious about the fire. The warmth was probably drawing her.

Naomi found herself circling around to stop the umbrek in case she kept going straight into the hearth. Instead, the umbrek stopped in the space before it, circled around and lay down. She even tucked her forepaws under her head for a cushion. Once the umbrek was settled, Mr. Squibbles wiggled out of her pouch.

"What are we supposed to do with her?" Naomi asked.

"She'd make an excellent guard dog. One whiff of her and most predators will steer clear."

"What are we supposed to feed her?"

"She's okay with vegetables and grain. She'd like meat, but she's had to get used to not eating it much."

"You've named her already, haven't you?"

"Named her? No, she's not my pet. She told me her name is Hip Hop."

"Really? And you didn't name her?"

"No, that's what she told me."

"Her parents didn't like her, huh?"

"I wouldn't bring that up with her."

Naomi shook her head. Having an umbrek by her side while she went into the forest would make her feel better. "Fine, Hip Hop can stay. I need to do this spell Agatha told me about. You can help."

"No, really, I'm all right. No need to fuss over me or thank me for selflessly leading the nasty, murderous umbrek away."

Naomi rolled her eyes. "That would've happened if you hadn't brought her home."

The three got to work and finished up the spell without any more interruptions. Naomi looked warily at the eyecups. "Okay, what didn't Agatha tell me?"

"How should I know?" Mr. Squibbles said.

"Because you know. Can I keep my clothes on to use this?"

"If you want to. It's not necessary."

"Any strange side effects?"

"No, you put the stuff in your eyes, and presto, you have excellent night vision."

"Okay." She still didn't completely trust him, but maybe this time the potion would actually do as promised. She leaned over the eyecups and put them up to her face. She pressed them until they had a seal, leaned back and let the potion go over her eyes. She opened and blinked them as instructed. The liquid stung a little, but it was pretty mild. She removed the cups finally from her eyes. She blinked open her eyes and immediately suffered an awful stabbing pain in her head.

She hunched over and covered her face. "Mr. Squibbles, what's going on?" she asked.

Yula knelt by her side. "Let me see," she said.

She sat up and let Yula pry open one of her eyes, but the terrible stabbing pain immediately returned as bad as before. She pushed Yula away to hunch over again with her arms folded over her face.

"Quit opening your eyes, and it might stop hurting," the mouse said in an unimpressed tone.

"How am I supposed to see in the dark with my eyes closed?"

"How are you supposed to see in the dark with so much light?" he countered.

"My eyes are light sensitive now?"

"How else are you supposed to see in the dark?"

"Great, so you've made me blind, too."

"When you're in the forest, you won't be."

Naomi sighed and stood up. "Then I guess I better get into the forest."

"Let me wake up Hip Hop."

"She just fell asleep. It's fine."

"Naomi."

"What if she wakes up grumpy?"

"Give her some food. That'll perk her up."

Naomi sat and listened to Yula bustle around the kitchen putting together a quick meal for the umbrek. Mr. Squibbles was given the task of waking the beast. She didn't know what he did, but Yula gasped, and it sounded like she tossed a bowl of food across the floor. She could hear Hip Hop chewing something.

"You still got all your fingers, Yula?"

"Yes," she said, but she sounded kind of dazed.

"What'd you give her?"

"A few apples and some nuts."

"Why'd you gasp?"

"It showed its teeth."

"It's okay. She was only smiling," Mr. Squibbles said.

"Something with that many fangs shouldn't smile," Yula replied. Naomi nodded in agreement.

"Are we ready?" she asked.

"Let's go, Naomi. Yula will guide us to the forest, and then she'll come back to the cottage."

"Are you sure this stream is close enough to get to in a few hours?"

"I think so."

Naomi was getting tired of all of the probablies, most-likelies, and I-think-so's. She wished someone was sure of something. Yula led Naomi to the forest and deposited her safely in the cover of shade. Mr. Squibbles was on the umbrek's shoulder. He preferred the beast's shoulder to the pouch. He said it sounded like digesting in there. When Naomi opened her eyes inside the forest, it was a completely different scene from before. She could see all the trees clearly. Small creatures she hadn't known were there earlier were clearly visible now. She turned around and took it all in. It was actually pretty amazing in there.

"Okay, which way?" she asked.

"Head west."

Naomi headed out with Hip Hop trailing her. The umbrek had been very docile so far. It surprised Naomi. She'd expected some growling or grunting. "Hip Hop isn't like other umbreks, is she?"

"I think she's brain damaged."

"Don't be mean," she said.

"No, seriously, that fall I told you about really did a number on her I think. She isn't normal at all."

"Oh, that's sad. I mean, I'm glad she isn't attacking me, but it's sad to have a beast so damaged she isn't herself anymore."

"Yeah, you're right."

They continued on in silence. Naomi kept a keen eye out for any possible danger, but the forest was relatively silent. She heard no loud beasts or saw any signs of them. Hip Hop seemed content enough following along behind her.

When they came to some rock outcroppings, Mr. Squibbles spoke up. "We need to start heading north now. We'll hit the stream eventually."

Naomi nodded. She started to head in that direction.

"Naomi, wait. Hip Hop hears something."

She stopped and turned back. The umbrek was standing up, utilizing all of her six feet of height. Her ears were flicking back and forth.

"Mr. Squibbles, do you know what she's listening to?"

"Not sure. There is a rustling, but I can't tell what it is."

Naomi began getting worried. "What should I do?"

"Get ready to run."

Naomi turned around several times searching for the threat. Hip Hop was pointed intently in the direction they had come. She peered down the path but didn't see anything, even with her newly enhanced sight. She went around the rock outcropping to try and hide. As she slid in among the rocks, a hand covered her mouth and jerked her back.

"Hip Hop!" Mr. Squibbles cried.

Naomi bit into the hand covering her mouth. There was a curse from a male voice. She was pushed away. She fell to the ground and immediately shot out a foot to sweep his feet from under him. He fell to the ground with a cry. Naomi jumped up with her little knife. Hip Hop came up beside her and growled in the direction of the fallen man. Naomi put a hand on Hip Hop's back and urged her forward with her. The man scrambled to his feet and held his hands up.

"Wait, don't hurt me! I have nothing to steal."

"Only because you wanted to steal something from me," Naomi said. Now that she could take a good look at her attacker, she wasn't impressed. He was in his forties with thinning hair, which he was valiantly combing over. His arms and legs were spindly, and he had a slight middle-aged paunch. It appeared he'd been roughing it for a few days. His clothes were ripped and stained.

Hip Hop crept closer with a low growl. The man backed up hastily and fell on his ass. "No, wait! I thought you were in trouble. The umbrek! I thought it was going to attack you. I didn't mean to hurt you. I don't want any trouble! Call off your umbrek! Please, I need your help, Unicorn Mistress. What are you doing with such a vile beast, anyway?"

Naomi relaxed and lowered her knife. "Because she's handy. Who are you? How do you know me?"

"I'm Lord Gerald. I'm Lady Naomi's husband. I need your help. Your husband Lord Tavik is trying to kill me!"

Naomi noticed now that while his clothes were ripped and stained, they were made of satin and silk in blue and gold. A gold chain swung across his chest. It had a large pendant in the shape of a rooster. He was as pitiful as Lady Crazy had described. "Why would Tavik want to kill you?"

"So he can properly marry my Naomi!"

That made sense and made Naomi's stomach twist, but it did give her an idea. If Gerald's life was stopping Lady Crazy from marrying Tavik, she should do everything to keep him alive. "I see. What are you doing out here? Shouldn't you be hiding at your cousin's castle?"

Gerald winced and looked away. "He ordered

me out. Once he heard Tavik wanted me dead, he banished me. He did not want the warlord at his gates. Really, I think he was just looking for an excuse to send me away. With only the clothes on my back and an old nag, he sent me out. It was awful. Then the nag ran off while I slept, I couldn't relight my lantern, and I've been wandering in here ever since."

"For all of a day," Mr. Squibbles said dryly.

"Your umbrek speaks?" Gerald exclaimed.

"No, my mouse does. That does sound terrible, Gerry. What do you want me to do about it?" Naomi was beginning to get Lady Crazy's decision to ditch her husband and go for Tavik, but that didn't mean she was going to just let her.

"Win him back! Trick him or slip him a potion or blackmail, maybe! I mean you're not as pretty as my Naomi or as refined, but you seem like a clever woman at least. It's rumored you defeated a god. I'm sure you can figure something out."

"Well, that's what I was trying to do before you grabbed me."

"Oh, you're not hiding like me?"

"Hiding like you? Why would I need to hide?"

"Because Tavik wants you dead, too."

"Where did you hear that?"

Lord Gerald reached into his doublet and pulled out a crinkled piece of paper. He unfolded it and held it out to her. It was a wanted poster with a drawing of him and her side by side. She'd been drawn with a really big nose. That bitch.

Underneath it was written, "Wanted Dead." They hadn't even bothered with the "or Alive" part. A hundred gold pieces to whoever presented their corpses. They also hadn't used her first name. She was only referred to as Taylor, probably to distinguish her from Lady Crazy, though Naomi preferred her method over theirs.

"I can't believe this. Haven't you people ever heard of divorce?"

"What's divorce?"

Well, there was her answer. Naomi crumbled up the piece of paper, dropped it, and ground her boot heel into it. Lady Crazy was definitely not taking any chances.

"I cannot believe this. Here I am risking life and limb to get him an antidote, and he's putting a price on my head. When this is over, he is going to do some serious groveling. I mean literal hands-and-knees groveling. This is ridiculous."

"Antidote?"

"For the love spell your bitch of a wife put on my husband."

Gerald sputtered. "Don't call her that!"

"Hey, I don't blame you. I wouldn't claim her as my wife either. Why the hell did you marry her?"

Gerald was growing red in the face. Naomi realized that he was actually upset about the bitch comment. Her estimation of him took an immediate nose dive.

"Lady Naomi is the sweetest, gentlest, most

beautiful woman I have ever met. How dare you disparage her!"

"Gerry, she's left you. And she's trying to steal my husband. That doesn't sound very sweet, and when she kidnapped me, she definitely wasn't gentle."

"It's Lord Gerald, if you please. And she's only trying to do what's best for our people in Harold's Pass."

"What are you talking about?"

"If she becomes their lady again, she can make sure the sick and the poor are provided for."

Naomi wasn't sure what to say to that. It was a good idea to do that, and she probably should've been trying to do something like that herself, but the statement just didn't ring true for Lady Crazy. From what she had seen, the woman was too delusional and full of herself to care about the sick and poor. "Fine, but does she need to marry my husband?"

"Do you think he'll give me back Harold's Pass?"

"That would be a big fat no," Mr. Squibbles said.

They were wasting too much time. She needed to get back on track to finding the fool-me-not. "Gerry, I gotta get going if I'm going to fix this. Do you think you can follow the path? There's a cottage at the end of it. Yula's there. She can take care of you."

"What path?"

Naomi turned and pointed, but remembered then that her night vision let her see much better than Gerry. She dropped her arm with a sigh. She'd have to lead him back if he was to go to the cottage. She didn't want to lose all that time.

Reading her thoughts, Mr. Squibbles said, "He's going to slow us down."

Naomi agreed, but for better or worse, she needed to keep him alive. She went to his side and picked up his hand. "Here, hold onto my arm." She placed his hand on her elbow, and began going down the path again.

"So you're collecting ingredients for a spell?" Gerald asked.

Deciding not to get into an argument with him again about who was under a spell, she agreed. "Yeah, I only need one more ingredient, and then I can get Tavik back."

Gerry nodded. "And then my Naomi can return to me."

"And then everyone's happy," Naomi said.

"Yes, I hope so."

Feeling like there was a lot left unsaid with that comment, Naomi asked, "Where were you two hiding?"

"We'd taken refuge in my cousin's estate, but his wife and my Naomi didn't see eye to eye. Naomi was used to being the lady of the castle, but Izzy would not relinquish her home to her." Naomi rolled her eyes. It sounded like they'd been living pretty easy lives, and Lady Crazy had still demanded more. This Izzy probably happily sent Lady Crazy on her way.

"Of course Izzy didn't let her. It wasn't her home."

"But Naomi is such an excellent woman, and after what had happened, Izzy should have been a little more understanding and generous."

Naomi thought Gerry really needed to sniff some fool-me-not, too. Had the woman used love spells on all the men? How many men were out there pining for her crazy ass? They walked for another half hour in silence.

"Um, miss?"

"What, Gerry?"

"I need to relieve myself."

As soon as he said it, Naomi realized she could use a bathroom break, too. "Okay, we'll stop here for a moment. You go that way to do your business, and I'll go over here."

"You won't go too far away, will you?"

"No, Gerry. I'll be in shouting distance."

He didn't seem very eager to let go of her arm. "Here, take Mr. Squibbles. He can see pretty well and can tell you if you're about to brush up against poison ivy or something."

"Wait a minute. I didn't agree to this," the mouse protested.

"I'm not taking you with me to use the bathroom."

"But I don't want to go with him."

"Tough."

"What about Hip Hop?"

"She can come with me."

"Why does she get to go with you?"

"The answer's in the question."

She pried Gerry's hand from her arm and put Mr. Squibbles on his shoulder. Gerry crept off the path to find a spot to relieve himself, with the mouse grumbling about humans and their strange hang-ups. Naomi went off the other side of the path with Hip Hop trailing behind.

She found a relatively secluded spot and squatted down. She peed and dried herself with a bit of rag. She put her clothes back to rights and made her way back to the path.

"Taylor!" Gerry yelled.

"Oh, what now?" she grumbled as she hurried back and went in search of the nobleman.

"Taylor!"

"Stop yelling!" she yelled back.

"TAAAYYYLOOORRR!"

What the hell was his problem? He was going to draw every umbrek and other nasty to them in a ten-mile radius. She broke through a line of brush.

"Taylor, thank goodness! Help!"

"Where the hell are you?" she said. He sounded close by, but she still didn't see him.

"Up here," Mr. Squibbles said.

Naomi looked up, and dangling head-down above her was Gerry.

CHAPTER FIVE

*Dragons love their hoards above all else and
guard them fiercely.*

"You have got to be kidding me," Naomi said
as she looked up at the hanging lord. It appeared
he'd gotten caught by a very large snare.

"Catch me, Naomi," Mr. Squibbles said.

She held out her skirt to catch the falling
mouse. He landed on the fabric with a little
bounce. He righted himself and climbed up onto
her shoulder.

"Thank you. Now let's go."

"What, and leave Gerry?"

"Yes, and quickly."

"No, please don't!" Gerry cried.

"We're not going to leave you, Gerry, but shut
up." She traced the rope holding him up. It was
attached to a wooden pole. She couldn't reach the
top of the pole, though, not without climbing up
it.

"May I make one observation?" Mr. Squibbles
said.

"What?" Naomi said as she tried to figure out
another way to get Gerry down.

"The people who set this trap were obviously hunting big game, and we probably don't want to meet them."

"We're not leaving Gerry."

"Fine. But he's going to get you killed. I just want to make that clear."

"Duly noted. Stay with Hip Hop while I try to cut Gerry loose."

"Fine."

Naomi tied up her skirts, put her knife between her teeth, and gripped the pole. She began pulling herself up. Her boots weren't very good for this, but she was able to manage a bit of a grip. She shimmied up and reached for the rope. She began sawing.

"Naomi!" Mr. Squibbles hissed.

She didn't stop to find out what he wanted. She kept sawing. The rope was very thick. She didn't want to imagine what the trap had been set for.

"Naomi, get down here now and run!" Mr. Squibbles cried. Hip Hop began to growl and scratch the ground with her feet and thump her tail.

She was halfway through the rope. Gerry had started blubbering. She tried to not listen to him. If she did, she might have left him to rot. She really didn't need a coward. She had no use for them.

"Naomi!"

"Shut up, Mr. Squibbles. I'm not coming down

until Gerry's free." She was starting to sweat, and her muscles quivered. Holding herself up on the pole with one arm was putting a serious strain on her. Finally the rope snapped, and Gerry fell to the ground like a sack of potatoes. The pole swung as it straightened further. Naomi couldn't keep her spot on the pole, but she held on well enough to slide down it rather than be launched into the air.

Her knees tried to buckle when she was back on the ground. She leaned on the pole to stay upright as she regained her balance. "What's going on?" she asked.

"A group of men from the east. We better hide."

"They could be help," Gerry protested.

"Anyone who's in these woods is risky at best and dangerous at worst. We should hide," Mr. Squibbles sagely said. Naomi was all in favor of hiding. She really didn't want to meet anyone new. Gerry may have been relatively harmless, but he was a hell of a pain in the ass.

"Come on," she said.

"No, I'm in charge, and I say we meet them."

"You're in charge of what?" Naomi asked incredulously. Maybe she should've left him hanging.

Gerry cupped his hands around his mouth and called out, "Hello, whoever's out there! Over here!"

"Dark Gods, just kill him now."

If Naomi didn't need him alive to keep Tavik from marrying Lady Crazy, Naomi would've taken the comment seriously. She turned to run, but it was too late. A crossbow bolt whizzed by her and embedded itself into a tree. She stopped and turned around.

A group of men dressed in dark clothes came into view. They uncovered several lanterns and ranged out around them. One looked at the snare trap. "You broke my snare," he growled.

"What were you trying to catch with it?" Naomi asked.

"Anything big enough to catch."

"Well, you caught me. So sorry, sir," Gerry chuckled. He stuck out his hand. "Pleasure to meet you, I'm sure. I am Gerald, the Lord of Harold's Pass."

The man crossed his arms rather than shaking Gerry's hand. "Last I heard, Harold's Pass was now the Demon Lord Tavik's."

"Yes, well," Gerry coughed and dropped his hand.

"Demon Lord?" Naomi said. She'd thought Tavik had lost that moniker by now.

"Haven't you heard of him?"

"Of course, she's heard of him. Why she's his—" Naomi turned and punched Gerry in the face with all of her strength. He needed to shut up and NOW.

Gerry fell to the ground and didn't get back up. She turned back to the men. "I know Lord Tavik.

He's the reason I'm out here. Same for you?" she asked.

"Yeah. What'd he do to you?"

"Threw me away. What about you?"

"Same."

She took a better look at the men. They were all fit, and she could see the remnants of armor. "You were in his army?"

"Yeah, nothing like being press-ganged to kill people and then set loose and told not to do it anymore."

"Sucks."

"As you say. Why'd you punch limp wrist there?"

"Because he's an annoying bastard. Weren't you about to?"

The soldier chuckled and stuck out his hand. "The name's Edgar. What's your name?"

"Yula," she said with a silent apology to her friend.

"Well, Yula, let's go back to camp."

"All right." She cast a quick glance around for Hip Hop and Mr. Squibbles. They'd somehow faded into the background. She hoped they stayed hidden. They were her only ace in the hole.

The ex-soldiers picked Gerry up and dragged him along. His head lolled. She hadn't realized she'd hit him that hard, but she couldn't feel guilty about it. The best thing for him at the moment was unconsciousness. They trekked through the forest, and Naomi wondered where they were going. It was definitely not in the direction of the river.

"So what have you been doing out here other than catching wimpy lords?"

Edgar smiled at her dig at Gerry. "Basically, that's all we've been doing. Catching rich fat merchants and making their loads lighter. It's a lot easier than schlepping across lands, ransacking towns."

Naomi let this sink in. She was with the brigands that Tavik had intended to capture. The reports had indicated the brigands were a nasty bunch. They didn't kill their targets, but they had no qualms over hurting their marks a lot. She really hoped Mr. Squibbles hadn't bugged out with Hip Hop.

"So, Yula, what were you doing with Gerry there?"

She shrugged. "I just met him. He insisted on us sticking together because he was scared."

Edgar shook his head at the man's weakness. "Hopefully we can ransom him and make a decent profit."

"His cousin sounds wealthy; maybe he'll pay for him."

"Doubt we'll get much for him."

They finally arrived at the camp. Naomi had to shield her eyes from the fire's glow. There were more men there and a couple of women. They all turned to stare at Naomi and the others.

"What's there to eat? I'm famished," Edgar said.

"There's stew," one of the women said.

"There's always stew."

"If you don't want stew, then you aren't hungry enough."

"I'd like some stew," Naomi said, thinking she might win points by eating with them.

"Hammond, get this lady some stew," Edgar said.

Hammond? Naomi swallowed and turned toward the man called Hammond and looked into bloodshot eyes framed by greasy hair. The man stared at her for a moment, too. He began to smile. His teeth were still piss yellow, except he'd lost one of the front ones since she'd last seen him.

"Well, aren't you a sight for sore eyes," he said.

Naomi smiled nervously and took a step back. "Imagine meeting you again. How've you been?"

"You two know each other?" Edgar asked.

"Oh yeah, this wench cost me my tooth." Oh shit, had she and Agatha done that?

"It was a crazy time," she said.

Hammond picked up a sword. Naomi backed up more with her hands raised. "Come on now, we're all friends. Down with Lord Tavik, right?"

"Hey, she looks familiar," one of the women said. Naomi turned nervously toward her. The woman pulled out a copy of the wanted posters. Naomi's stomach dropped. The woman held up the ragged piece of paper. Everyone looked at it, then at her.

"See? Tavik hates me way more than all of you," she said, tensing up to run.

After a moment, Edgar's face broke into a smile. "That he does, and any enemy of Tavik's is a friend of ours. I guess wimpy there is a friend, too. Can't believe he's done anything to warrant someone wanting him dead. Punching him sure, but dead takes passion."

"No, this bitch needs to be taught a lesson," Hammond said.

"Oh, shut up, Hammond, and put that sword away. You aren't gonna do anything with it."

Hammond clenched his jaw. He sent Naomi a nasty look but put away the sword.

"So what'd you do to make Tavik want you dead?" the woman asked.

Naomi scrambled for something to tell them. "Oh, you know the usual. Kidnapped him, poisoned him. Almost killed him a couple of times."

She could tell the brigands were impressed. She was such a fraud.

"So why does he want sleeping beauty dead?"

"Oh, he's married to Lady Naomi, and Tavik can't marry her properly without killing him first."

"Humph, I'm almost inclined to help the demon lord out with that."

Still needing Gerry alive to keep the marriage stalled, Naomi said, "Oh, why make things easier for him?"

"You're right. Might be fun to annoy Lord No Tomatoes."

"Lord what?" Naomi asked. She could easily understand Demon Lord, but what the hell did tomatoes have to do with anything?

"Yeah, no tomatoes," Edgar said grabbing his crotch.

"Oh, tomatoes are balls," Naomi said and then frowned, finding the metaphor gross on both sides.

"He may come back looking for us, though, if he knows we got both of them. We barely kept ahead of him when he was last here," the woman said.

"I'd be happy to kill 'em both," Hammond offered.

"Shut it, Hammond. You ain't harming the woman. I like her." Naomi smiled nervously at Edgar and hoped he'd meant that in a totally platonic sense.

"Then what's the plan?" the woman asked. She hadn't appeared too thrilled with Edgar's declaration either, and the female brigand was wearing a lot of knives. Naomi couldn't afford to make any more enemies. She edged away from Edgar.

"We keep doing like we are, Zettie. The scouts saw a caravan coming. It should be in range tomorrow."

Everyone smiled at each other. Their grins reminded Naomi of sharks. She tried to smile with them, but it was strained. She couldn't stay the night. Where would she sleep? She had a nasty idea that Edgar and Hammond would both offer her space in their bedrolls.

There was a rustling on the edge of camp. "What's that?" one of the men asked, reaching for a sword.

"Probably a squirrel."

The rustling increased.

"I'm going to check it out."

"If you catch it, we can throw it in the stew pot," Zettie said.

The man sneered and rose to check it out. He left the light of the camp fire. Naomi could still see him pretty clearly.

He crept into the surrounding brush. Naomi hoped it was Mr. Squibbles and Hip Hop and that the rustling had been intentional.

"Don't see anything," the man called back.

"Told you," Edgar called.

The man began coming back, and the rustling began on the other side of camp. All heads swiveled in that direction.

"Maybe it's a dog scrounging for food," Hammond said. He reached into the stew pot and pulled out a bone. He threw the bone in the direction of the rustling. They waited. There was a bit more rustling, then the bone came flying back into camp. Everyone jumped up.

"Fan out. Find whoever that is," Edgar ordered.

Naomi rose, too. She picked up an unclaimed sword and moved out. She didn't want to be obvious, but she moved steadily away from everyone else. "Mr. Squibbles," she whispered.

She didn't receive a response. She kept going out.

"See anything?" Edgar called.

Everyone called back in the negative. Naomi hunched down, trying to get out of sight. "Mr. Squibbles, where are you?" she called out in a whisper.

She spared a moment's thought for Gerry. But she needed to get away, and it'd be impossible with him in tow. The idiot still hadn't woken up yet, and he probably wouldn't want to go with her after she'd clocked him. She hoped Edgar would stick to his idea of keeping the nobleman alive to annoy Tavik. She just had to hope Gerry didn't annoy him enough to make him reconsider that idea.

Naomi was well out of view of the fires, but neither Hip Hop nor Mr. Squibbles had materialized yet. She looked all around and kept a keen ear in case the others found them before her. She hadn't headed in the direction that the rustling had come from, figuring they'd already moved from that area. She was walking along on tiptoes when an arm reached out and grabbed her. A familiar hand clamped over her mouth.

"Taylor, what have you been up to?" Tavik asked.

She froze.

"I'm going to remove my hand, but don't scream or I'll silence you," he told her and pressed a knife against her throat.

"Tavik, what the hell do you think you're doing?" she whispered.

"Surely, you've seen the wanted posters by now."

Naomi pushed away from him and turned to glare at him. "You put a price on my DEAD head. That's—" Her hand flashed out and struck his face. Was slapping him going to become a daily occurrence? Her hand stung, but the tears that pricked her eyes weren't due to that pain. Was she becoming abusive? She knew she shouldn't keep hitting him, but look at what he was doing to her! First he tossed her into a dungeon, then came and told her he'd never loved her, and now there was a price on her head, plus they drew her with a big ugly nose! And she'd noticed he'd called her Taylor rather than Naomi. So along with everything else, Tavik was giving Lady Crazy all rights to her name, too? But still, she shouldn't keep smacking him. She should switch to kneeing him in the balls. Or rather, the tomatoes.

Tavik's head swung back toward her slowly. She waited for him to speak. He sheathed his dagger and flexed his hands. Illogically, she was happy to see him, but things were so messed up. And she still hadn't gotten the fool-me-not.

When he didn't speak, she tried again to reach

him but with words rather than hands. "Does any of this make sense to you? One day you're checking to see if I'm pregnant and the next you're putting me in the dungeon while you plan a wedding to another woman."

"You're only angry because my eyes are finally open."

"Open? More like cross-eyed. Think about it, Tavik! You meet Lady Crazy, and after making you drink something, you're all gaga for her. Does that sound normal?"

"We're in love."

Naomi couldn't help protesting. "No, you're not!"

Tavik sighed. "And even if she hadn't appeared, we were doomed."

Naomi's eyes widened. "What are you talking about?"

"You are determined not to have my child."

Naomi's frustration exploded. She threw her hands in the air and turned away from him. "I want to have children, dammit! I just want an ob-gyn available when I find out the good news."

"A what?"

Naomi scrubbed her face and made herself take deep breathes. "Never mind."

"Lady Naomi is eager to have my children."

It was like a cold bucket of water was upended over her. How could he say this to her? This was all so surreal. It was like Lady Crazy was her doppelganger determined to take over her life. "She doesn't love you."

"We were fated for each other. If my mother hadn't interfered, we'd be expecting our first child by now."

"Tavik, that's not true. What about Errilol? If you'd married her instead of me, you'd most likely still be in service to him. You'd still be hiding your face, you'd still be pillaging cities, you'd still be placating a bloodthirsty, insane god, and you'd still be a virgin. Don't you get it? I was the best thing that ever happened to you, and the only reason I did all of that is because I love you. You stopped listening to Errilol and put away your sword because you love me."

"And yet here we are," he said.

His short, sardonic reply to her impassioned argument made Naomi scowl. "You're under a spell," she said flatly.

Tavik didn't reply.

Naomi's shoulders slumped. "Just let me go. I'll go away, and you won't need to worry about me anymore. If you do see me again, then you can take action, but you won't. I promise." She was lying. She had no intention of giving up, but she could see that while Tavik was under this spell, reasoning with him wasn't going to do any good. She just had to hope she could get him to show her mercy.

"You'd leave and never come back?" he asked.

Even though it made her chest ache, she nodded. Tavik's brow lowered, and an angry glint came into his eyes. Naomi took a step back in fear.

"No, I'm not going to let you just leave," he said.

Tears began running down her face. She'd hoped he'd still have some soft feelings for her underneath the love spell. She tried reasoning with him. "Why not? You don't have to kill me. They told me the marriage to Lady Crazy would supersede ours. That once you marry her, our marriage would be null and void. You don't have to do anything to me."

It was stupid of her keep pleading with him. The love spell had too strong a hold on him. He reached out and grabbed her again. "No, Lady Naomi said you have to be dealt with if we're to be happy."

"Tavik, you don't have to do this!" Naomi begged, staring into his eyes, trying to convince him.

"I'm sorry, Taylor."

"I am, too." She kneed him in the tomatoes and ran.

Tavik let her go to double over.

"Mr. Squibbles, help!" she screamed.

She could hear Tavik crashing through the brush behind her. Her night vision gave her an advantage, as she could navigate through the foliage and trees while he had to bump through them.

She could hear the brigands calling out now

and the clash of swords. Tavik hadn't been alone. She had to get away. If she got caught up in the fighting, she could get killed or captured by either side.

She was looking over her shoulder keeping track of Tavik when an arm clotheslined her. She went down choking. She looked up and suffered a nasty twist of déjà vu as Hammond lowered a sword to touch the tip of her nose.

"Where do you think you're going, girlie?"

She couldn't reply around the kink he'd put in her throat.

"Get up. We're to regroup at the river, and I think the others will be real interested in hearing about your chat with Lord No Tomatoes. Can't much want you dead if he had his dagger at your throat and didn't take the easy kill."

This was a quandary. She still desperately wanted to get away from the brigands, but she needed to get to the river, and if Hammond could take her to it, that put her that much closer to getting to the fool-me-not. She got up warily, keeping a close eye on the sword.

"If you were watching, you saw him grab me and me kicking him."

"Yeah, but it looked real cozy before that. You ain't what you claim."

A figure rose up behind Hammond.

"So who are you?" he asked, raising his sword to keep it leveled on her.

"She's my wife," Tavik said.

Hammond tried to turn, but Tavik stabbed him before he could strike out with his sword. Blood bubbled up between Hammond's lips. His teeth changed from yellow to pink. Naomi couldn't muster any sorrow, but she had revulsion in spades. Hammond crumpled to the ground. She raised her eyes to Tavik.

He reached out and grabbed her arm. He turned and started striding through the forest, dragging her behind him. "Tavik, what are you doing? Let me go!"

"I need to take you back and dispose of you properly."

"Dispose of me? I'm not a piece of garbage for you to put in the proper recycling bin." He didn't even comment on not understanding what she was talking about. This was bad. She tried to pry his hand off her, but it was impossible. His grip was too strong. It hurt a lot. She tried to dig her heels in, but he just dragged her along. It reminded her of their wedding day. The two days did have a lot in common. She was being unwillingly taken somewhere by Tavik, and there promised to be a lot of pain waiting for her at their destination, except this time, it would be worse than branding.

Naomi started trying to reason with him again. "Why do you need to kill me? I'm just your war bride. You said war brides have no standing. You can just take another. Why not just marry Lady Crazy and be done with me?"

"Because Lady *Naomi*," and Naomi's jaw clenched at him using her name for other woman, "does not wish for you to cast a pall over our wedding."

Now, Naomi's jaw dropped. "And my death won't cast a pall?"

Tavik didn't reply.

Naomi slumped her shoulders. "Tavik, just let me go. You can lie and say you killed me. Everyone will believe you."

"No, I can't," he said.

The situation was appearing more and more hopeless. She was pleading with the man she loved not to kill her. She was pleading with him to let her go. She was even giving her blessing for him to go marry some other woman. It was ridiculous, and she didn't want to be hopeless. Pissed off seemed much healthier.

"Then just kill me, you dumb ass. Go on, chop off my head and take it to the crazy bitch. You can mount it to the wall and put underneath it: First wife."

"Stop calling me dumb ass!"

"Oh, I'm sorry, LORD Dumb Ass!"

Tavik let go of her arm with an angry yell. Naomi looked around and thought about which way would be best to make a dash for it.

"Why do you have to be so infuriating?" he shouted.

She didn't reply. She was judging the opening in some brush.

He turned to her with exasperation. "Just accept what is. I'm marrying the real Lady Naomi, and you are no longer my wife."

She rolled her eyes. "You are so going to regret all of this once the spell is broken. You are not going to escape this guilt, and I'm going to use it for years after this because seriously, this is too much."

He glared at her. She glared back.

"Naomi, don't you know the swiftest way to a headache is to argue with someone under a spell?" Mr. Squibbles said from behind Tavik. Tavik didn't turn around. He should have. Hip Hop kicked him into a tree. He hit the tree hard and bounced off it. He fell onto his back in a sprawl. He tried to get up, but he appeared to be disoriented.

"Naomi!" he yelled.

Well, at least he was calling her Naomi again. She paused, torn between going over to make sure he was okay and running.

"Naomi, let's go before he draws anyone else," the mouse said.

Mr. Squibbles was right. "Tavik, I'll see you later. Don't do anything stupid until then, okay?" Tavik only snarled her name and swiped in her direction. They were going to need serious marriage counseling when this was over. Hip Hop turned around and began bounding through the forest. Naomi ran as fast as she could to keep up.

They ran for a long time. Naomi finally had to

stop when she developed a stitch in her side. "Do you think we've lost all of them?" she panted as she leaned against a tree.

"I think so. Are you all right?"

Naomi nodded. "I'm fine. Tavik didn't hurt me. Where were you two?"

"We were following you and watching for the best time to get you out. We spotted Tavik and his men creeping up on the camp. We had to fall back or else be seen by them. We figured the resulting confusion from the confrontation would be our best chance. I didn't figure on Tavik zeroing in on you and breaking from the others to catch you."

"Yeah, he has it out for me."

"Hmm, I'm not so sure. Like that dead brigand said, Tavik didn't kill you outright, even when you told him to. Maybe the spell doesn't have as strong a hold on him as Lady Crazy hopes. Maybe that's why she's insistent on your death."

Naomi could still feel where Tavik's fingers dug into her arms. She wasn't sure he didn't have it out for her. "Where are we in relation to the river? Please tell we were running toward it."

"Yes, we were. It's not too much further now. You ready to keep going?"

Naomi nodded and pushed off the tree. "I hope Yula's all right," she said.

"I'm sure she's fine. She could move the cottage if danger appeared. Let's go and get this straightened out finally."

They continued through the woods. Naomi

caught a branch before it could whop her in the face. "Where's the river, Squibbles?"

"Just up ahead," he said.

Naomi's lips thinned. He'd been saying the same thing for the last half hour.

She continued walking and walked right into Hip Hop. "What now?" she asked.

"Um, well, you know, it's like this, don't get mad, and please don't hurt me, it'll upset Hip Hop."

Naomi gritted her teeth. "What is it?"

"The river's dried up."

"What?"

She shoved past Hip Hop and found herself on a small embankment that bottomed into a sludgy path. "That's supposed to be the river?"

"Well, at best, it was only ever a stream."

She looked up and down the gully. She didn't see any flowers. "Where's the fool-me-not?"

"Well, since there's no water, I figure the flowers have all died."

"Mr. Squibbles," Naomi said in a dangerous tone. Her heart had begun pounding, and her hands were beginning to shake. She clenched her fists and jumped down into the gully. Her shoes sank into the mud. "What happened to the river?"

"I don't know. How am I supposed to know that?"

"Could it be dammed up somewhere upstream? Maybe we should follow it and see.

Maybe we'll find some flowers along the way."

"I suppose we'll have to," the mouse said.

Naomi gave a definitive nod and started going up the gully. She'd follow it all the way to the source if she had to. "Naomi, what about your eyes?"

"What about my eyes?"

"The night-vision potion will wear out eventually, and then you won't be able to see the flowers when we do find them."

"I'm sure we still have plenty of time. It hasn't been a day yet. And it shouldn't take us that long to follow the river."

"There's also the danger of Tavik and the bandits."

"Hopefully they've canceled each other out. I'm sure it'll be fine. We have to get the flowers. Unless you know somewhere else they grow?"

Mr. Squibbles didn't answer her. Naomi started marching. Everything was going to be okay. There was nothing to worry about. This was just a minor setback. So she'd been captured by brigands and threatened by Tavik. It would be okay.

"Naomi, are you sure about this?"

Naomi wanted to scream. "What else am I supposed to do? If I don't get this fool-me-not, how am I supposed to get Tavik back? And if I don't get Tavik back, what's left for me?"

"You could return to your parents."

Naomi stopped dead and turned to the umbrek

and mouse. "What the hell did you just say?"

"You could return to your parents. The unicorns will send you back. It wouldn't be a problem."

"You want me just to give up?"

"You don't have to give up, but it is an option. If things get any worse, keep it in mind."

"I'm not giving up."

"Okay, then let's keep going."

They trudged through the forest in silence. Naomi wondered how big the forest was but didn't want to ask Mr. Squibbles. His suggestion to return to Earth had left her rattled. She hadn't considered going back, but if this didn't work out, was that what she'd have to do? She hated the thought, but if she really lost Tavik, what else was there? Agatha was barely teaching her anything about witchcraft, everything she owned was Tavik's, and if they didn't have divorce, they sure as hell didn't know a thing about alimony.

Naomi kept herself occupied as they trudged by thinking about what she would do once this whole ordeal was over. She'd make Tavik grovel, of course. Then she'd take a trip to Harold's Pass and figure out how to make things a little better there. She'd tell Agatha either to teach her real witchcraft, or she'd contact that wizard and get him to take her on as an apprentice. And she'd get Snowflake to send her to Earth for a visit so she could stock up on neonatal vitamins and sign up with a good ob-gyn. That was good. No more worrying about stuff but taking charge. She liked it.

"Uh, Naomi."

Naomi turned to Hip Hop and Mr. Squibbles.

"What now?" she asked.

"I think we're being stalked."

"Stalked? Can you tell by who?"

"I think the better question is by what."

Hip Hop was scratching the ground and snorting in a stressed manner. She obviously could smell whatever it was out there and didn't like it.

"Can Hip Hop tell you what it is?"

Mr. Squibbles said something to Hip Hop in animal speak. Hip Hop's reply didn't make any distinct sounds to Naomi's ears, just some growls and grunts.

She waited tensely for Mr. Squibbles to clue her in. "She says it's big. She says it's not an umbrek. It's a solitary hunter. Likes to bite—" Mr. Squibbles cut himself off as Hip Hop made some motions with her paws. "Oh shit."

"What is it?" Naomi asked, her stomach clenching. She looked around the forest. She could see clearly, but it was only as good as human sight during daytime. She didn't have superior hearing or scent.

"It's a dragon," Mr. Squibbles said.

CHAPTER SIX

Hardly anyone has ever met a dragon. Those who have, regret it.

Naomi looked for the dragon. She couldn't see anything unusual past the surrounding trees. She did notice that a hush had fallen over the forest. "Are you sure it's a dragon?" she whispered to Mr. Squibbles.

"It's big, scaly, smells like bad eggs. Scares umbreks. Can't think of anything else."

"Are you sure it's stalking us? Could it be just strolling in the same general direction?" Naomi asked.

"It could be, but it's been strolling with us for a quarter mile now and creeping closer."

"Wait, let's make sure your dragons are the same as my dragons. Do they breathe fire?"

"Some do, especially the ones that smell like bad eggs," Mr. Squibbles replied.

"They're big and scaly with mouths full of fangs?"

"Yep. And talons as long as your hand."

"They have a penchant for eating damsels in distress?" she asked.

"So they're the same on both worlds. Good to know."

"Except they don't really exist on Earth," Naomi said, still looking around for signs of the dragon. Nothing was apparent except for the tense silence of the forest.

"Well, there's a big difference. They definitely exist here."

"What can we do?"

"Scream, run, get chomped."

Naomi's body broke out in a cold sweat. "Oh, that sounds easy." Her voice cracked on "easy."

"Maybe we should keep going and not wait for the dragon to kill us."

Naomi could agree to that. She picked up the pace. She kept looking over her shoulder expecting to find dripping jaws with razor-sharp teeth. When she kept finding nothing, it only made her look more. She started jogging without realizing it. Hip Hop wasn't hanging around. She quickly outpaced her and disappeared among the trees.

"Mr. Squibbles, don't leave me!" Naomi called.

"Can't help it. Hip Hop knows the dragon's out there, and she's not hanging around for it. She can outrun it if need be."

"No, she knows she just needs to outrun me," Naomi grumbled.

"Do your best, Naomi."

"Mr. Squibbles!" she shouted, but there was no answer. Hip Hop had bounced out of shouting range. Naomi could distantly hear her through the trees, but that was all. Naomi still hadn't really heard any evidence of the dragon. She wondered if maybe he'd gotten tired of stalking them and wandered off.

She figured that she couldn't appear that appetizing. She wondered how she could make herself less appetizing. Maybe she should fart. The thought made her smile. And before she'd really consciously decided, a big one ripped out. That stew from the brigand camp had made her gassy.

"Dragon, I just want you to know, that I'm not good eating. I'm very stringy, and I'll probably give you heartburn. Just saying."

She didn't hear any noise in reply. "I mean it. I've got bad cholesterol. I'm sure you'd much prefer a nice cow or sheep."

"And where am I supposed to find a cow in these woods?" asked a deep, raspy voice.

Naomi stopped and looked all around, but didn't see any large, hulking monster. "Dragon?"

"Yes."

"You can talk?"

"Not very smart, are you?"

"Right, stupid question." She turned all around looking for the dragon, but still did not see it. The disembodied voice, though, sounded like it could belong to a dragon. Along with deep and raspy, his voice was loud. Not like yelling loud, but like something with a mouth much bigger than hers was talking, so his voice was louder. For something that sounded so big, she still couldn't spot him. Her night vision didn't appear to be faulty. She could still see everything else clearly, but she could not spot the dragon. He had to be invisible. That seemed a bit unfair. She was afraid to try running away in case she actually ended up running toward him.

"Um, I've never met a dragon before," she said, hoping to keep the polite chatter going. Maybe he'd let her go, or she'd at least figure out where he was.

"Most people never do, and if they do, they never meet one again."

"And why's that?"

The disembodied voice didn't reply.

Naomi looked around at the dark woods, and the answer came to her. "It's because you eat them, isn't it?"

"You're not clever, but you eventually catch on."

"Right. Um, well, we haven't officially met, so I'll just be on my way."

"Oh, how terribly rude of me, I am Grisbek, Green Dragon of the Darkon Forest. And you are?"

Naomi didn't reply.

"Oh, don't be that way. I'm going to eat you whether you tell me your name or not."

Unhappily, she said, "Naomi. How do you do?" She even dropped a slight curtsy for him. She couldn't help it. The dragon might be about to eat her, but he was being so well-mannered that she felt compelled to be equally polite.

"I'm very well, thank you. And how are you?"

"Not good. Pretty terrified, actually."

"Perfectly understandable. Now that the formal introductions are out of the way, would you like to begin running?"

Naomi looked around again but still didn't spot him.

"Where are you?"

"Right here."

She turned to the direction his voice came from but still didn't see anything. Her heart was racing, but her body was exhausted. She'd run so much already that day. She knew she couldn't go very far.

"I don't see you," she said.

"You don't need to see me."

"I would like to see the thing that's going to eat me."

"Very well." There was some rustling. She was looking in that direction and couldn't see anything. Then all of a sudden there was a dragon. It was like looking at one of those magic eye posters. At first, there were just branches and trees and leaves and bushes in her view, then a little shift, and suddenly, there was a dragon.

He looked just like the fairy tales. Size and all. He was as tall as a house. He had a long scaly head with spines that started on his neck that went all the way down his back that tapered off at his whiplike tail. His claws had massive talons that were each bigger than the dagger Tavik had been threatening her with earlier. He was an iridescent dark green, which helped him fade into the forest without any effort. His eyes were the size of grapefruits and were a dark plum color, which made the slit pupil difficult to discern.

Naomi had held out a slim hope that this had still been a trick. That he'd appear and be actually the size of a house cat, but as she craned her neck back to look up at him, she knew complete and total terror. She couldn't move. She knew she should run, but her body and brain had gone offline. What use was doing anything? A big, freaking dragon was planning to eat her. There was nothing she could do.

The dragon sighed. "I knew it. Now that you've seen me, you won't even try to flee, will you? Frozen in terror. I was hoping to have a little fun with you before eating you."

Naomi couldn't reply. She just stared at the dragon and hoped that chomping was a swift death.

No, she is under our protection.

Naomi turned and found Snowflake standing by her. His alicorn glowed brightly and made her eyes hurt. "Snowflake, get out of here. Don't let the dragon get you!"

Grisbek snorted. "As if I would sully my tongue with that thing's blood. Unicorns are one of the foulest-tasting creatures in the land, and killing them always generates such terrible ill will from the other creatures. It isn't worth the trouble."

Naomi is under our protection. I will not let you kill her.

"Oh, and what are you going to do about it?" Grisbek asked.

The unicorn turned to Naomi. *Think of somewhere safe.* Snowflake's horn dipped and lightly touched her arm. She didn't have time to think of anywhere clearly. The darkness rose, and when it receded, she flailed back and fell on her ass. Her backside hit the cement stoop hard. Her vision was normal again. Snowflake's alicorn must have neutralized the night-vision potion. She still rubbed her eyes and blinked a lot because she couldn't believe what she was seeing. She grabbed the railing and pulled herself back to her feet. She stared at the door before her and gulped. This couldn't be happening.

"Snowflake!" The unicorn didn't appear at her desperate shout. She stared at the brass door knocker in terror. How was she supposed to explain her sudden appearance? How was she going to get back? She looked down at her peasant dress. How was she going to explain what she was wearing?

She didn't get a chance to think up any answers because the door opened, and she looked into the eyes of her mother.

"Naomi? Oh my God! You're here!" Barbara, Naomi's mother, pulled her into a massive hug.

"Hi, Mom. I was in the neighborhood and

thought I'd drop by," Naomi joked.

"How long have you been back?"

"I just got here," she said. She winced at how truthful that statement was.

Barbara looked over Naomi's shoulder and up and down the street. "Where's Tavik?"

"He couldn't make it."

"No? That's too bad! But I'm so happy to see you!" She pulled her in for another hug.

"Yeah, it has been a while," Naomi said, not knowing how long it had been actually for her parents. It'd been four months for her, but unicorn travel could turn back time along with the instant relocation. It made things hard to predict.

"It's been four months! And not an e-mail or a postcard. What have you been up to? How was your honeymoon?"

Naomi sighed in relief. So the time difference was the same this time. She could deal with that. "Oh, you know, honeymoon's over," she weakly chuckled.

"Well, get in here. How long are you staying?"

Naomi let her mother pull her inside. "A few days. Sorry for not warning you."

Barbara waved off the apology. "You know you can show up at any time. There's always a place for you here. So what have you been up to? How's Tavik?"

When Naomi saw Snowflake again, she was going to have a long talk with him. If she saw him again. Did he even know where he'd sent her?

Had he gotten away from Grisbek? What was she supposed to tell her mother?

"Tavik's well." And Naomi bit her tongue from saying more.

Barbara took them to the living room. It looked the same. Barbara pulled her down to the sofa. She sat close enough for their knees to touch and held onto both of Naomi's hands. She couldn't stop smiling. Naomi smiled back but wished it was due to true happiness and not nervousness and panic.

"Well, you tell him he has to come with you next time. That's an order," Barbara said. Naomi had to look away from her. The next time she saw Tavik, he could be married to another woman.

"You still haven't said what you've been up to. Did you get a job?"

Naomi shrugged, trying to stay relaxed. "I've been helping my mother-in-law with her business."

Barbara's eyes widened. "Really? What does she do?"

"She makes herbal remedies. She's highly respected."

Barbara nodded and didn't question this odd career choice. "Oh, that sounds nice. It's pretty different from the bank."

"Yeah, but it's good. Agatha and I get along really well, except she's desperate to be a grandma."

"Well, who isn't?"

Naomi rolled her eyes. "I'm not pregnant."

"But you're trying?"

Naomi thought about that. If having unprotected sex was trying, then yes, they were, but if birth control were available, she'd be using it. "We're trying, but I don't feel ready to have a kid."

Barbara nodded. "Well, you haven't been married that long. Waiting a year would be perfectly okay."

"Yeah, but—"

The front door opened, and Naomi's father stuck his head in. "Barbara, I thought you were going to wait for me on the sidewalk?"

"Phil, look who's here!" Barbara said.

"Naomi?" While Naomi's reunion with her mother had felt natural and old hat, seeing her dad and hearing the little catch in his voice put tears in her eyes.

"Hi, Dad. How've you been?"

He came over to her on the couch. He reached down and picked her up by the biceps and crushed her in a hug. "Missed my little girl," he said. Naomi hugged him back and couldn't say anything for a minute. When they finally parted, both had to wipe the corners of their eyes.

Remembering what her father had said, Naomi asked, "Were you guys going somewhere? Mom, you should've said."

Barbara waved off her question. "We were thinking about going out to eat, but this is better.

I need to call your brother and get him over here."

"How is he?" Naomi asked.

Barbara answered while she dialed. "He's doing well. Straight As this semester. We're very impressed."

Naomi's eyebrows rose. "Yeah, that is really good. Has he picked a major?"

Phil snorted. "Yeah, he's picked five different ones so far. It seems like every month he discovers a new life calling."

Naomi smiled. "Well, he's still a freshman. He doesn't need to settle on anything right away. He'll know by the time he finishes all his prerequisites."

"Hope so," Phil grumbled. "He's not even staying in the same discipline. One week it's chemistry, the next English, after that sports medicine. Now he thinks he'll be a world-famous photographer."

Naomi smiled. "He's trying new things. Remember when I wanted to be a police officer?"

Phil shuddered. "Don't remind me. The only thing worse would've been if you'd enlisted. And you talked about that briefly."

"With the idea of it paying for college, but yeah, I'm glad I decided against that."

"Bobby, you're coming over for dinner tonight. I don't care if there's a slammin' party at whoever's house. Your sister's in town, and we will have dinner together."

Naomi felt guilty about dragging Bobby away from a college party. She remembered how good those could be. "Mom, it's all right. I can see him tomorrow."

"No, everyone is eating here tonight. We'll be sitting down at six thirty," she said to Naomi and into the phone.

Naomi looked over at her father. He was determinedly looking down to better not get any spillover of Barbara's irritation.

Naomi got up and wandered into the kitchen. She looked in the fridge to see what might work for dinner. She didn't care what they ate, but if her mother was going to make such a big deal about the whole family being there, she'd probably want to make something special.

She heard the kitchen door swing open. Barbara came in sans phone.

"Bobby on his way?" Naomi asked.

"With bells on."

Naomi smirked. "What do you want to fix?"

Barbara went over to the stove and turned it on. "I was thinking lasagna. Pull it out of the freezer. Do you want to help me with the salads?"

Naomi nodded and did as she was told. Together they began chopping vegetables while the oven heated up. "So where are you staying?" Barbara asked.

The question startled Naomi. Her knife slipped and cut her thumb. She hissed in pain and sucked on the wound.

"Oh dear, let me see," Barbara said, grabbing a handful of paper towels.

Naomi let her take her hand. She hadn't hurt herself on purpose, but it gave her a few precious moments to figure out a lie. Of course, she could stay with her parents, but they would wonder where her luggage was. "I got a room at the Ramada," she lied. She had no money or ID. All she had was literally the clothes on her back. She didn't know what she was going to do.

"Well, next time, you're staying here, capisce?"

Naomi nodded. That talk she was going to have with Snowflake later was getting longer and longer. Teleporting to her parent's doorstep was not something to be done lightly. One needed like a week to prepare!

Bobby called out from the front door. Naomi quickly cleaned up her part of the salad making and went to greet him. She went straight to him, bypassing her father to give her brother a hug. His face cracked into a big smile. Her eager greeting surprised him, but she needed to be close to whisper in his ear, "You're taking me back to the apartment tonight, but Mom and Dad will think you're taking me to the Ramada Inn. Understand?"

"Huh?"

"Just nod your head or I tell them what makes college parties so *slammin'*."

He nodded his head.

"Good," she said and released him. She stepped back and looked him over. "Dad says you're into photography now."

He nodded. "I got my gear in the car if you want to see it."

"Maybe later. How's the apartment?"

"Great."

"Good, you got a girlfriend yet?"

"Nope. You pregnant?"

"Nope."

"Excellent. I'm too young to be an uncle." Naomi laughed. It was the first real laugh she'd had in days.

"Okay, everyone, I want a picture tonight. If you want to spruce up beforehand, do so now."

Naomi looked down at herself and wondered if she had any old clothes still in the house. "I want to wash my face," she said and went upstairs. She couldn't believe no one had commented on her medieval dress yet. And the thought of her mother insisting on a family portrait was surreal. How long was she going to be stuck here? How was she going to get back to Terratu? Her reflection stared back at her. She waited a moment, hoping Agatha would appear to answer all her questions. The mirror didn't change. When she went back downstairs, everyone was gathered in the living room. Bobby was fiddling with a fancy camera on a tripod.

"That yours, bro?" Naomi asked.

"Yep, Mom wants a super-nice picture, and her

point-and-shoot wasn't going to cut it."

Phil motioned for her to come stand with him and Barbara in front of the fireplace. Bobby checked the viewfinder and set the timer. He came over to join them. Barbara and Naomi were in the middle while Bobby and Phil stood on either side. "Next time, we'll take one with Tavik," Barbara said right before the camera clicked.

Naomi barely held her smile. She couldn't imagine Tavik there. That troubled her. She should be able to imagine her husband meeting her parents, but their worlds were so different. She'd given up everything to be with him, but she didn't know if he could handle visiting her childhood home. That didn't seem right. If she could deal with his world, he should be able to deal with hers. But her musings seemed silly considering that at the moment, Tavik wanted her dead and planned to marry another Naomi. The happy couple could very well be putting up wedding decorations at the castle and making up a guest list. She wondered where they were registered.

The kitchen timer went off. "Okay, all of you set the table while I get the food," Barbara ordered.

As Naomi grabbed glasses from one cabinet, and Bobby grabbed the plates, he whispered to her, "You're not in trouble are you, sis?"

She shook her head, but the words that came out of her mouth belied the negative. "I'll explain after we leave." Bobby nodded, and they finished setting the table.

They all sat in their usual seats. Being at the family table made Naomi's heart constrict. She'd unconsciously assumed she'd never sit here again. Being back showed her how much she'd missed it. While Barbara dished out the lasagna, Naomi caught up on everyone's day-to-day life. Her dad had gotten a promotion. She could tell he was very proud about it. Her mom had started volunteering at the local food bank. She seemed to really like it. Naomi relayed to everyone her apprenticeship with her mother-in-law, the "herbalist." They chatted amiably through dinner and for an hour after.

When it reached eight o'clock, Bobby got up, saying he had homework that he needed to do and asked Naomi if she needed a ride back to her hotel. She said good night to her parents and made plans to go out shopping with her mother the next day. Naomi wouldn't be doing any buying, of course, but it would be nice to spend time with her mother, and she didn't know what else to do. She had no talking mouse to give her a list of ingredients to gather for a spell. She hoped Snowflake hadn't abandoned her.

Naomi left the house with Bobby and got into her old car with him. She felt strange sitting in the passenger seat.

"You gonna tell me now what's going on?" Bobby asked.

"I didn't plan to come back."

"What do you mean? You didn't just pop here magically."

"Actually, I did."

Bobby snorted and pulled onto the street.

Naomi had decided that she needed to tell someone everything, and that someone would have to be her brother. Her parents weren't an option because they wouldn't be able to let her go back if they knew all the danger involved, but her brother wouldn't think of stopping her. He would probably believe her more easily, and if he didn't, she'd make him believe her.

"Do you remember me telling you about marrying the King of Mars?"

Bobby chuckled. "Yeah, what about it?"

"I'm now the Queen of Mars."

He raised an eyebrow and looked over at her. "I know. You married him. Way to go. It has a much nicer climate than Venus anyway."

"No, what I mean is, I married a man on another planet."

Bobby laughed. "What's he doing that's so weird?"

Naomi didn't know where to start. "You're not getting it. Where did you think I went when I left?"

He shrugged. "One of the 'Stans. Can you pull it up on Google Earth for me?"

Naomi shook her head. "Our castle is not on Google Earth."

"I wouldn't be so sure," Bobby assured her.

"I'm sure, because the castle isn't on Earth."

"Yeah, then where is it?"

"I don't know where it is on a star chart."

Bobby gave her a look. "Sis, seriously, what's up?"

Naomi sighed and rubbed her forehead. "Don't you think it was strange that I left with only the clothes on my back?"

He shrugged. "Thought you didn't want to bog yourself down with a lot of luggage."

"I took no luggage, and I didn't come back this time with any either."

"Oh come on, no one would build a spaceship without plenty of storage compartments."

"I didn't travel by spaceship."

"Then how can you travel from one world to another?"

"By unicorn."

Bobby was quiet a second and began snickering. "Does it gallop on rainbows and have butterfly wings?"

Naomi scowled and crossed her arms. "No, it uses its alicorn, which is the proper name for a unicorn horn. By thinking of the place I want to go and touching me with its alicorn, a unicorn can send me anywhere. I was being menaced by a dragon before, and a unicorn sent me here to get away from it."

"Wait, there are dragons, too?"

"Apparently. This one's name is Grisbek. Mr.

Squibbles and Hip Hop abandoned me to it, though I can't really blame them. The thing is terrifying."

"Wait, what? How does hip-hop music figure in, and who's Mr. Scribbles?"

"Mr. Squibbles is a talking mouse and Agatha's familiar. Hip Hop is a blind umbrek. Those are like kangaroos on steroids. I was with them before the dragon showed up. They ran away and left me with the dragon."

She could tell Bobby didn't understand half of what she was saying and didn't believe the other half, but he was humoring her anyway. "But the unicorn saved you?"

"Yeah, Snowflake showed up out of nowhere, which he does, and told me to think of somewhere safe, and when he touched me with his alicorn, I found myself on Mom and Dad's doorstep."

"Why didn't you go home to Tavik?"

"Because he currently wants me dead."

The car screeched to a halt. Naomi grabbed the dashboard to keep from slamming into it. "Bobby!"

"Tavik's hurting you?" he shouted.

Naomi quickly tried to explain. "He's under a spell. I'm supposed to be getting the antidote, but stuff keeps getting in the way. First it was Hip Hop, which turned out to be not such a problem; next it was the brigands; then Tavik caught me, but I got away from him; and then Grisbek showed up and was planning to chomp me, but Snowflake sent me here."

Bobby just stared at her. Naomi realized she could've eased him into this a little more slowly. "Naomi, are you on drugs?"

"No, got any?"

"I wish I did."

He started driving again, and Naomi tried to think of a way to explain the insanity that was her life. "Tavik and I were doing okay. We were happy, but then the real Lady Naomi showed up, and she slipped Tavik a love potion, and the next thing I know, he's put a price on my head, and I'm running through a dark forest looking for some flower called fool-me-not. Tavik does love me, and he was so excited about having a kid. Even now under the spell, that's all he can talk about."

"Naomi, are you listening to yourself?"

"I know it sounds completely preposterous, but it's all true. I didn't know about dragons until today. It surprised me, too."

"And you're back here. For how long?"

She slumped back into the car seat. "I don't know. Snowflake didn't give me any info before he teleported me here."

"Wait, that unicorn horn Grandpa left you— are you trying to tell me that it was real?"

She nodded. "I accidentally pricked myself with it and ended up on Terratu, in a place called Harold's Pass, which was under attack by Tavik's army. His mother, Agatha, found me and took me to him. I ended up married to him, and well, the rest, as they say, is history," she said, quickly wrapping it up because she didn't know if it was worth proving how insane she was to Bobby by telling him all that she had done.

Bobby didn't say anything for a few more blocks. Naomi was willing to let it all rest. She was pretty tired and ready to sleep. They pulled into the apartment parking lot and got out of the car. Naomi looked around at the familiar setting. It was still so strange to be back. To see cars everywhere and electric lights. She'd gotten used to castle life.

"We're lucky that Roy and Mike are out this weekend at a festival. I can sleep in their room, and you can have my bed," Bobby said.

Naomi nodded. "Thanks. This means a lot, Bobby."

He waved off her gratitude. "You did a lot for me when you left. I mean, geez, paying the rent up and giving me the car, that was a lot."

"I'm glad you could use them."

Naomi and Bobby went into her old apartment, but it didn't seem familiar. Bobby and his room-mates had rearranged furniture and put different stuff up on the walls. It was actually a relief that it wasn't the same. It made it less likely that she would fall back into her old life.

"Do you want to watch TV?" Bobby asked.

Naomi shook her head. "I'd like to take a shower and just collapse."

He nodded and pulled out clean towels for her. It amused her to watch her brother play host. It was strange being grown-ups with him.

She greeted the indoor plumbing with gratitude. She took her shower and went into Bobby's bedroom. It was her old bedroom. Bobby had even left a clean T-shirt and a pair of pajama bottoms for her on the bed. She was grateful for his forethought. She crawled into the bed and lay there staring at the ceiling. It was strange being in her old room, but the pillow smelled like her brother. She'd given him her old life. She couldn't have it back, which meant she had to fight for her new life with Tavik even harder.

She closed her eyes and turned off her brain. She needed to rest, and tomorrow she'd try to figure out what she could do to get back.

"Naomi, come out here. I don't think you want me to come in."

Naomi eyes snapped open. She looked around the dark bedroom, then at the digital clock. It said it was one fifty-seven in the morning.

"Bobby?" she called.

"No, Naomi. You know who it is. We've been introduced properly."

Naomi sat up and turned on a light. No one was in the room. She pinched herself hard. She was definitely awake.

"Grisbek?" she said in disbelief.

"Come out, Naomi, or I will come in."

She went to the bedroom window and opened

the blinds. The window frame was filled by a pair of dark purple, reptilian eyes that looked back at her. He was leaning up against the building, peering in at her. She jumped back but couldn't stop staring. She pinched herself again and felt it this time as well.

"What's going on? How can you be here?"

"You've been marked, and I will have my dinner."

"What? How did you get here?"

"Unicorns aren't the only ones who can blink travel. I have to say it's been ages since I've had a quarry run to another world to flee me. I'm quite impressed."

"You can't be here! Dragons don't exist here."

"Come now, Naomi. We may not live here anymore, but we obviously exist."

"You have to leave. If you're discovered, you'll be killed."

Grisbek snorted. "That would be a worry if I planned on being discovered. You forget I can make myself invisible. Only you can see me right now. But it is very sweet of you to worry about my safety. It's not often a meal does that."

Naomi shook her head. This couldn't be happening. "You have to go."

"I will once I've eaten you. I don't like the air here. It's foul."

"And I'm supposed to just let you?"

"You might as well. I'm not going to let you go."

There was sound of footsteps from the hall. "Sis, who're you talking to?"

Naomi rushed to the bedroom door and slammed it before Bobby could come in. She quickly locked it. Bobby rattled the doorknob.

"Who's that, Naomi? Aren't you going to introduce us?" Grisbek said. And the way he said it chilled her. She was not putting her brother on the menu.

"Sis, what's going on? Let me in."

"Go back to sleep, Bobby. Sorry if I woke you," Naomi said through the door.

"Who are you talking to?" Bobby demanded.

"Come out, Naomi. Or I will come in."

Naomi pulled the dresser in front of the door to keep Bobby from possibly bursting in. She also effectively trapped herself. Her only way out now was through the window, and Grisbek was just on the side. Naomi was afraid again. But she wasn't frozen in panic like before. Her worry for Bobby kept her focused.

Bobby was pushing on the door trying to open it, but he wasn't getting anywhere quickly due to the dresser.

We feared this would happen. Naomi turned, and Snowflake was in the room.

"Do something!" she cried.

"Naomi, who's in there with you?" Bobby demanded.

"Don't you dare help her. She is my rightful prey," Grisbek said.

She is under our protection, dragon. You should hunt elsewhere.

Grisbek shook his massive head. "No, she is my prey. I have never interfered with your affairs; you should not interfere with mine."

Naomi is under our protection. Snowflake repeated.

"Naomi!" Bobby shouted and started throwing himself at the door.

"Snowflake, if you get me out of here, will Grisbek follow?"

Yes, but it will take him time to catch up with you.

"You won't get away from me," Grisbek said.

"Oh yeah, come and find me," she goaded.

She held out her hand to Snowflake. She had the image of Agatha's cottage firmly in her brain. Snowflake dipped his horn and touched the tip of her finger. The world went dark, and when she raised her eyes, she was standing before the door of Agatha's cottage. It was still on the edge of the Darkon Forest. She quickly turned to look behind her, but there was no unicorn or dragon with her.

She prayed that Grisbek immediately left Earth. She'd taunted him in the hopes of making him chase her. She was worried about what might happen to Bobby. If he got hurt, she wouldn't be able to handle it.

She knocked on the door. Agatha opened it. "There you are," the witch said.

"Agatha, what are you doing here?" Naomi asked.

"That woman has come searching for Tavik, who is searching for you. There wasn't any point staying at the castle," Agatha said.

"Lady Naomi, I'm so glad you're back," Yula said. She'd been sweeping the cottage.

"Thanks, Yula. Agatha, I'm glad you're here. I need your help with something."

"What? Have you not found any fool-me-not?"

"Nope, but that's not what I need help with."

Agatha waited for her to continue.

Naomi took a deep breath. "We encountered a dragon in the woods, and he's decided to eat me."

"What?" Yula cried. She rushed to a window to look outside.

"He's not out there. Yet. Snowflake said we have some time, but Grisbek will show up again."

"How is the unicorn involved?" Agatha asked.

"He's saved me twice by teleporting me away."

"Thank Calax," Yula said, but her eyes were still glued to the window.

"Where did you go?" Agatha asked.

"Back to Earth. I—I saw my parents and brother. But Grisbek followed me there. Snowflake had to teleport me back. I'm scared the dragon might do something to Bobby."

Agatha looked around the room. "Did the dragon speak to you?"

"Yeah, he said I was his rightful prey."

Agatha shook her head. "Once a dragon has chosen his prey, he won't pursue any other. He won't eat anything else until he's had you."

"Are you sure? Bobby's safe?"

Agatha looked at her, and she looked so sad. "I'm sure. The dragon will pursue you and none other until he has you."

"Well, we'll have to do something. What can kill a dragon?"

"An army."

"Well, we have an army. I mean Tavik does. Has he been to the cottage? I saw him in the forest."

Agatha shook her head. "He hasn't been here."

"Huh, well, what should we do? Should I go after the fool-me-not again?"

"Naomi, we have to hide you from the dragon. He won't stop until he eats you!" Agatha exclaimed.

Naomi shrugged. "It's okay. I mean as long as he won't go after anyone else, I'm fine."

Agatha grabbed Naomi and shook her. "You don't understand. You have a dragon after you."

Naomi pushed her away. "I do get it. Grisbek is going to chase me until he gets me or until we kill him. Fine. You say the only thing that can slay a dragon is an army. Tavik has an army. But Tavik won't help until he gets the antidote so that means we have to get the fool-me-not."

Agatha threw up her hands and stomped away. Yula tried to reason with her. "Naomi, it doesn't matter if you get the fool-me-not if the dragon kills you."

"Then what should we do instead? Do you have

an army in your apron pocket? Let's make more of the night-vision potion. I'll put it on and go back into the forest. I'll get to the river this time. I won't let anything stop me. I'll get the flowers to Tavik and break the love spell, then we can gather the soldiers to slay the dragon."

Yula shook her head. "Naomi, you're not being reasonable."

Naomi shook her head. "If you're not going to help me, I'll do it alone."

"You'll do nothing of the sort," Agatha said. She held up a handful of powder and blew it into Naomi's face. Naomi tried to avoid it, but the cloud enveloped her. Her entire body grew heavy.

"Agatha, you can't keep throwing—" She began to slump.

"Catch her so she doesn't hit her head," Agatha said.

She felt hands grab her and ease her to the floor.

"She's not going to be happy when she wakes up," Yula said grimly.

"Especially when she discovers she's tied up," Agatha agreed.

Naomi wanted to complain about everyone knocking her out and tying her up, but she slipped completely into unconsciousness before she could form the words.

CHAPTER SEVEN

You cannot outrun a dragon.

"I will get you, you know."

Naomi looked around her bedroom at the castle and got up from the bed. She went to the window, but didn't see anyone in the courtyard. She didn't remember returning home. A large green scaly head rose up on the other side of the window.

She rushed to the bedroom door, but it was locked. She banged on it and called for help, but no one answered her. She turned from the door and looked for a weapon.

"It's only a matter of time, Naomi. You can't escape me," Grisbek said.

"The unicorns will protect me," she said, grabbing a fire poker. She could gouge out one of his eyes at least.

Grisbek shook his massive head. "They'll grow tired of coming to your defense, and one day, they'll just be too slow."

"My husband commands an army. He'll defeat you."

Grisbek snorted. Smoke came out of his nostrils. It filled the room, hiding everything from her. The room disappeared. Grisbek rose above her and looked down at her with glowing, purple eyes. She clutched the fire poker harder. It was the only thing she had.

"Is that the husband who wants you dead?" the dragon asked.

"It's a temporary thing. He'll come to his senses soon."

"Before or after I eat you?"

Naomi held up of the fire poker. It wasn't enough against a dragon. She knew it was futile, but she wasn't going to do nothing. "You haven't eaten me yet. Why don't you go find a herd of sheep or some cattle to munch on? I'm sure they're much better for you."

His massive head dipped toward her.

"It's true that they taste better than human, but think what the other dragons would say if I let you go?"

"I'm sure they'd understand. I'm just one puny human. I'm not worth the effort."

Grisbek shook his head again. "All true, except they wouldn't understand. They'd think I was weak. Unable to kill one puny human? They'd laugh at me."

"They don't need to know."

Grisbek's eyes narrowed. "They'd know, and I would never hear the end of it."

"Who's going to tell them? And why would

they believe it? You're a big, ferocious dragon. They'd figure if you decided to trouble yourself with one puny human, you'd eat one puny human."

"You obviously don't know dragons very well. We're consummate gossips. I'm sure they've already heard about my thwarted attempts to snap you up on two different worlds, and I'm already in for a good ribbing. But if I fail completely..." The dragon shuddered. "It doesn't bear contemplating."

"Is there any other way out of this?" Naomi asked.

"I am afraid not, my dear. Sleep well. You will be seeing me again."

"Sleep w—" Naomi closed her eyes and shook her head. She didn't feel right. She tried to move but found she couldn't. She opened her eyes and found herself on her back, looking at the ceiling of the cottage.

She was tied to the bed in the loft.

"Agatha!"

Yula appeared at the top of the ladder. "We did it for your own good."

"You knocked me out and tied me up. How is this worse than the dragon again?"

"Because we won't eat you?"

"Let me go."

Yula shook her head and disappeared back down the ladder. Naomi craned her neck and looked out the window. Clouds were going by, level with the cottage.

"Agatha!" she shouted again, louder.

This time the witch appeared at the top of the ladder.

"Yes, dear?"

"Where are you taking us?"

"Somewhere safe. We have to deal with this dragon, and that means we need time to think, and we need to be somewhere safe to think."

"And where's that?"

Agatha went back down the ladder. Naomi struggled to get out of her bonds. They'd tied her up tightly. She lay there and wondered how Tavik was doing. Was he picking out china patterns with that woman? She wanted to cry, but she was too pissed off. She struggled harder to escape her bonds. Her wrists and ankles became bloody due to the ropes. They slicked her limbs, and she was able to finally pull one hand free. She quickly worked her other hand free and undid the ropes holding her feet. She stood up from the bed gingerly. Her wrists and ankles burned. She took a better look out the window. They were flying high in the sky over water. Moving further and further away from any hope of finding any fool-me-not. Where were they going? She crept down the ladder.

Yula was at the hearth tending to a bubbling pot, and Agatha was at the ship's wheel.

"You didn't have to keep me tied up. Or were you afraid I'd dive into the ocean and swim back?"

Yula and Agatha turned to look at her. Yula looked guilty, but Agatha merely raised an eyebrow.

"Before I sedated you, you were acting like you would."

"Naomi, your hands," Yula said. She came over and carefully examined the rope burns that Naomi had given herself. She let Yula tend the wounds while keeping an eye on Agatha. She was beginning to get why Tavik had issues with her.

"You don't always know what's best," she said to the witch.

Agatha shrugged. "Maybe, but neither do you," she said.

"Where are Mr. Squibbles and Hip Hop?" Naomi asked, realizing she hadn't seen either animal since Grisbek.

"They never came out of the forest," Agatha said.

"You left them?" Naomi asked, a pang of worry for the animals going through her.

Agatha shrugged. "Squibbles is very capable of taking care of himself, and he has an umbrek with him. He'll be fine."

"Still..." Naomi said, not liking the thought of the familiar on his own. Umbrek or no umbrek.

Agatha waved off her concern. "We'll meet back up eventually. He's my familiar. He has to come back to me."

"Where are we going?"

"You'll see. We're almost there."

"What about Tavik and Lady Crazy?"

"Everything is fine."

Agatha was being far too sanguine. Naomi started looking around the cottage. A large lump in the corner caught her eye.

She moved over to it. The lump was covered by a large quilt. She pulled it back and found Tavik hogtied underneath.

"See, at least we gave you the bed," Agatha said.

Tavik looked up at Naomi with murderous rage. "I had nothing to do with this!" she said to her husband. She pulled up her sleeves and showed him her ankles. "See, I was tied up, too!"

He said something from behind the gag. She reached out and pulled it off.

"This will never work, Taylor. I'm going to marry the real Naomi."

Ignoring Tavik's delusion, she turned to Agatha and Yula. "You lied to me. You said you hadn't seen Tavik."

"No, we said he hadn't found the cottage. And he didn't. I found him, and he got a face full of sleeping powder, too."

"I'm surprised you didn't knock him out."

"I thought about it, but thought you might disapprove."

"Untie me, Mother."

"No."

"Agatha," Naomi said, feeling she was being

too strident with Tavik.

"Naomi, Tavik *will* jump out that door and try to swim to back. Trust me on that. The love spell is too strong. We have to keep him bound."

"You can't keep tying up family! If we have kids, are you going to hogtie them as discipline?"

"If?" Agatha said.

"When, when, when!" Naomi said, though she hated having to say it.

"I'm never sleeping with you again, Taylor. We will never have children."

"Oh, put the gag back on him. I can't listen to him spout such nonsense without wanting to hit him," Agatha said.

Naomi decided gagging Tavik was probably for the best. "I'm sorry," she said as she slipped the gag back over his mouth. He just stared murderously at her. "I do still love you," she whispered and bent down to give him a kiss on the forehead. He flinched away. His reaction pained her heart.

"We're almost there," Agatha said.

Naomi peered out the open door. An island was in view. It appeared to have a large central volcano, which was smoking. "Uh, that doesn't look like the safest place to hide out."

"Don't worry; the volcano is managed."

"Managed? How can anyone manage a volcano?"

From the mouth of the volcano, something with leather wings rose. It was a dragon.

"You're taking me to Grisbek?"

"No, I'm taking you to Torreng. Grisbek won't trespass on another dragon's territory, especially Torreng's."

"Why?"

"Because Torreng is the king of the dragons."

Naomi paused a moment to absorb this. "Okay. But won't he want to eat us?"

"No, he owes me."

"How does a dragon owe you?"

"How else do you think he became king?"

Naomi was getting the urge to strangle Agatha. The witch maybe should have kept her knocked out. "Are you going to give me a straight answer or are you going to draw this out for as long as you can?"

"Draw it out."

"Just as long as we're clear."

Naomi took a seat near Tavik. He was still staring at her in murderous rage. She figured he'd get tired of doing that eventually.

Agatha set the cottage down on the edge of the beach. Naomi went outside and took in their new location. It was a tropical paradise. The water was crystal blue. She wanted to take a swim and wondered if Terratu's oceans had sharks. Or something else bad in the ocean. Maybe they had horrific dolphins. It wouldn't surprise her.

"Naomi, don't wander off. Lunch is almost ready," Yula called from inside.

Naomi went down to the water and let the waves lap at her toes. She looked up and down the beach. It was an unspoiled paradise. She turned her back to the ocean and looked up at the volcano. It still smoked, but Agatha said Torreng was "managing" it. She wondered if another dragon was enough to keep Grisbek away. She remembered her dream, and though she had no proof, she was pretty sure he had really been in her dream. So he could track her anywhere, awake or asleep.

"Naomi, lunch is ready!" Yula called.

She walked back from the beach to the cottage. The small home didn't look right in its new set-ting. It was perfect for woodland scenes, but something more hut-like was needed for the beach. She went back in and stopped short at the familiar sight of Yula, Agatha, and a tied-up Tavik sitting at the table ready to break bread, and the spot by Tavik was empty. It appeared she was to feed him again.

She slid into the seat. "Tavik, I am really sorry about this. I don't want to keep you tied up."

"Then untie me."

"I would, but Agatha seems pretty adamant that you'll try to do something stupid, and I kind of believe her."

He didn't respond.

Their lunch was boiled vegetables and fried venison. She began cutting up the meat for Tavik. She fed him before taking a bite for herself. "Agatha, what exactly are you going to do while on this island? I mean, I get that I'm supposedly safe from Grisbek, but we can't stay here forever."

"And why not? We have everything we need," she asked.

Yula's back stiffened.

"Agatha, Yula's sons are back on the mainland. Are you going to make her abandon them? You get to have your son. What about her?"

Agatha cast a guilty glance at the other woman. "Yes, well, I wasn't really planning on staying here forever. I think we should first seek audience with Torreng and see if he can call Grisbek off. And if he can't or won't, we'll hopefully think of something else."

As plans went, it wasn't much, but having Tavik beside her made Naomi more willing to consider the dragon problem.

"What are you all talking about?" Tavik asked.

He didn't know. *Maybe that was for the best*, Naomi thought. "Oh, um, it's nothing," Naomi said and offered him a bit of potato. He ignored the offered morsel.

Agatha told him the truth. "She's been chosen by a dragon as prey. He's pursued her from the forest to her home."

Tavik turned back to Naomi. "When did you return to the castle?"

Naomi blanched. "Not that home."

His eyes narrowed.

"Snowflake said to think of somewhere safe, and Squibbles had mentioned I should consider going back to my planet, and POOF! I'm in front of my parents' house. It wasn't a conscious thing, and I don't think of it as home. And you want me DEAD! Why am I the guilty one?!"

"Maybe you should go back to your parents," he said.

Naomi dropped the fork that she'd been still holding up for Tavik. "Yula, please feed Tavik. I have to go get some air."

"Naomi, you need to eat more, too," Yula said.

"I've lost my appetite." She left the cottage and went back to the beach. She walked until her toes hit water again. She stood there taking deep breaths, telling herself that he didn't mean it, that he was under a spell, that he still loved her, and she would make him grovel for forgiveness for each and every thing he'd said to her.

"Are you enjoying my beach?"

Naomi turned, but she saw no one. But there were large tracks leading up to her. "Torreng?"

"Oh, I'm sorry. I forgot to shift into view."

And like with Grisbek, one moment there wasn't a dragon before her and then with a little hop to the left, there was. Torreng had similar body to Grisbek's, but he was larger and had yellow gold scales and large green eyes.

His scales glinted in the sunshine, dazzling Naomi's eyes. "Oh, you're very handsome," she said.

Torreng dipped his head. "Thank you. I take it you are a companion of Agatha's?"

"Yes, actually I'm her daughter-in-law. I'm

married to her son, Tavik."

Torreng nodded. "I remember Tavik. But he must be full-grown now. When we met, he was quite small by human standards."

Naomi smiled and nodded. "He's a man now. Do you know why we're here?"

Torreng appeared to sniff the air. She wondered what he smelled. "You've been marked."

"Come again?"

Torreng's black tongue flicked the air. "Grisbek, I believe. He has marked you as prey."

"What do you mean marked? When? How?" She looked down at herself. She hadn't noticed anything on her, and Grisbek had never touched her.

"He probably marked you when he first saw you. It's what we do, so if prey does escape, we can track it down."

"How am I marked? Can I remove it?"

Torreng sighed and shook his head. "I can't tell you that. I may be king, but I cannot interfere with the rightful hunt of another dragon."

Naomi's shoulders slumped. "So Grisbek can track me here? Agatha was thinking you'd keep him away at least."

"Being on my island will deter him for a while. This is my domain, but eventually, he will have to swallow his pride and ask permission to stalk you, and I will have to allow him."

"Thanks, I guess that's the best we can hope for."

Torreng bowed his head again and turned. He walked back into the jungle.

Naomi guessed she should let Agatha know the situation. She walked back to the house.

"Tavik, if you speak to Naomi like that again, I will hex you. If you can't think of anything nice to say to her, then you shut up. Are we understood?"

"You'll like the real Lady Naomi, mother. She's very strong willed, too."

"She's a money-hungry former barmaid. She will ruin you."

"Don't speak of my beloved like that. If you have nothing nice to say, then you shut up."

"Agatha, remember he's be-spelled," Yula said.

"I'll show you be-spelled."

Naomi sighed, and her shoulders slumped. "Knock, knock, friendly coming in."

She stuck her head in cautiously and looked around. Yula was standing between Agatha and Tavik. Agatha's eyes snapped to her. "Are you all right?" she demanded.

Naomi shrank back but nodded her head. "I met Torreng. He said he can run buffer for us for a little while, but eventually, Grisbek will come to get me."

Agatha put her hands on her hips and looked at the floor. "Very well. I was hoping for better, but we'll have to work with what we have."

"Are we sure there are no better ways to defeat a dragon?"

"No, and I doubt Torreng will tell us."

"You're right. He did tell me that Grisbek has marked me, but he couldn't tell me how to remove the mark."

Agatha's eyes lit up at this news.

"He said he couldn't tell you how, not that it couldn't be done?"

Naomi nodded.

"Then that means that there must be a way to remove it. I need to study this mark. Take a seat on the stool."

"I'm not going to like this am I?"

"I promise not to hurt you, much," Agatha said.

"Not comforting, witch."

Agatha pulled out a stool and pointed at it for Naomi to sit. She reluctantly took a seat. Agatha started off by plucking a few strands of Naomi's hair. She didn't warn her before doing it. Naomi scowled and massaged her scalp.

Agatha sniffed the strands and tasted them. It was vaguely unsettling.

"Take your clothes off," she ordered.

Naomi straightened with a start. "What?"

"Torreng said Grisbek marked you. I have to make sure it isn't an obvious physical mark."

"And if it is?"

"It'll help me figure out how to remove it. Why are you balking?"

"Because I don't like getting naked in front of just anyone."

Agatha shook her head. "Squibbles is right; you are weird about nudity."

"Then why don't you get naked?"

"Fine, if that'll make you undress quicker."

Naomi suddenly had an image of herself and Agatha naked, in the same room as her husband who was tied up. "No, no, no, I'm even weirder about that." She grabbed the bottom of her T-shirt and paused. She cast a quick glance at Tavik. He was watching, and he didn't look murderous, which was something. She thought about saying something to him about him watching her get naked when he was "in love" with Lady Crazy, but the potential dig depressed her.

She turned her back and lifted off the shirt.

He gasped. She turned around with her breasts covered by her hands. "What is it?"

"Oh," Agatha said.

"Oh, Lady Naomi!" Yula cried.

Naomi turned to them. "What is it?" she asked.

Agatha turned her around to look at her back. "There is a physical mark."

Naomi tried to look down her own shoulder. "What is it?"

"I believe it's *G* for Grisbek," Agatha said.

"What?"

Yula pulled her to the mirror and turned her back to it. Naomi looked over her shoulder. On her back, was a large stylized letter *G*. It was colored green and shaped like a dragon. Her hands dropped from her breasts as she tried to wipe her own back.

"How the hell did he do that without me noticing?"

"Naomi?" Tavik said.

She turned to him. "It's okay, Tavik. We'll figure it out."

He stared at her a moment and then dropped his eyes, his cheeks growing red. She looked down at herself and realized her breasts were exposed. She began putting her clothes back on.

"Any thoughts, Agatha?"

"It's too large to cut off."

"Well, all I can say is I'm very happy to hear you say that."

"Maybe strong soap and extra-hard scrubbing?" Yula offered.

Naomi shuddered and shook her head. "No, I don't think that'll work."

Agatha had her head bent in thought.

Naomi didn't know what the witch was thinking, but she could hear the ocean waves, and they were calling to her. It was a beautiful day and a beautiful place. She was doomed, might as well enjoy it. "I want to go for a swim. Is there anything that is likely to eat me in the water?"

"Not with a dragon after you," Agatha muttered.

Naomi's eyebrows rose. "What was that?"

"No other predator will approach a dragon's prey."

"Seriously? Nothing is going to chomp me because of Grisbek?"

At Agatha's nod, Naomi grinned. "Then I am definitely going for a swim. Yula, you want to come, too? Let's go play on the beach."

Yula looked unsure. She glanced from Agatha to Tavik. Naomi rolled her eyes. "We can bring Tavik. Agatha, do you have any sunscreen?"

"What's that?"

"Lotion that keeps the sun from burning your skin."

Agatha nodded and reached onto a shelf and handed her a jar. "Rub that on all exposed skin, especially your nose."

"Will the ocean wash it off?"

"Not for hours."

So it was waterproof. Agatha always had a lotion, a tincture, or an oil for everything. Naomi grinned. "Yula, grab some towels and let's go." She went over to Tavik and put a hand under his arm. "Come on, big guy. You don't want to stay in here all day, do you?"

Tavik got up reluctantly. Yula's arms were full of towels, and she followed the pair out. Naomi looked over her shoulder at Agatha.

"You coming?" she asked.

Agatha shook her head and shooed at them. "No, you go enjoy yourselves. I'm going to see what I might have here to help with our predicament."

Naomi's eyes softened at the use of the inclusive pronoun for what was clearly Naomi's problem. "Okay, but don't work too hard. Sometimes it's good to take a break from a problem. It'll become easier to solve."

Agatha nodded absently while she took a book down from a shelf. Naomi helped Yula spread out the towels. She slipped off her pants, but left on her T-shirt and panties. She would've liked to have a swimming suit, but wasn't going to worry about it. She slathered up with the lotion Agatha had given her, marveling at the fact that the witch could make sunscreen. When she was done, she looked critically at Tavik. His arms were bare as were his bald head and face. She scooped up some of the lotion and started rubbing it on his head. He stiffened under her touch.

"I don't want you to burn," she said as she switched from his head to his arms.

He didn't comment. She kept her touch impersonal and her face blank, but her hands ached to stroke and fondle him, maybe give him a tickle. She didn't do any of this though. She didn't want him to flinch from her again. When she was done, she looked at Tavik's face and found him staring at her. His gaze was dark and unreadable. She reached up and gently spread the lotion on his nose and cheeks. His eyes fluttered closed at her touch. She wanted to dip down and kiss his mouth, but didn't want him to flinch again. When she was done, her hands fell away listlessly. Tavik opened his eyes again and his gaze was still unfathomable.

She swallowed the lump in her throat and turned away. "Yula, are you going to swim?"

"No, milady. I don't know how."

"Oh, I could teach you. It's not that difficult."

Yula smiled but shook her head. "Maybe another time," she said.

Naomi shrugged and went down to the water. She waded in and let the waves wash over her. She dipped down to get her body wet. She continued walking out and finally lifted her feet off the sand to start swimming. She turned her body to be parallel with the beach and swam until her muscles began to burn. She rolled onto her back and looked up at the sky.

She had to admit, as vacations went, this wasn't too bad. Sure, she wasn't technically on vacation, but this was the closest she'd gotten to one since marrying Tavik. She watched the clouds drift overhead and sighed. It was a shame that Tavik wasn't able to enjoy it with her. They definitely needed counseling. She tried to imagine going to a marriage counselor with Tavik and couldn't even come up with an amusing scenario. She turned over in the water and started swimming back toward the others.

She'd felt fine, but as she was swimming back, she could feel a cramp beginning to develop in her calf. She slowed down and tried to stretch it out to loosen up the muscles. She started swimming again, but the cramping crept back into her leg. She stopped and tried to wade in the water while massaging her calf. She told herself to keep calm. Freaking out would make her drown surer than the cramp.

She started swimming again and began angling herself toward shore. As she got closer to shore, she found herself battling breaking waves. They started trying to roll her. She put down her feet to ground herself, but her weakened leg quickly buckled and she went over. She rolled head over heels and couldn't stop.

She dimly heard Yula screaming, and then she flipped over again. Her head must have hit a volcanic rock. She felt a sharp pain, and everything went dark.

CHAPTER EIGHT

Green dragons stalk the forests, blue dragons guard the sea, black dragons have the mountains, but there is only one gold dragon.

"You won't escape me that easily, human."

It felt like a gust of fire shot through her, and Naomi's eyes snapped open. She sat upright and started coughing up seawater.

Someone was rubbing her back. She turned and found Tavik dripping wet beside her. It was his hand on her back.

"Naomi, are you all right?" Yula asked.

Tavik kept rubbing her back as her coughing petered off. She nodded her head. "I think Grisbek just saved me from drowning."

"What? Why?"

"He said something about me not getting away that easily like I meant to drown, and whoosh, all this heat went through me and here I am."

"You need to be more careful," Tavik grumbled and sat back.

Naomi finally noticed that he was untied. "You came in to save me?"

"Oh, milady! He demanded that I untie him, and then he ran into the water—"

"It doesn't mean anything," Tavik said and got up. He walked away from them toward the jungle.

Naomi and Yula shared a look. Naomi hurried to follow him as he ducked into the jungle. She wasn't sure if he knew she was following or if he cared. He obviously cared if she died. She got a little flutter in her chest thinking about that. He'd rushed into the water to save her. He must care about her deep down. At least enough not to want her dead, bounty on her head notwithstanding. She decided not to push her luck, though, and kept back, only following him. He tramped through the jungle without comment. She wondered if they should worry about anything like snakes, spiders, or jaguars.

"Tavik, are you sure this is safe?" she called.

He didn't acknowledge her query and kept going. Naomi barely kept from getting slapped by a palm frond. Her lips thinned, and she didn't call out again. If he wanted to sulk, fine. But he wasn't going to get away.

They continued walking for another half hour. Naomi didn't hold onto her anger. She decided to pretend it was a hike like she'd take on an actual vacation and looked at the unusual plants and kept an eye out for birds and insects. She saw one plant that made her stop and squat down to better view it. It had a truly disgusting-looking flower. It was the color of dried blood and had a vaguely decaying smell coming from it. She remembered a story from the newspaper about a

149

similar flower on Earth. It was called a corpse flower. It was much bigger though and only bloomed every hundred years. She thought she was looking at its smaller cousin.

A shadow fell across her and the flower. She looked up and found Tavik had doubled back to her. "Do you know what this is called?" she asked.

He squatted down and took a closer look. "No, but it is truly repugnant."

"I think it's neat," Naomi said, grinning.

"Neat? It smells like death."

"Yeah, it's different. Most flowers smell sweet and look pretty, while this one goes for the exact opposite. It's neat."

Tavik shook his head. He straightened and held out his hand to help her up. She took it without thinking, but when she was standing, she realized what he'd done. He realized it as well and quickly dropped her hand.

"It's getting dark; we should head back," he said.

"Okay," she said. They walked back together. She kept stealing glances at him, but she never caught him looking at her. Maybe she was making too much of his chivalry, but it was hard to ignore it.

Yula had already packed up everything from the beach and was in the cottage fixing dinner. Agatha was immersed in a stack of books. Naomi went over to her and began closing books. Agatha's head jerked up. "What are you doing?" she demanded.

"You need to take a break. Come out to the beach, and let's look for shells and watch the sun set."

"I will find a way to remove that mark," Agatha said.

"I'm sure you will, but I don't want you going crazy to do it. Come on; let's go." Naomi tugged on her arm to urge her out of the cottage.

Agatha sighed and got up from the table. Naomi cast a quick look at Tavik, not sure what he would want to do. He took a seat on the bench against the wall and stretched out his legs. Yula waved good-bye and said dinner would be waiting for them.

Naomi led Agatha down to the beach. "Did Yula tell you what happened?"

Agatha sighed and nodded her head. "You can't even escape that dragon in death."

"You know, having a dragon's mark seems to have a lot of benefits."

Agatha gave her a sharp look. "Except for the dragon planning to devour you."

"Yeah, but otherwise, I mean, it's pretty neat. Other beasties won't touch me, and if I have an accident, he'll bring me back to life. That's pretty good."

Agatha sighed and shook her head. "I'll figure out a way to remove the mark, Naomi. Don't worry."

Naomi shrugged. "You don't get it. I'm not

worried. I know we'll work this out. I believe in you."

They looked out at the ocean. The sun was just touching the horizon. "You know, this is a really nice place."

"Yes, I suppose."

"The real reason I brought up the thing on the beach is because Tavik came to save me. That's pretty special."

Agatha nodded. "He still loves you. The love potion doesn't change that."

"But he's head over heels for Lady Crazy."

Agatha sighed and nodded. "You need to understand how the love potion works. When a love potion is given to someone already in love with another person, their love is in essence cleaved in two. The happiness and admiration of the original love is supplanted by the love potion's designee, but the darker parts of the first love— the insecurity, the fear, the doubt—are all still firmly rooted to the first love. He still loves you, but all he can focus on is the bad parts of your relationship."

"I didn't know there were bad parts to our relationship."

Agatha sighed. "There's always a dark side to any love. We battle it with the good, but the love potion has stolen away all of Tavik's defenses against it."

"If we don't find the fool-me-not soon, could he stop loving me?"

Agatha didn't answer.

Naomi breathed slowly and blinked back tears. Agatha's silence upset her more than anything Tavik had said. They continued to watch the sunset.

"What do you think Mr. Squibbles is doing right now?" Naomi asked.

Agatha sighed and shook her head. "I really have no idea."

"I hope he's okay."

Agatha nodded and went to the cottage. The sunset wasn't over and was really pretty. Naomi stayed to watch it. She found herself still standing there and unwilling to head back in when the sky was purple and the stars were twinkling down on her. The ocean breeze felt nice. She thought about grabbing the towels and sleeping out there.

"Naomi, are you coming back inside?"

She turned to look at Tavik. He looked calm. He wasn't staring angrily at her. Agatha had said that he still loved her but he only had access to the bad parts of their love. If he stopped being angry with her, should she worry? Agatha had basically told her that Tavik could stop loving her. If he could only express his love with anger and sadness, then being calm and courteous could mean his love for her was fading. He'd saved her earlier. She'd taken that as a good sign. Maybe that had been naïve. If the bad parts of their relationship were all he could experience, then maybe he shouldn't have run into the water but instead watched her drown. This was all so confusing. She didn't want Tavik to hate her. She shook her head. Trying to determine the state of her marriage was giving her a headache.

"I think I'll sleep out here," she told him.

He nodded and came to stand beside her.

"Thanks for saving me earlier," she said.

He nodded again.

"I didn't know Agatha was going to kidnap you. I would've told her not to."

"You would have?"

"Well, yeah. I mean there's only so many times you can kidnap someone to show that you love them."

Tavik snorted.

"Do you want to sleep out here, too?" she asked.

He shrugged.

Naomi turned and went back into the cottage. She gathered some sheets and an old quilt. Yula cast her a questioning look. "I'm going to sleep outside. It's really nice. You and Agatha can share the bed."

"What about Tavik?" she asked.

"Still on the beach. I guess he might sleep out there, too."

Yula gave her a small smile and nodded. "That would be good," she murmured.

Naomi went back outside and spread everything out. She lay down. Tavik still stood off to the side. The quilt was big enough that he could lie down too, but she figured it wiser not to point that out. He could see that on his own.

She looked up at the sky and played connect the dots with the stars. She made a duck and a horse and then traced the letters of her name.

Eventually her eyelids grew heavy, and she fell asleep.

"Naomi, I will get you. There's nothing you can do."

She was on the beach. Tavik lay beside her on the quilt. She looked over and could make out the dark outline of Grisbek, but she knew this was a dream, mainly because he wasn't attempting to chomp her right that second. "Oh, just leave me alone. I know about the stupid tattoo on my back. You're lucky I'm not on my home planet, or I'd get it lasered off."

"Removing my image won't remove my mark."

"Whatever. You know I've killed a god, right?"

"Yes, I've heard about your defeat of Errilol. But I don't believe in gods."

Naomi had to admit that was a pretty good comeback. "So, what's your plan? Are you going to keep coming into my dreams to threaten me until you eat me? Don't you need regular sleep, too?"

Grisbek didn't reply.

Naomi looked out at the dream sea, then over at Tavik. She wondered if he were really beside her. She reached out and stroked the dream Tavik's head. He murmured and rolled toward her.

She turned back to Grisbek. "You might as well leave. You know where I am, and I know you can find me wherever I go, and really, what else can you possibly accomplish with this?"

Smoke rose from Grisbek's nostrils.

Naomi lay back down and turned her back to the dragon. "Go get some regular sleep," she said.

Grisbek began to growl. The sound crawled across her skin and made her shiver. "I'm getting very hungry, human."

"And what do expect me to do? Give up and let you eat me?"

"It doesn't matter what you do. I am coming and you cannot escape."

"Blah, blah, blah," Naomi replied.

Grisbek roared and fire shot across her. Even though the fire wasn't real, it frightened her so bad, she woke up. She sat up and looked around the dark beach. There was no dragon, only Tavik, softly snoring beside her. She sighed and lay back down. She closed her eyes and determinedly went back to sleep. She was half-asleep when she wiggled over to Tavik's back and snuggled into it. She thought dimly she shouldn't be doing that but was too tired to wiggle back.

The next day, the sunrise woke her. She sat up and looked blearily around. She looked to the other side of the quilt but found no husband. She turned and peered at the cottage. She thought she saw evidence of life inside it. She got up and walked unsteadily to it, brushing sand off herself as she went. She walked into the cottage to find Tavik drinking what appeared to be tea while Yula prepared breakfast.

"Morning, everyone," Naomi said, going over and slumping into the seat by Tavik. He nodded to her.

"Good morning, milady. Would you like some tea? Breakfast should be done soon. How did you sleep?"

"Not great. Grisbek showed up in a dream and threatened me some more."

"That's just awful. He shouldn't do that."

"Oh, I agree. I think he's going to talk to Torreng soon. I think he's getting impatient."

"We can ask Torreng to delay him," Agatha said, coming down the ladder from the loft. "I need to see the dragon king eventually anyway."

"Why do you need to see him?"

Agatha shrugged. "To pay my respects, politely ask about his last clutch, that sort of thing."

"Clutch?"

"A group of hatchlings. He fathered a clutch with Lilatiq."

"Oh, and how exactly do you know that?"

Agatha shrugged. "It's good to keep up with these sorts of things."

The group ate breakfast, and except for Tavik's only mild interest in their talk and lack of attentiveness to Naomi, the meal was relatively normal.

Yula begged off going to see the dragon. "I'm very happy not to make his acquaintance. Be careful, Naomi."

She nodded and looked to Tavik. Agatha saw her glance, too. "Oh, Tavik's coming with us."

Tavik stiffened slightly. "What if I don't care to make the dragon's acquaintance either?"

"Well, you already have."

"He did mention you when I met him on the beach," Naomi said.

Tavik sighed and shook his head. "Fine, I'll go, but know that I don't want to."

They set out from the cottage and traveled through the jungle. They arrived at the foot of the volcano, and Agatha led them to a narrow footpath up it. When Naomi asked her about the path, the witch said that they weren't the first or the last humans who would seek audience with the King of Dragons.

They didn't go to the top of the volcano but to a large opening on the side. A warm breeze emitted from it. They walked into a large cavern. Everything was black rock. Naomi wondered if they should have brought torches. The lava rock absorbed all of the light.

As they walked farther in, Naomi soon became aware of a glow up ahead. They walked further, and Naomi tripped over something. She stumbled and looked down. A gold goblet rolled away from her. She looked around more and saw gold coins peppering the floor.

"Whatever you do, don't pick anything up and make sure nothing leaves with you when we go," Agatha said. They rounded a bend, and the source of the glow became apparent. Only a few torches were lit, but they reflected over mounds upon mounds of gold. There were piles as tall as Naomi of gold coins. There were hundreds of gems. One pile appeared to be all crowns. Her eyes were dazzled by all the shimmering riches.

"Welcome to the hoard of the King of Dragons," Agatha said.

"It's good to be the king," Naomi murmured as she looked at a pile of rubies that were spilling out of a bag.

"It is very good to be king," Torreng said. The gold had distracted her so much that Naomi hadn't even noticed the large gold dragon sitting in the center of it. Or maybe he'd done that shifting invisibility thing. He could easily be lost within the gold. Naomi looked to Agatha for her cues. The witch gave the dragon a perfunctory bow. Naomi dropped a small curtsy.

"You appear well, Witch Agatha."

"I am. Thank you, King Torreng, and thank you for allowing my little cottage a respite on your beautiful island."

"It's the least I could do. Is this your son, Tavik? He has grown since I last saw him." Agatha glanced back at her son.

"Yes, this is my son. And you have already met his wife, Naomi."

Torreng's massive head turned slightly to acknowledge Naomi with a slight dip. "She is the one marked by Grisbek."

"Indeed. Has Grisbek contacted you yet for permission to approach the island?"

"No, and I am quite surprised he has waited this long."

"He hasn't spoken to you? I saw him last night. Well, it was in a dream," Naomi said.

Torreng nodded. "The dream realm knows no boundaries. He may come to his prey that way no matter where they may rest."

"Can he harm her in her dreams?" Tavik asked.

Naomi's eyebrows rose. She was surprised Tavik was showing an interest in her plight. Again, she didn't know if that was a good or bad thing.

Torreng shrugged his massive shoulders. "He cannot physically harm her, but fear can be a very deadly thing."

Naomi didn't like the sound of that. Agatha stepped forward. "Do you have any recommendations to block the dreams?"

Torreng dipped his head. When he raised his eyes to them again, Naomi knew he couldn't help them. "I'm sorry, if you had asked when none of you were marked, I may have given you the information, but as this information would clearly cause interference in an established hunt, I cannot answer you."

"What can you tell us about Grisbek?" Tavik asked.

Again, Naomi glanced in surprise at her husband. Torreng looked to Tavik. "He is a green dragon, which means he favors forest and fields. Green dragons love the hunt above all else. They can pursue a single prey for years."

"Is there anything green dragons do not like?" he asked.

Torreng shook his massive head, making the long spikes running down the ridge of spine sway. "Green dragons—like all dragons—have few if any weaknesses."

Agatha gave them a wry look at that.

Tavik appeared to want to ask something else, but the witch touched his arm and gave him a small shake of her head. "Thank you, Torreng, for seeing us and for your kind hospitality. We will show ourselves out."

"As you wish, Mistress Witch. You are welcome to come marvel at my hoard whenever you like."

Agatha bobbed her head and motioned for Naomi and Tavik to go. They filed out of the cave and headed back down the path on the side of the volcano. "I take it you know of a few dragon weaknesses," Naomi said once she thought they were well clear of Torreng's hearing.

Agatha grinned. "Well, greed is obviously one weakness. Show a dragon something shiny or sparkly, and they'll want it. They also have a colossal amount of pride. They will never admit that they are wrong. And they're massive. They can't squeeze into small spaces."

"I can see all of that, but how can any of that help me with my current dragon problem?"

"It'll come to us," Agatha said.

They trekked back through the jungle to the cottage. Yula had a late lunch waiting for them. Naomi began to wonder how much longer they had on Torreng's island or if they had any more time. What the King of Dragons had said about dreams had her unsettled. She suspected that eventually if she fell asleep, Grisbek could terrify her to death. He didn't have to be anywhere near her. Nowhere then was safe.

She went out with Tavik again to lie on the beach, but she couldn't enjoy the idyllic setting like the day before. She needed to take action. She needed to do something. She couldn't wait for Agatha to bail her out. And it wasn't fair to keep all of them in danger like this, because if Grisbek did finally ask permission of Torreng to hunt on his island, the king would grant it—and then they were all dragon kibble.

Tavik fell asleep in the sand, and Yula was dozing as well. Naomi got up and went into the water. She wasn't going for a swim. She wandered along among the waves. She was walking away but didn't want to appear blatant about it. She walked for a bit and veered back onto dry land. She made her way to the jungle and found her way through to the volcano. She took the path up to the cavern and went in. Torreng was napping upon his mountain of gold when she approached. She was afraid to wake him up because a cranky dragon was not something she wanted to deal with. She looked around at the treasure a bit more and marveled at all of it. She looked back at Torreng and saw one eye cracked open watching her. She turned to him and dropped a little curtsy, though she was only in her oversized T-shirt and panties.

Torreng raised his head and stared silently at her. "Can you teleport me back to the mainland like a unicorn?" she asked, going straight to the point.

The dragon blinked and stared at her a moment longer.

"I need to get back so I can deal with Grisbek without endangering everyone else. Can you send me there?"

"No, I don't believe I can. If you were riding me, I could teleport both of us, but such an action would be a clear interference with Grisbek's hunt."

Naomi frowned and stared into space, trying to think of another solution.

"You said the unicorns teleported you before?" Torreng asked.

Naomi nodded. "When Grisbek threatened me, Snowflake would appear to rescue me."

"Then I believe I may know a possible solution." Smoke began to drift out of dragon's nostrils. Naomi watched him curiously. The smoke grew thicker and blacker. It began to fill the treasure room and made Naomi cough.

"Your Highness, what are you doing?" she asked as she coughed harder.

"Is that a gold coin in your hand, Naomi? How dare you try to steal from me," he said with a deep reverberating growl. The sound went straight to her heart, and it began to pound.

She held up her empty hands and waved them to show how empty they were. "No, I didn't pick up anything. I wouldn't dare steal from you!" she shouted.

"Run," Torreng growled.

Not sure what was happening, she turned and sprinted to the mouth of the cavern. She looked over her shoulder at Torreng and saw his head lower and his huge mouth open. From between his jaws, a fire built. Naomi knew she wouldn't make it out of the lair.

As she ran, Snowflake appeared on the side of the tunnel like a water volunteer at a marathon, but instead of a paper cup, he held out his alicorn. She barely had time to think of where she wanted to go as she reached out and grazed the alicorn with her hand. She squeezed her eyes shut and pictured the Darkon Forest.

CHAPTER NINE

A dragon's breath is so foul, it burns.

When Naomi opened her yes, she looked around the dark forest in relief. She understood what Torreng had done. He must have known that if he threatened her overtly that Snowflake would appear to save her. She had to admit it was a clever idea, but she would've liked not to have gone through the quaking fear of almost being dragon barbecue. But maybe that was required. She may have to truly believe her life was in danger for the unicorn to take notice and offer her an escape. Still there had to be better ways to going about this. She'd have a talk with Snowflake.

She didn't have the benefit of night vision as before. She looked around her and wondered how she was supposed to find her way to the river without light. Everything was such a mess. Tavik, Yula, and Agatha were on the Dragon King's island. Who knew where Squibbles and Hip Hop were, and she was all alone in a dangerous forest. Naomi really knew how to get into very fine messes.

Feeling overwhelmed, she sat down on a log and wondered how exactly she was going to get out of this particular mess.

You really should avoid dragons. They are very powerful creatures.

Naomi looked up in surprise at Snowflake. "I didn't expect you to show up here. You seem to just zap me and be done with it."

The unicorn's horn glowed and gave her some light to see by. *I feel maybe you need more direct help in your current predicament.*

"I need all the help I can get. Do you know exactly what my problem is?"

A green dragon has chosen you as prey.

"That and the problem with Tavik. He's under a love spell and thinks the 'real' Lady Naomi is his true love. I'm supposed to get a bouquet of fool-me-not to counteract the spell."

I am familiar with the flower. Shall we go?

Naomi stood up from the log. There were butterflies in her stomach. "You know the way to the river? You'll lead me there?"

Snowflake nodded his head. *I will escort you to the stream. I fear that if I'm not with you, the green dragon will kill you before I have a chance to save you.*

Naomi wanted to hug the unicorn, but he pranced back at the very thought in her mind. Naomi stayed but and simply said, "Thank you. Please lead the way."

Snowflake turned and began making his way through the forest. Naomi followed in his wake.

He glowed gently, allowing her to see where they were going.

"How far is it to the river?"

Not far. We will reach it soon.

Naomi nodded. "Thank you."

Snowflake didn't respond. One thing about unicorns was they weren't chatty. They continued on in silence for another twenty minutes. Naomi's pace quickened when she heard the sound of running water. She broke through a wall of bushes and found herself on the bank of a burbling brook. She quickly began looking for the small yellow flowers. Snowflake went down to the water and dipped his horn into it.

"Do you see any fool-me-not?" Naomi asked.

Snowflake lifted his head and cast his gaze up and down the banks. *No, I do not.*

Naomi continued to root around for the flowers, but didn't see any. She had a nasty thought. "Could this be the wrong time of year for them to bloom?"

Snowflake shook his head. *No, it should be blooming. None may be on this section of river.*

"Okay, should we move up river or down to look?"

Snowflake looked up and down river and finally turned toward where the river was flowing from. *Up river is most likely where we will find the flowers.*

"Okay, lead the way."

Snowflake snorted and scraped his hoof across

the ground, but he did begin walking. Naomi realized her mistake. Unicorns didn't like orders. She'd have to be more careful with how she spoke to him. She didn't want to annoy him so much that he winked out on her and stopped protecting her from Grisbek.

They continued walking along the river. Naomi wondered what everyone else was up to. She wasn't worried about the cottage gang. Agatha, Yula, and Tavik could look after themselves. The extended absence of Mr. Squibbles was worrying, though. Yes, he had an umbrek, but it was an undersized, blind umbrek. She hoped they were all right.

There's the flower you seek.

Naomi stopped and looked to Snowflake. The unicorn dropped his head and pointed with his alicorn at the bank. She went over to him and crouched down. There nestled in the undergrowth were little yellow flowers with blue centers.

"Finally," she breathed. She reached out and plucked a flower. She brought it to her nose and sniffed it. It had a light, pleasant smell. She began searching for more. As she found another clump, Snowflake reared back and turned. She jumped up as well and turned to face whatever had spooked him.

"What is it?" she asked.

Snowflake didn't respond, and suddenly the forest became very dark. The unicorn was gone.

Why had he done that? She crouched down and tried to hear whatever it was out there. Was it Grisbek? But why would Snowflake have left her now? He'd appeared by her side whenever Grisbek had appeared before.

She clutched the single fool-me-not flower she'd plucked. She didn't know what to do. She had no weapons. She couldn't see, and she was now alone.

"Naomi!" sounded distantly.

She stood up in relief. That had been Agatha's voice. They must have flown the cottage back to the forest to look for her.

"Aga—" A hand covered her mouth, and another wrapped around her waist. She instinctively struggled, but soon realized the arms were familiar. She relaxed.

"Don't call out again," Tavik said into her ear.

She nodded, and he took his hand off her mouth and moved his hand from around her waist to her wrist. "Tavik, what's wrong?" she asked.

"What's wrong? You, Yula, and my mother kidnapped me again. That's what's wrong. I'm taking you back to the castle and putting you in the dungeon."

Naomi rolled her eyes. She held up the single fool-me-not that she'd plucked. "Smell this. It's very nice."

Now that she was facing him, she could see the silvery sheen of the night-vision potion in his eyes. He had to see the flower fine.

He took it from her, but didn't bring it to his face. "A flower is not going to fix this," he said.

"You never know. Come on, take a moment and smell it." She watched his silhouette. She couldn't see him clearly now, but she could make out general shapes and movements. Tavik shook his head and jerked her behind him as he began trudging through the forest.

"No, Tavik, just smell the flower. It's good for you!" she said as she struggled to stop him.

"We don't have time for this, Naomi. Hopefully, my men are still camped at the forest's edge. We'll ride back with them, and then I'll deal with you."

"You really expect me to just go along with your plan to put me in the dungeon? What'd you do with the flower?"

"I dropped it."

Naomi dug her heels in. "No! You need to smell it, and then the spell will be broken."

Tavik wheeled around and grabbed her by the arms. "You expect me to believe that? I'm under no spell. It's more likely that flower will put a spell on me. This has all the hallmarks of one of my mother's schemes."

"That may be, but you're under a spell. I swear it. Tavik, please believe me."

It was hard to tell in the darkness, but she thought he wavered. She didn't know how to convince him. She slipped up to him and put her arms around him. "If you insist on me going back with you, I will. But think about us and this other Lady Naomi. Really think. Why do you love her? Why did you love me?" She could feel the tears coming and moved to let him go, not wanting to become a weeping mess on his shoulder, but Tavik pulled her back. He buried his head in the crook of her neck and just breathed deeply against her. She wasn't sure what it meant but stroked his back to ease him. His hold tightened on her and became almost painful.

"Tavik?" He jerked his head up at her voice and pushed her away. He stepped back and scrubbed his face with his hands.

"We need to get going," he said and grabbed her by the arm again. He began going through the woods, and Naomi tried to keep up. She wasn't sure what that had been, but it gave her hope. If only he hadn't thrown the flower away!

Naomi followed Tavik as best she could, but without any light, she kept getting tripped up by the forest's undergrowth. She would've done a face-plant several times if not for Tavik's tight hold on her arm.

"Slow down; I can't keep up," she finally said. She'd barely managed not to sprain an ankle, but if they kept on like they were, she surely would.

"We have to hurry. If the dragon reappears, I won't be able to fend him off. I need my weapons and men."

"Snowflake will save me. He already has several times."

Tavik stopped and spun around to face her. "You would rather rely on a unicorn?"

Naomi scrunched her eyebrows together. She didn't get the question or Tavik's sudden hostile tone. "Well, he can teleport, and Grisbek hasn't really made any move to attack him. Whenever the dragon has threatened me, the unicorn has appeared and sent me away. He's watching me or something. If Grisbek shows back up, he'll help me."

"You don't think I can protect you?"

Naomi really didn't understand his questions. "You want to throw me in the dungeon. Is that your idea of protecting me?"

Tavik growled and began walking again, dragging her behind him. Naomi followed along in a bit of a daze. What was going on with him? Was the spell making him generally crazy as opposed to crazy in love?

"You know they were worried."

Naomi had been focusing on her feet and was caught off guard by Tavik's comment. She stumbled, and Tavik caught her. She said thanks, but the motion, the care, it all seemed so normal. She repeated his words back in her brain.

"Sorry to make you worry. Torreng sort of sprung that idea on me without really consulting me. And you know what? Dragons can't pretend to breathe fire. Either they do or don't, and Torreng did. I'm lucky he didn't singe my hair."

Before she knew what was happening, Tavik had her pinned to a tree. "You're lucky he didn't singe your hair?"

His closeness flustered her. "Yeah, it was a near thing."

"A dragon breathed fire at you, and you were only worried about your hair?" he ground out.

"Well, no. At the time, I didn't know what exactly was going on, so I was worried about becoming a crispy critter, but afterward, I realized he did it to help me. It got Snowflake there to teleport me back to the forest. All the good that's done me." She muttered that last part more to herself. Why'd she only pick one flower? She should've pulled the entire clump from the ground.

Tavik shook his head and let her go. "Why did you come back to this forest? There's nothing for you here."

Naomi hugged herself and nodded. "Yeah, I'm starting to feel that way, too."

"Let's go," he said and took her by the wrist again. When they reached the edge of the forest, Tavik stopped and took out a canteen. He began washing his eyes out to get rid of the night-vision formula.

For some reason, watching him do this made Naomi's chest ache. She really didn't know anymore what she could do. She'd lost the flower, the only one she'd managed to gather, and Tavik was still be-spelled. Tavik dried off his face and turned to her. He caught her staring and quirked an inquiring eyebrow in return.

"I do still love you, you know," she said. "Even though you've decided you have to marry another woman, I still love you."

Tavik's shoulders drooped, and he turned his eyes to the ground. "I-I still care for you a great deal as well."

"Tavik!"

Both of them turned, and Naomi wished she knew a few of Agatha's hexes because she would've cast all of them at what was coming toward them.

Across the meadow, Lady Crazy had her skirts hiked up and was running full tilt in their direction. Tavik dropped the canteen, grabbed Naomi's arm, and started running toward the other woman. Naomi's eyes widened as she was pulled along. Was Tavik really making her a part of his happy romantic reunion with Lady Crazy? She couldn't even slow down. Tavik was sprinting so fast; all she could do was try to keep up. They ran across the meadow toward Lady Crazy. It was like a scene out of a cheesy romantic film, except for Naomi. For her, it felt like she was in a horror film. Tavik collided with Lady Crazy and threw his free arm around her while still holding onto Naomi's wrist. Lady Crazy rained kisses onto Tavik's face. The sight made Naomi throw up a little in her mouth.

Lady Crazy finally took note of Naomi. Her

eyes widened. "Dear Calax, you're a brazen slattern," she exclaimed. She unhooked her embroidered cape and flung it at Naomi. Naomi realized she was still in only her T-shirt and panties. She caught the cloak and looked at it. She recognized it. It was actually her cloak. Lady Crazy had raided her wardrobe. Naomi flung it on. It did cover her more than her oversized T-shirt.

Tavik coughed in embarrassment. "Yes, she is quite brazen."

Naomi narrowed her eyes at him. He hadn't seemed to have any problem with her wardrobe before now.

Lady Crazy rolled her eyes and huffed. She lifted an arm off Tavik and pointed at Naomi. "Guards!"

Naomi was surprised when Tavik stepped back and pulled Naomi behind him.

Lady Crazy noticed the protective action as well. "My love?" she asked.

The guards rushed to them. They stopped short and looked back and forth between Lady Crazy and Tavik. They were unsure as to what to do. They very well couldn't attack Tavik. Naomi was wondering what her husband was thinking as well. She wished she could get him alone to talk to him more. It seemed like there were chips appearing in the love spell. Maybe it was wearing off?

Tavik shook his head as if remembering he was supposed to not like Naomi and pulled her out from behind him. "Put Taylor in one of the wagons. Make sure to tie her up well."

Naomi sighed at the loss once again of her name. "I really wish you wouldn't call me Taylor," she said.

Tavik's eyes slanted to her, but dropped them when they met hers.

Lady Crazy sniffed. "Your name is whatever we say it is."

"Tavik," Naomi pleaded again.

Lady Crazy looped her arm through Tavik's, pulling him away from her. "That's Lord Tavik to you."

With Tavik away from her, the guards stepped in and flanked Naomi.

Lady Crazy smirked and squeezed Tavik's arm. "Darling, shouldn't we gag her?" she asked.

Tavik's focus had shifted firmly back to Lady Crazy. "Yes, my dear. An excellent suggestion."

Lady Crazy mouth widened to a predatory smile. She pointed toward the nearest wagon. "Toss her in there and make sure she can't get out."

Naomi didn't try struggling. She could see it would be futile, but as the guards pulled her away, she called out, "Tavik, is this really what you want?"

He turned to look at Naomi, but Lady Crazy placed a hand on his cheek and turned his face back to her. Naomi was too far away to hear whatever she said to him, but whatever it was, he simply nodded and drew Lady Crazy closer. Naomi's chest clenched at the sight. She turned away to save herself more pain.

The guards took her over to the wagon and proceeded to tie her ankles and wrists. They finished up by gagging her. She was hauled into the wagon and left there while a guard stayed outside to keep watch.

She lay in the wagon and wiggled her arms and legs to see if there was a possibility of slipping her bonds. She hadn't managed to get them to leave much slack in the ropes. The guards were Lady Crazy's, not castle guards. They held no allegiance to her, so there was no possibility of them looking the other way while she snuck out. She wiggled more to try to force the ropes to give. She wasn't getting anywhere very quickly.

"Well, this is a fine pickle," said Mr. Squibbles.

"Mmffer mffiffles!" Naomi exclaimed.

"Hello, Naomi. It's good to see you, too. Well, maybe not good, considering the circumstances, but maybe we can make them better."

"Mffefe mf Mffamfa?"

"Agatha and Yula are in the woods. There are too many men for them to sneak in."

"Mfaf mffof mf mf?"

"You can lie there while I'll try to get the ropes undone, but you know they're really thick."

"Mfmf. Mfefef mfef mfef?"

"Hip Hop's hiding out. No point getting everyone freaked out by a blind umbrek."

"Mfefef mfef mfaf?"

"I don't think that's a good idea. If I remove the gag and the guard sees it's gone, it'll give us away for sure."

"Mfef."

"I'll just get to work on these ropes."

Squibbles started on her wrist bindings and gnawed on them. Naomi lay like a statue to not bother him. She didn't know how long this would take. She was afraid it would take decades. Maybe she'd get free by Tavik and Lady Crazy's tenth anniversary. She could get them a gift.

"It's no good, Naomi. I can't get this rope to break at all, and I think I'm allergic to it. My tongue's swelling."

"Mff mfmf?"

"Jus' si' 'igh'. I'll see wha' else I can do."

"Mf! Mf mf!"

"Is'll be 'ine, Naomi. Don' worry."

Mr. Squibbles left the wagon, and Naomi slumped. She just seemed to be accumulating problems and not solving any. Where was Snowflake? At least Grisbek wasn't there. She wiggled around in the wagon, trying to find anything to help her, but of course, they'd put her in an empty wagon. Had they brought it just for her? She rolled around and tried to at least get to her feet.

The canvas flap was pulled back, and the guard looked in on her. "What the hell are you do—" He suddenly flew out of view. There was a distant crash. Naomi fell back and started scrambling as best she could to the front of the wagon.

A large purple eye peered into the wagon. "Hello, my dear. You have certainly made it very easy for me. But you didn't quite finish the full motif. You're supposed to be chained to a stake in a clearing."

"Mf-mff." No one outside was screaming or running. Was Grisbek cloaked? Or had they abandoned her? She fell into the front of the wagon and quickly fell out of it. She tumbled to the ground and struggled onto her knees. Several nearby guards saw her and quickly began approaching to recapture her. She looked to the back of the wagon. Grisbek was still there. He was three times the size of the wagon, but no one was paying any attention to him. She tried to tell them, but being still gagged, she wasn't very understandable.

"Taylor, you need to give it up. You're not getting away," one guard said.

She shook her head and tried to point at the dragon, but again, with hands tied behind her back, all she could point with was her head, and as she tried to do that, the guards didn't seem to understand what her flinging hair meant.

The guards flanked her and grabbed her by the arms.

"Back into the wagon, Taylor."

"Why do they call you Taylor?" Grisbek asked.

The guards hauled her to the back of the

wagon. "Where'd Sam go?" one guard asked the other, standing in the shadow of the dragon.

"Probably had to piss. He has the bladder of a rabbit."

Naomi tried again to alert the guards of the dragon that was standing on the other side of the wagon. "Mfffmfff! Mffaffmf!"

"What's she saying?"

"Probably cursing us. Just put her back in the wagon."

The dragon shook his head. "I can't understand a thing you're trying to say. Take that stupid gag off."

If looks could kill, Naomi would have slain the dragon right then. If looks could kill, she would've done that a long time ago to quite a few people, but at the moment, if looks could kill, Grisbek would have been a former dragon.

"Well, make them take the gag off. Aren't you their lady?"

Naomi looked back and forth between the guards. They weren't hearing any of this? They didn't sense the big green talking dragon? The guards put her back in the wagon.

"I guess we should stay until Sam gets back."

Naomi shook her head and again tried to point out the big damn evil-looking green dragon that was standing right behind them. The guards didn't pay any attention to her.

"Your unicorn hasn't appeared. I guess he grew weary of saving you."

The dragon was right. Snowflake had always appeared within moments of Grisbek's arrival. She didn't want to think about what Snowflake's absence meant. He'd been her only hope against Grisbek. She hunched over in the wagon and hoped Snowflake was just running late.

"Now I wonder if I should roast you or eat you raw. I don't like the taste of hair, but I don't want to burn off what little meat you have. If there was a pond nearby, I could put you in that and boil you. But we'll just have to work with what we have."

Naomi glowered out of the back at the wagon at dragon, who was cheerfully contemplating her death.

"Mfumf mfou," she said.

"I don't know what you said, but I don't think it was very ladylike," the dragon chided.

The guards paid no attention to her.

"Smf."

"I would rather not deal with all these men. I'm not that hungry. Can't you send them away?"

"Mff, mf mfaff."

"Oh, will you take that gag off already?" Grisbek said in irritation.

Naomi kicked her heels and cursed everyone and everything in all her muffled glory.

"She's a feisty one," one guard commented to the other.

"Yeah, can't believe Lord Tavik married her."

"Mmmf."

"I guess I could burn them," Grisbek said thoughtfully. "I'd have to shift into view, but either way, they have to go."

Naomi shook her head desperately. "Mf! Mfou mfif mfumf mfafmfmf!"

Grisbek sighed. "It will draw the others though."

Naomi rolled her eyes.

"What are you men doing here?"

Naomi stiffened.

"Guarding the prisoner, milord. Like you ordered."

"But two of you?"

"Sir, she's already gotten out of the wagon once."

Tavik chuckled. "And it hasn't even been an hour yet. Well, you can both go tend to other duties. I want to have a word with the prisoner."

"Oh, yes, sir. Of course."

Naomi tried to slide back to the front of the wagon again as Tavik climbed in. "Mff-mf-mf-mf?"

Behind him, a large scaly head dipped down to look into the wagon and at her. "He's your husband, correct? The one you killed a god for? And he's holding you captive?"

"Mf-ffou."

"What was that, Taylor?" Tavik asked sharply.

She shook her head. "Mf mfou."

Where the hell was Snowflake? Why hadn't he swooped in to whisk her away? Had she irritated

182

him enough to abandon her? Why not? She was doomed. She was going to die, and no one cared. She hated herself at the moment and hated the tears that began leaking out of her eyes even more.

"What's wrong, Taylor?" Tavik asked.

What was wrong? He was so damn lucky she was tied up or she'd slap him. She turned her face away from him and tried to stop her tears with willpower alone. Tavik sat down beside her and turned her to face him again. What did he want now? Did he think it'd be fun to gloat? Did he want to finally find out about the joys of divorce?

He reached up and wiped her tears away and slipped the gag from her mouth. "What do you want?" she asked.

"I want to know what my mother is doing."

"How should I know? You saw her last."

"She will try to rescue you. We can't keep doing this. I will marry Lady Naomi."

"So I shouldn't escape if she gives me the chance?"

"Why draw this out any further?" he asked. And there was a weariness in his voice that hadn't been there before.

She stared at him. Her heart had been strong through all of this. No cracks. No doubt. She loved him, and he loved her. There'd been no question that she would fix this and all would be well again, but looking at him now with his shoulders slumped, the first shadow of doubt nestled in her chest. "Tavik?"

"It's not good anymore, Naomi. We can't make each other happy. We want different things."

"No, goddammit. It's the spell! That woman gave you a love potion, and it's made you see her the way you used to see me. You still care about me. You can't deny that, and if your mind wasn't clouded by the love potion, you wouldn't be doing any of this."

Tavik pressed his lips together and shook his head. "You aren't happy with me."

Naomi wished her hands were free so she could touch him. Hold him. "I'm very happy with you, Tavik. We'll get through this."

Tavik shook his head again. "You're not happy."

Her knee-jerk reaction to his statement would have been to say that of course she wasn't happy. He had her tied up and was planning to marry another woman, but that little shadow of doubt that had entered her heart suggested that maybe Tavik was messing up his pronouns. It wasn't that she wasn't happy with him; it was that he wasn't happy with her. He didn't seem to care that he was under a spell. Even if she had gotten him to sniff some fool-me-not, he very well would still marry Lady Crazy. She shuddered and clenched her jaw to stop the sob that wanted to escape. She didn't have time to weep. There was a dragon still outside.

Tavik wiped the fresh tears that leaked out of

her eyes. "He's back," she murmured.

"Naomi, I wouldn't tell him if I were you. I'm willing to wait to watch how this plays out, but if they become aware of me, I will kill them all."

"What did you say?" Tavik asked, moving his head closer to hers.

She looked into his eyes. She still couldn't accept the idea that they were over, that he loved another woman. She leaned in and kissed him. It felt so natural, though she knew he wouldn't like it, but Tavik didn't immediately jerk away. He stayed still, and he pursed his lips and gave her a small kiss back. She opened her mouth to deepen the kiss, but he leaned back and pushed her gently away.

She wished he'd never left the castle. Then Lady Crazy would never have gotten her hooks into him, and Naomi wouldn't have ended up with a stalker dragon, and maybe things would be a little simpler. Heck, she might even be pregnant by now.

Tavik stood and wouldn't look at her. "I need to get back to Naomi."

Naomi turned away. Tavik hopped down from the wagon. He called back the pair of guards. Grisbek still lingered outside.

At least, Tavik hadn't replaced the gag. Suddenly there was a lot of whinnying and hoof stomping from outside. "Hmm, good. The wind changed," Grisbek said.

CHAPTER TEN

A nest of baby dragons is called a clutch.

The horses sounded like they were going crazy, but then again, they were getting a strong whiff of dragon. It would freak anyone out. They weren't settling no matter what their handlers did. She heard shouts and figured some horses had broken loose and were galloping away. She wished she was on one of them. She wondered how Stomper was doing. She hoped someone was giving him his daily allotment of apples and carrots. Geoffrey had constantly complained that she was spoiling the easygoing draft horse, but she'd seen no harm in it, and the way the big black horse would perk up when she came by had given her delight. Lady Crazy wouldn't do that. She wouldn't take time out every day to spoil a big draft horse.

Because of the commotion with the horses, one of her guards was called to help calm the remaining steeds. Naomi wasn't sure how far the departing guard got before Grisbek sent the remaining one flying. All she saw from the wagon was the dragon's massive body, and then she heard a muffled, startled oath from the guard, who retreated at high speed. She hoped the two guards weren't killed. With the second guard gone, Naomi was alone with Grisbek. Her stomach lurched. Screaming for help would do her no good. Only she and the horses knew Grisbek was there. He stuck his snout into the wagon. Naomi tried to squirm back instinctively, but his jaws closed around her feet. She froze. Her ankles disappeared between his massive green jaws. She feared that she no longer had feet, except she could still wiggle her toes, and she wasn't in massive, life-threatening pain. Grisbek delicately sawed his jaws and let go. The ropes binding her feet were in tatters. But her feet were still there. She didn't have a single scratch.

"Jump out, Naomi."

"Why the hell would I do that?"

Grisbek snorted and filled the wagon with thick, black smoke. Naomi coughed uncontrollably. She had to jump out to breathe again. Once she scrambled out of the wagon, she gasped for fresh air. When her coughing subsided, she looked up at the dragon. He hadn't immediately lunged, but he did lick his fangs. They were alone, no one was near to help her. Naomi began to shake. It was dinnertime.

"I've decided on flambé. Your fingers and toes will burn away, but also all of your hair and clothing, so I won't have to cough it up later."

"I hope I give you indigestion," Naomi said. Her false bravado was ruined by a tiny whimper.

Lady Naomi, you are needed.

"NO, NO, NO! Stop interfering!" Grisbek shouted.

A unicorn had appeared at Naomi's side, but it wasn't Snowflake. She was still relieved though. She vaguely recognized the unicorn from when the blessing came to tell her how to kill Errilol. This unicorn had been at the front and had seemed to be in charge.

The unicorn dipped his alicorn to Grisbek.

I am sorry, he told the dragon.

"You can't save her forever," Grisbek said.

Without comment, the unicorn turned and tapped Naomi with his horn, teleporting her away.

When Naomi opened her eyes, she found herself beside a small, burbling spring in a small clearing, surrounded by tall trees that were old and thick. Everything seemed vibrant and had an inner glow to it. There was a quiet hum in the air as well. Magic imbued everything here.

The unicorn that wasn't Snowflake stood before her. All unicorns looked basically the same. They were all white with golden horns. She'd asked Snowflake once if there were different unicorns like black or palomino ones. He'd answered no and hadn't elaborated. She'd gotten the impression that he wasn't allowed to tell her more. So though this unicorn was white with a golden horn, she knew he wasn't Snowflake because his face was longer, and his mane was very straight whereas Snowflake's had a touch of wave to it. She also got the impression that this unicorn was important like a leader or elder among the magical beasts.

Do you know why you are here? The unicorn asked.

"Is it because Grisbek was going to eat me?"

The unicorn shook his head. *No, you are here because the one you call Snowflake is trying to start a war.*

The statement alarmed Naomi. "What do you mean?"

By helping you, he will put us at war with the dragons.

"You mean by rescuing me and sending me back and forth to Earth?"

The unicorn shook his head. *No, by removing the dragon's mark.*

Naomi's jaw dropped and her heart lifted. "He can remove it?"

The elder's eyes bore into hers. She realized her happiness was not appreciated. *By interfering with a dragon's hunt, he threatens to break magical law.*

"And that'll put you at war with them?"

Yes.

Knowing many unicorns were murdered by Errilol's priests because they had helped her, her gut twisted at the thought of any more dying because of her. Naomi shook her head, "I don't want you to go war because of me."

Then stop him.

"How?"

Tell him to let you die. The request was so simple that Naomi at first wanted simply to nod, but then the full impact hit her. Her chest constricted, and she stared at the elder unicorn wordlessly. He simply turned his head. *He is through there.*

When Naomi turned in the same direction, there was an opening in the trees that hadn't been there before. Snowflake stood at the center of a small clearing. His horn blazed blindingly.

Naomi entered the clearing, but the light of Snowflake's alicorn hurt her eyes. She held a hand up to shield them. "Snowflake, stop whatever you're doing. We'll figure something else out."

No, this is the only way. Snowflake's words skittered through her mind like dead leaves. They made her wince.

"Just stop for a moment. Let's talk about this."

No, if I don't do this, you will die. It's the only way.

You are bringing shame to the unicorns. By choosing another to die in her place, you are attempting to play god.

"Wait. What are you talking about?" Naomi asked, looking back and forth between the unicorns.

Snowflake didn't answer. He continued to

stand still with his alicorn blazing so brightly, it caused tears to run down Naomi's face. Naomi turned to the elder unicorn.

He is attempting to transfer the dragon's mark.

"Transfer?" Naomi repeated.

The elder explained. *The mark cannot be destroyed. He is trying to transfer the mark from you to the other Naomi.*

Naomi blinked. She was ashamed to admit it, but a little part of her liked the idea and wanted to cheer Snowflake on. She knew it was wrong. That while Lady Crazy had done wrong to her, that did not give her the right to do wrong to Lady Crazy. If Snowflake succeeded, Grisbek wouldn't just kill Lady Crazy; he would eat her. Dead was dead, but eaten just seemed worse.

It is an evil act, but I will do it. Snowflake was resolved. Nothing she or the elder could say would change his mind. Peering past the brightness, Naomi looked into his clear blue eyes. A wave of determination and love washed over her. She'd never known how much he cared for her. He'd always seemed so aloof.

"But how is it even supposed to work?" she asked him.

When I transfer the mark, Grisbek cannot know that it is on a new target.

"But he's met me. He'll notice that the mark is on someone else."

He won't if he doesn't remember you.

"How can he forget me?"

If I erase you from his memory and substitute the other Naomi, he will be fooled, but the spell is easily broken. If he sees you again, then the memories will come crashing back, as will the mark.

"So Grisbek forgets me and all's well?"

She got the distinct impression of scorn from the elder unicorn. *He will hunt the other Lady Naomi, and you both know it is not fair that this hardship should be placed upon her.*

Naomi was properly cowed by this reminder. "So Snowflake does this spell. How does that put you at war with the dragons? It sounds like Grisbek won't know anything has happened. He'll forget me, and I'll make sure to never cross paths with him again."

You think it so simple? Whatever opinion the elder may have held of Naomi, she suspected that it just kept dropping precipitously.

Snowflake shook his ponderous head. *Naomi, it isn't only Grisbek who must forget.* A wave of sadness and remorse washed over her from him. He was supposed to shepherd her, protect her, and he had failed.

"Shh, it's not your fault." She looked to the other unicorn. "What does he mean?"

For the mark to be fully transferred, Grisbek cannot be the only one who forgets. We shall have to forget you, as well, and everyone who knows you on Terratu must be made to forget. The deeds you accomplished will become the work of another. Your friends will no longer know you. Their lives will no longer be what they were. Once this spell is completed, it will be as if you had never come to Terratu.

"But how am I supposed to live?" Naomi asked in alarm.

You will return to your home world. You will remain there and live out the rest of your life. Snowflake explained.

"But what about my life here?"

The elder stepped forward. *Exactly. You are taking this woman's life from her. You may not like how her life has gone, but it is her life. You have no right to interfere with her fate. We owe her nothing.*

Naomi didn't know who to side with anymore. She didn't want to leave Terratu, but if she kept the dragon's mark, she would surely die.

The elder unicorn stamped his hoof. It shook the ground. Naomi jumped and moved in front of Snowflake protectively.

You would have us go to war?

"I'm sure we can talk this out. Torreng seems reasonable. I'm sure he would understand."

Torreng may not care, but the other dragons will. Interference with a dragon's mark is unprecedented. If they learned unicorns could transfer their marks, they would clamor for our blood. They would view us as threats. And we have already lost too many in service to you, human.

Naomi swallowed painfully. He was right. The unicorns had already helped her so much, and it had cost them dearly. She couldn't be the cause for any more of them dying.

Snowflake would not be dissuaded. *If the spell is a success, the dragons will never know.*

They will know! The spell is doomed to failure.

The elder was so emphatic that Naomi believed him. "Stop the spell, Snowflake."

No, I will not let you die.

But the spell will not work! The elder unicorn's exclamation made Naomi wince. She watched worriedly as the elder unicorn's alicorn began to glow brighter.

"What does he mean?" Naomi asked Snowflake.

Snowflake wouldn't meet her gaze. *He thinks Tavik will be immune to the spell.*

"Why Tavik?"

True love. His answer was tinged with guilt. She understood why.

Are you Tavik's true love? The elder demanded.

Naomi didn't know how to answer.

The spell will work. Snowflake's declaration made tears sting Naomi's eyes.

"He's under a spell, that's all."

The elder's eyes flared. *If you do this, you will be banished. No unicorn will know you. You will be alone.*

I know, and I accept.

Naomi put up her hands. "Wait, banished? Snowflake, stop. Please, you don't have to do this. I'll figure something else out."

Neither unicorn acknowledged her.

Very well. You are outcast. You are stranger. You are no brother of mine.

The elder's alicorn flared brighter than Snowflake's, but only for a moment. When the light faded, the elder was gone. Naomi blinked to clear her vision, but it was screwed up. She was seeing things in negative. Or rather just Snowflake.

She understood now why Snowflake hadn't wanted to tell her about nonwhite unicorns because he was now a black unicorn.

"Oh, Snowflake," she said, her hand covering her mouth.

Her juvenile name no longer fit him. It would be cruel to call him Snowflake now. From pearly white, his coat was now a glossy black. His tranquil blue eyes were switched to fiery orange. He was still beautiful, but while the old coloration had instilled peace and trust, the opposites inspired suspicion and anxiety. She reached out and touched his cheek. Though it was now black, it felt the same. He was still her friend. Snowflake leaned into the touch. His orange eyes briefly closing in pleasure.

I will transport you home and then complete the spell.

"Will you help the other Lady Naomi?" she asked. The reality of Grisbek going after Lady Crazy and chomping her was beginning to sink in. It was a terrible thing to do to a person. She wouldn't have survived without Snowflake.

No, once the spell is done, I won't be able to help her. But do not fear, Naomi. She will have protection.

Naomi didn't know what Snowflake meant but

did not question him. Unicorns could not lie. "Thank you for everything you've done for me."

Unicorns do not regret.

She held out her hand. "I'm ready when you are."

Snowflake dipped his horn and touched her finger. With a small flick, they were in the backyard of her parent's home. It was the middle of the night. Her parents' home and the houses around it were all dark and quiet. Snowflake swayed on his hooves, and the glow of his horn faded in and out. *I am sorry, Lady Naomi. I want you to know that. If there had been another way, I would have done it.*

"I know, Snowflake. You should go now. You have to forget me, too."

No, I won't forget you.

Snowflake's head dropped, and he slowly got down onto his knees. Naomi hovered over him, feeling helpless. "Snowflake? What are you doing?"

It is time to complete the spell, but I need your help.

"Anything. You don't have to ask," she said.

But I do need to apologize.

"You have nothing to be sorry for. This is my fault, not yours. You've helped me so much, saved my life multiple times, and I will forever be grateful."

Please accept my apology, Naomi. I give it now because I won't be here to extend it after.

"Snowflake, what are you planning?"

His eyes flared, and while she felt traitorous for feeling it, suspicion and unease had her drawing back or at least trying to. She couldn't move her feet. She was frozen in place.

"Snowflake, what are you doing?"

Take my alicorn, Lady Naomi.

"What?!" Naomi strained to move away, to run from Snowflake, but she couldn't move a muscle. She didn't have control of her body, but Snowflake did. Like a marionette puppet, her knees collapsed from under her and she found herself eye level with Snowflake. Her hands rose up and circled the base of the alicorn. She tried to fight it, but she couldn't even cause her fingers to twitch from around Snowflake's alicorn.

"No, Snowflake, don't do this! I beg you, please!"

The spell will be done when the alicorn is snapped off. It was a pleasure knowing you, Naomi. I will dream of you when I am among the stars.

"No, Snowflake!"

Her grip tightened on the alicorn, and her arm strained. She couldn't stop herself. She was powerless. The alicorn's glow turned blinding, and then there was a crack like lightning, and she went flying through the air.

She skidded across the grass, rolling over and over, not stopping until she hit the back fence. She pushed herself upright with a groan. Lights were coming on in the house. Her father's voice rang out from the backdoor. "Who's out there?

I'm calling the police!"

Naomi tried to get up, but her knees were weak. Her hand still clutched the alicorn. She wanted to let it go. She wanted to throw it from her, but as if Snowflake's will still controlled her body, she couldn't let it go. "Dad?" she called. A flashlight beam touched her face. She blinked and held up her empty hand to block the light. The beam dropped.

"Naomi? What are you doing back here?"

She managed to get up. She turned her eyes to where Snowflake had been, dreading the sight of his corpse, but nothing was there. The only indication that there had been a unicorn was the grass pressed down in a large circle and the alicorn in her hand.

Naomi's father had come off the back patio and was in front of her. "Naomi, are you all right?" He shined the light up and down her.

"No, Dad. I'm not all right," she said.

CHAPTER ELEVEN

Dragons can live for hundreds of years.

Naomi didn't have to really lie to her parents. She told them that Tavik and she had split. When they asked why, she said he'd fallen in love with another woman. Again, none of it was lie. Her father's face had grown very dark, and he began muttering that he'd still like to meet Tavik. Five minutes alone in a room with him was all he needed. Naomi's mother couldn't stop hugging her and stroking her hair.

She'd told them that she'd tried to enter the house quietly so as not to wake them but got turned around in the dark. She asked if she could stay with them. They said of course. She had to break down and say that she didn't have anything but the clothes on her back. She kept the cloak closed so they wouldn't see how little she was wearing. She felt so ashamed. Her mother told her not to worry about it. They would go to Wal-Mart the next day and pick up everything she needed.

She'd gone up to her childhood bedroom and

lay down. She stared up at the ceiling with its glow-in-the-dark stars and let the tears slide. She hugged the alicorn to herself and wondered what there was for her to do now. As she slept, she dreamed of strong arms circling her.

The next morning, she showered and dressed in some clothes borrowed from her mother. She'd figured out that it had been only a day since she'd left. Her previous oddness was understandable to them now. Her parents thought she'd been putting on a brave front. Bobby had explained that she'd insisted on staying with him because she hadn't had anywhere else to go. They didn't know where she'd been all day and had gotten worried. She'd again told the truth that she'd been trying to talk to Tavik and convince him that they could work it out. And of course, they hadn't worked it out.

She'd gone to Wal-Mart with her mother and picked up new clothes. Being in the big box store had been surreal. The florescent lights had given her a headache, and the feel of the synthetic fabrics had felt so strange to her. They'd gone grocery shopping as well. The produce section had really thrown her. She'd gotten used to market day at the castle. She'd often gone with Yula and helped her friend make the purchases. She wondered what her friend would have said if she could see the huge swath of vegetables and fruits from all over the world. More produce there than on five market days. Her friend probably would've fainted.

But her friend would never see it, and she would never see her again. When the alicorn had broken from Snowflake, the spell had been cast. No one on Terratu knew her anymore.

They went back to the house, and Naomi helped her mother bring everything inside. They found Bobby waiting for them.

"Sis! Are you all right?"

She set the bags of groceries on the counter and nodded. "Yeah, I'm doing better. Sorry for disappearing on you other night. I had a lot on my mind."

Bobby's face darkened, and he motioned for her to follow him into the hall. Barbara waved at her to go. "I can finish the rest."

She followed Bobby up to his old room. "Bobby, I'm sorry. I didn't mean to freak you out."

He closed the door and grabbed her. "What happened the other night? I heard something talking to you. It was threatening you. I heard it. Then I get into the room, and you're gone! What the hell is going on, sis?"

Wow, so much had happened since that night. She hugged her brother. "Don't worry, everything's okay now."

"Are you going to tell me this was more unicorns and dragons stuff?"

Naomi smiled. "No more unicorns and dragons. The fantasy's over."

Bobby shook his head. "Are you really all right?"

"I'm safe. Don't worry."

"So you're staying here now?"

Naomi nodded. "Cat's out of the bag. I got nowhere else to go."

Bobby shuffled his feet. "Hey, if you want any of your stuff back like your car, you can have it."

She smiled and ruffled her brother's hair. He scowled and jerked back. "Don't worry, little brother. You can keep the car. Maybe I'll just borrow it once in a while, but I want you to keep it."

His shoulders relaxed. She could tell he really hadn't wanted to give up the car or the apartment. "What are you going to do now?" he asked.

She didn't know. She said the first thing that occurred to her. "Maybe I'll go back to school."

Bobby's eyebrows rose. "Really? I guess that could be a good idea. What will you study?"

"Don't know. Maybe computers, maybe nursing. I can't stand the thought of going back to the bank."

He nodded. "Well, if you need any help studying, let me know."

She smiled. "Same for you," she said and ruffled his hair again. He scowled and ducked away. "Let's see if Mom needs any help putting stuff away," she said.

They went back into the kitchen, and Naomi thought about what she'd told Bobby. The idea of going back to school had been something she'd come up with on the fly, but it might be a good idea. She needed a change in her life. She couldn't go back to what she had. She tried to stop the next thought, but it formed anyway. She couldn't go back to what she had because she had nothing.

No one remembered her. Not Agatha, not Yula, not Mr. Squibbles, not Tavik. She realized that she hadn't gotten a divorce. She'd gotten an annulment. She'd effectively never been married. Tears sprang to her eyes, and she willed them away, but she didn't seem to have any control.

Her mother slid a bag of cans toward her. "Honey, can you put these away?"

She surreptitiously wiped her tears away. She needed to pull it together. What could she say if her mother asked why she was crying? She took a deep breath and exhaled through her nose. She opened the cabinet and began stacking the cans inside. She'd get through this. Everything would be okay. She'd rebuild her life.

By the time dinner was ready, Naomi had a pounding headache. Trying to keep up a cheerful front for her parents and brother was wearing her out. She just wanted to go up to her room and hide underneath the covers. She didn't have any appetite and could only push around her food.

As Bobby was telling his parents about an anthropology assignment, she got up from the table. "I'm sorry, but I'm not feeling very well. I'm going to lie down."

"Of course, sweetheart. Do you want me to

bring you any medicine?" her mother asked.

Naomi shook her head. "I'll take something when I go upstairs. Thanks."

She left the table and went up to her room. She didn't bother with the aspirin. She crawled underneath the covers and willed herself to sleep, but she wasn't sleepy in the slightest. All that was left to her was thinking, and she didn't want to think. She didn't want to wonder what everyone in Terratu was doing. She didn't want to wonder if any of them noticed anything as odd. She didn't want to wonder how Lady Crazy was handling the dragon's mark or what Tavik might be doing for her. The elder had told her that Lady Crazy would be given her story. Everything Naomi had done would be done by Lady Crazy, with only minor changes enacted. Her mind toyed with what those changes might be. Had Tavik captured Lady Naomi at the beginning, and had she'd slipped him the love potion then? Had Lady Crazy faced down Errilol in her birthday suit, too? The unicorns had described the spell as not changing the past. Things that had happened, like Errilol's defeat, remained the same, but everyone's memories had to be altered to make sense of what had happened. Since she couldn't be remembered, Lady Crazy had to step into her role.

She wondered how other things were explained, like her kidnapping of Tavik. Lady Crazy wouldn't have needed a unicorn. Maybe she'd still kidnapped him, but to convince him to let Harold's Pass go or to spare the people? But if she'd used the love potion, then Tavik would've agreed to all that without the need for kidnapping. Maybe that whole incident had been forgotten. She sort of hoped it was. She'd rather the whole thing be forgotten than Lady Crazy be remembered in her place as she fell in love with Tavik.

She shook her head. She needed to stop wondering about it. It didn't do her any good. She couldn't know. She was out of their lives now.

There was a tap on the door. She dug her way out from underneath the covers. "What?" she called.

Her brother opened the door. He grinned. "Love the new look."

She raised her hand, and her hair crackled with static electricity. She smoothed it down. "What?" she asked again.

"All your talk about unicorns and dragons got me thinking. Where do you think Grandpa picked up that unicorn horn?"

"At flea market or something?"

"Yeah, but if it was real, and I'm still thinking you need your head checked for suggesting this, but if it was real, what's the likelihood he'd find a real unicorn horn at a flea market?"

"Dumb luck?"

"That's a lot of dumb and a lot of luck."

Naomi scowled and pushed the covers away. "What are you suggesting then?"

Bobby shrugged. "I don't know, but Mom

saved a lot of his old stuff, like his journals and whatnot. Maybe he mentions it in one of them?"

Naomi frowned. "Don't you think that would be kind of gross? I mean reading Grandpa's private journals?"

Bobby laughed. "What do you think you're going to find? Grandpa's private sex journals or something?"

Naomi shuddered. "Don't say Grandpa and sex in the same breath."

"Like you just did?"

Naomi shuddered again.

"It might be a good thing to check out, though. It'll give you something to do at least."

Naomi had to concede that it would be something to do. Without a car, a job, or money of her own, she didn't really have much on her plate. "Fine, I'll look in the attic and see what I can find."

"Cool. You can tell me all about it."

Naomi's eyes narrowed. "You don't have a genealogy project or something due, do you?"

Bobby looked far too affronted when he replied. "What? Me? Nooo. I'm just looking out for you, sis, but if you could take notes on what you read, I can look them over."

"Uh-huh, you're a sweetheart, bro. A real sweetheart."

"Like I said, just looking out for you, sis. You know me."

Naomi couldn't help grinning. "I'll look tomorrow and see what I can find. Just remember this when I need help with quadratic formulas."

"No problem. Quadratic formulas and I are like this." He held up a pair of crossed fingers. Naomi groaned and tossed a throw pillow at him.

Bobby let himself out of her room, and Naomi flopped back onto her bed. Helping Bobby out with his studies would be something to do, and he might be onto something. Where had Grandpa gotten that alicorn? It wasn't something someone would just stumble across. Not a real alicorn at least.

She still had a real alicorn. It was tucked underneath her bed. She didn't know what else to do with it. It had been Snowflake's dying gift to her. She had to honor his sacrifice in some way. She wondered what had happened to the case the other alicorn had been in.

She drifted off to sleep in a better mood. Family really was a good antidote to most of a person's ills. She was grateful that she still had them, though she wished she still had her other family as well.

She dreamt that night of Tavik. He was holding her. Kissing her. They were in their bed. The bedcurtains were drawn. When it was like that, she'd always felt like they were in their own little world, the safest, best little world. She was underneath him, and he was laying kisses down her neck. She was running her hands over him, glorying in all of his muscles. They rippled so amazingly under her hands. Everything was perfect in their little oasis of darkness. His hands were on her hips, kneading them as he laid down kisses between her breasts. He seemed to be on his way to bypassing them.

"Hey, buddy, what's the rush?" she chuckled and pulled on him to come back up.

"Naomi?" he asked.

"Come on, Tavik. You know I like it when you show my breasts some loving. No need to rush by them."

"Naomi?" he asked again.

"Uh, yeah, are you expecting someone else, handsome?"

He grabbed her wrists and pinned them to the bed. He rose up over her. "Who are you?" he asked harshly.

"Your wife, idiot." She arched up to kiss him. He turned his head and wouldn't let her meet his lips.

"You're not my wife. You're not Naomi."

"Yes, I am. What's wrong with you?" She tried to break his hold on her wrists.

"Stop your outrageous lying. Who are you?"

Naomi blew out a frustrated breath. "It's me, Tavik."

Tavik growled and pulled back the bed-curtain. He grabbed the candle that was burning there. "Who are you?" he demanded again as he swung around with the candle.

She sat up and opened her eyes. "I'm Naomi,

your wife," she said to her childhood bedroom. "Oh for Pete's sake, that was just cruel," she told the array of stuffed animals on the shelf beside her and collapsed back. It was morning. The room was bright with sunlight. She wasn't going to be able to get back to sleep or return to her dream. She got up and stretched. She could smell the lovely scent of coffee from the kitchen. She shuffled down the stairs, silently telling her subconscious that she should at least be able to dream about Tavik in peace. The spell hadn't affected her as well. She should be allowed to dream about the man she loved without him getting angry and accusatory. What would she dream about next? Maybe they could talk about babies and how she was so awful for not already popping out three of them. If Grisbek had really wanted to get to her in her dreams, all he had to bring up was motherhood. She probably would've chained herself to a stake to make him stop.

Naomi's mother was in the kitchen when she came in. "Sleep well, darling?"

She grunted and made a beeline for the coffee and poured out a cup with anticipation. She hadn't had any proper caffeine in ages. As she took her first sip, she almost sputtered as she remembered something else. Something marvelous. Something that might make being banished back to her parent's house worthwhile. Chocolate! Okay, maybe chocolate didn't make up for her failed marriage and banishment, but copious amounts would surely dull the pain.

"Chocolate!"

Her mother laughed. "No, that's coffee."

"No, I mean I haven't had chocolate in a long time. Is there any?"

Her mother gave her a bemused look and reached into a cabinet. She pulled out a chocolate bar and handed it over. Naomi ripped it open and took a huge bite. She moaned as it hit her taste buds.

"Ooh, this is good. I should've dreamed about this last night instead of Tavik," she said.

Barbara's eyes softened. "Oh, was it a good dream?"

"Not really. He didn't know who I was."

Barbara gave her a half hug and moved past her. "I have my volunteering job today. Will you be all right here by yourself?"

Naomi held up her coffee and chocolate bar. "Yeah, I'll be fine. Got everything I need. Would it be all right if I looked through Grandpa's stuff in the attic? I promised Bobby I'd help him with a project."

Barbara nodded. "Sure. It's a little messy up there, though."

Naomi shrugged. "Not a big deal. Maybe I can clean it up some."

Her mother's eyebrows rose. "Maybe you need to finish that coffee and have another. You're obviously not fully awake. You just volunteered to clean the attic."

Naomi smiled, but she could feel it was wilted a little on the edges. "Yeah, but it's not like I have anything better to do."

Barbara shook her head. "Don't do that. You need a little time. That's all. Bobby told me about your idea to go back to school. I think it sounds like a good idea."

"Yeah, but it's just an idea. I don't even know what I want to study."

Barbara sighed while shaking her head again. "You need time. That's all. Let yourself deal with what's happened before plunging into the next thing. The end of a marriage is a very hard time for anyone."

Naomi wished she could let loose the bitterness that rose in her throat at her mother's statement. Oh yes, this had been very trying for Tavik. He had a new wife to deal with and an old one to get rid of. Scratch that. He hadn't even needed to get rid of her. She'd gotten rid of herself. All he had to worry about now was living the rest of his life with his new wife. He didn't even know he'd had an old wife. And she had to come up with a better term for herself than old wife. First wife. Best wife, rather.

"I'm going to be okay, Mom. Don't worry. I'll give myself time to process this."

Barbara nodded and picked up her purse. "I'll be going. Don't get in over your head in the attic. Bobby should do his own schoolwork."

Naomi grinned and herded her mother to the

door. "I'll take it easy. Now go make the world a better place."

Barbara gave her a kiss on the cheek and finally left. Naomi finished her cup of coffee and refilled it. The pot was almost empty. She debated making another. She'd seriously missed coffee, but she did want to go to sleep that night. She turned off the coffeemaker and wandered up the stairs. She pulled down the ladder to the attic and climbed up. She looked around the space while still sipping her coffee. Her mother hadn't been fully truthful with her. It wasn't a little messy. It was absolute chaos up there. Cushioned chairs leaned back against coffee tables. Boxes were stacked everywhere. She wryly wondered how her mother had been able to tell her with a straight face to only keep three things of her grandfather's when she'd kept three hundred. Hadn't they'd had a yard sale? She hadn't stuck around for the actual sale, but she wondered if it had been a big bust. She had no idea where to begin. She had no clue where Grandpa's old journals were. She started with the closest box and opened it. Lumpy mounds of newspapers greeted her. She unwrapped the mysterious lumps to find glass vases. She repacked the box and moved to the next.

She worked steadily through the morning. She didn't have a watch on, but eventually stopped when her stomach began threatening to defect. She fixed herself a sandwich and ate it at the kitchen counter. She'd found everything but journals. Old tax forms, water bills, bank statements. She'd even found a pile of love letters of Grandpa's and Grandma's. She'd set those aside to make sure her parents saw them. Maybe Grandpa had thrown away his old journals. She remembered coming upon him writing in one when she was little, but that didn't mean he'd held onto it or any others.

She couldn't eat the last bite of her sandwich as she contemplated the possibility that she wouldn't find anything. She might never know where he'd picked up the alicorn. *That's the spirit*, her memory of Mr. Squibbles said. She cleaned up the kitchen and dragged her feet back up to the attic. The boxes were stacked a little more neatly now, and she'd sorted out knickknacks from useful items. She'd made a stack of the papers like those old water bills that should be shredded. She'd gone through about half the attic.

She squared her shoulders and mustered her determination. The attic would be organized by the end if nothing else. She could claim that as an accomplishment. If she didn't find any journals, Bobby would have to make do with the old tax forms. She started opening boxes and peering inside them again.

She was on the last group of boxes when she opened one and found a stack of old composition books with the dates written on the covers. Her heart gave a little flutter as she took the top one out. These were it. She knew it. She remembered her grandfather writing in these very notebooks. She sorted through them. There were thirty-eight in the box.

She sorted them by date. The notebooks spanned her grandfather's adult life. She wished there'd been a date on the alicorn's case to give her a place to start but no such luck. She opened the earliest book. She figured it was as good a place to start as any.

May 7, 1958

It's strange how familiar everything has become. Motor cars, the radio, light bulbs. I once viewed these things with amazement, but now my hand automatically shoots out to flip the light switch when I go into a room. I like it here. I don't want to ever go back.

"Go back?" Naomi wondered aloud. She turned the page and skimmed the next entry and several more. He'd always said he was born and raised in Atlanta. His southern drawl had been as thick as any other good ole boy's. Grandpa never mentioned the mysterious place he'd come from again anywhere else. He talked about his job at the newspaper and what he and his buddies did on the weekend. She found the entry detailing his first time meeting her grandmother. She bookmarked that page for her father, thinking he'd like to read how his parents met. She began looking through the next book, hoping to find something more. As she flipped through pages, a strange word caught her eye. A big swashing X began the entry.

November 16, 1961

Xersal found me. I should've expected it, but I'd held onto the impossible hope that he would not. I won't let him drag me back. He can have all of it. Father always favored him. He was gifted. Not me. I'm happy here. Beth Ann is expecting. I'm going to be a father. What do I care about inheritance when I'm about to create a legacy?

"Now who the heck is Xersal?" Naomi asked the empty attic. It was an unusual name, and she would've remembered it if she'd heard it before. She turned to the next entry but almost threw the book across the room with a growl when she saw no mention of Xersal. It was like her grandfather was being purposefully coy. She'd never heard of anyone named Xersal, and she wanted to know more!

She flipped through the journal and picked up the next. She was on the fifteenth notebook when she finally saw the big slashing X again.

July 19, 1988

Xersal appeared! He just popped into my living

room this evening. He about gave me a heart attack. I demanded to know what he thought he was doing, and he said I had to keep something safe for him. I cannot believe him. He just pops into my home without invitation or warning and expects me to help him. I don't care if he is my brother, we haven't spoken in over twenty-five years. He does not know my family, and I don't want him to. I'm a grandfather now, for Pete's sake! I can't be bothered with his foolishness. He didn't give me a choice, though. When he disappeared, I found he'd left the alicorn, the very item I'd used to escape all those decades ago.

Why would he leave it with me? I don't want it. I'm happy. I have the life that I want. I don't want anything to do with home or him.

Naomi stared at the entry after she finished it. She was in shock. Her grandfather had used the alicorn to come to their world, but from where? She flipped through the pages, again searching for the swashing X. She was flipping through the last notebook when she found it again, along with the answers to her questions.

May 6, 2010

Lord help me, I spoke to Xersal again. I am old, and my health is failing. I can't keep this damnable alicorn any longer. He said he couldn't take it back. I asked him why he left it with me. He said he'd hoped I might return. He wanted me to have the option. I told him clearly I never wanted it, and so now he should take it back. He again said no, that it was safest with me. I asked why. He's a big, powerful wizard. He should be the one keeping the alicorn. He shook his head and said no, it wasn't safe. There's some warlord wreaking havoc across the land, and he's afraid it would fall into his hands. He says that the warlord is on his way to Harold's Pass. He was packing to leave. He said the entire castle was fleeing. He was about to be an out-of-work wizard. As if there is such a thing. He said he'd contact me when he was resettled. I told him I might be gone before that happened.

He looked at me then. I think he finally really saw me, and you know what that idiot said? He said, "Dear Calax, you've gotten old!" If I could've reached through that mirror and punched him, I would've. I asked him what I was supposed to do with the alicorn. He shrugged his shoulders. He said I could hide it. Tuck it away somewhere and forget about it. I told him again that my health is failing and that I might be gone soon. He had no answer. Lord, forgive me, but all I can think is to leave it behind and hope no one ever finds out what it truly is. I've written a note saying it's for Naomi. I know she'll keep it safe even if she thinks it's a worthless bauble. Damn Xersal. I left to get away from all of this.

Naomi closed the notebook. She had her answers, but now, she had more questions as well. Her grandfather had been from Terratu. He'd known the alicorn was real. If he hadn't wanted to keep it, why hadn't he simply broken it? She'd managed to do it within a day of receiving it. She'd also managed to get herself whisked away to Terratu in the process. And everything else had happened. She'd met the warlord. She'd fallen in love with him. She'd found a unicorn. She'd come home. Gone back to Terratu. Killed a god. Lost her husband. And killed a unicorn.

Her grandfather was right. Damn Xersal. If he hadn't left the alicorn with her grandfather, he wouldn't have left it to her. She would never have pricked herself with it, and none of the rest would've happened.

There was a creak on the attic ladder. She quickly closed the journals. She didn't put back the ones that mentioned Xersal. She kept those. She wanted to read them again, and she didn't think it was a good idea for Bobby to see them.

"Naomi, are you up here?" her mother called.

"Yeah, right here," she said and went to the attic ladder. Barbara looked around the attic.

"You've been up here all day?"

"Yeah, there was a lot to do. What time is it?"

"It's after seven. Dinner's ready."

Naomi nodded and made to follow her mother down the ladder. Barbara stopped her. "Dear, have you been crying?"

Naomi froze and raised her hands to her face. Her cheeks were wet. She wiped them dry. "It's nothing," she said.

She joined her mother and father at the dinner

table. Bobby was out with his roommates having pizza. Naomi cut into her steak and listened to her father talk about his day at work. She didn't understand most of it, and it bored her anyway. Her parents' chitchat finally died down. She finished her last bit of steak and stared at her empty plate. Neither had tried to draw her into conversation. She'd nodded along with what they said, but hadn't added anything. She suspected her mother had told her father about her crying. They were treating her like glass. And she probably needed that. She got up from the table. "I'm going to my room," she told them.

"Okay, honey. Let us know if you need anything," Barbara said.

She nodded and left the dining room. She didn't want to go back to her room. She found herself pulling down the attic ladder without realizing that was where she was going. She climbed up and pulled the ladder up after her. She turned on the bare bulb dangling from a rafter and looked around the attic. It looked very different at night. Gloomier. It matched her mood. She went back to the journals and contemplated looking through them one more time, but the idea of cracking them open again made her feel sick.

She sank down into a battered chair and stared into space. She should be excited about her discovery. Her grandfather was from Terratu. She had a great-uncle who was a wizard. Her arrival at Terratu wasn't so random. It was still pretty random, but it wasn't completely random, but she didn't know what good the information did her. She was still exiled. She should probably look for that enchanted mirror. It wouldn't do for Mom or someone to accidentally trigger it. If they still had it. What if it had been sent to the Goodwill? The idea sent a fissure of despair through her, but then she looked again at all the items her mother had kept, and she was comforted. She began searching. She had no idea what the mirror would look like. Agatha's had been rather plain. She flipped through frames looking for any mirror. She came up with three mirrors finally. All three showed her reflection like a normal mirror would. She wished she'd had time to ask Agatha about her mirror. She felt around trying to find maybe a hidden button to turn it on. The mirrors didn't have any hidden buttons or controls. She propped the mirrors up and stared at herself in triplicate. She looked tired.

"Naomi, are you up there?" her father called.

She should just give this up. She'd done everything she could. She picked the mirrors up to put them away. As she slid the last one in back among the pictures frames where it had been stored, the reflection caught her attention, or rather the lack of reflection caught her attention. She crouched down in front of the plain wooden mirror and stared into another room.

CHAPTER TWELVE

Most dragons don't live past infancy.

"Naomi?" her father called again.

"Yeah, Dad. I'm just finishing up," she yelled back.

She picked up the mirror and stared into the strange room. It was dark with moonlight coming in. She couldn't see any sign of anyone there. There was a worktable with items similar to what she'd seen strewn about on Agatha's worktable. There was a cold fireplace and dimly she could see a tapestry of a woman standing among flowers. She felt around the frame, thinking she had pushed a button to turn it on. Her fingers passed over a carved bit on the back of the frame. She hadn't paid it much attention initially because it had just felt like a defect in the wood. She turned it over and saw a glyph that looked like an eye. She pressed it, and when she looked into the mirror again, she saw herself. She tucked the mirror under her arm and made her way to the attic ladder. She climbed down and found her father waiting.

"Hey, kiddo. What you got there?" he asked.

"Just a mirror. I need one for my room."

Her father nodded. "You feeling better?"

Naomi nodded. "Yeah, Dad. I just wanted to get this before I forgot. I'm going to my room now."

He gave her a smile and put the ladder back up for her.

Once she was back in her bedroom and away from parental prying eyes, she laid the mirror down on her bed. As she stared at it, a little voice in her head was telling her to hide it in her closet and leave it there. Too bad she wasn't listening to that little voice.

She took down a framed Monet poster and put the mirror up in its place. She touched the carved mark again and activated the mirror. The strange room reappeared. It had to be her great-uncle Xersal's room. She wondered where he'd moved to after leaving Harold's Pass. It looked like he'd found a new residence. Those were definitely stone walls. The flickering light of a candle entered the room. Naomi quickly slid her fingers over the glyph to turn off the mirror.

The little voice came back, a little louder this time. She shouldn't use the mirror again. It was a bad idea. If Xersal met her, what could she say to him? There was the issue of the forgetting spell. He hadn't known her before the spell. So to her understanding, it shouldn't be a problem if he met her now, but she couldn't tell him about Tavik, the unicorns, or Grisbek. No one could know. Better to leave him alone. Better to leave everything involving Terratu alone. The little voice had some good points. Naomi sat on her bed and stared at the mirror.

Dammit, she couldn't *not* use it. She couldn't imagine having the mirror and never contacting her great-uncle. The little voice told her to break the mirror to get rid of the temptation, but she actually began to shake as she contemplated the idea. She knew she couldn't destroy it, and what's more, she *just had* to use it. The little voice huffed and went silent. She checked the hallway and listened for her parents. She could hear the television in the living room. She locked her door and stood before the mirror. She couldn't help checking her reflection and primping a bit. She should at least try to make a good impression on her great-uncle, even if she had no idea what she was going to say to him. She was set on this path and wasn't stopping. It was her only link to Terratu, and she was desperate to know how things were. To know that Tavik was all right. She passed her fingers over the glyph, and her reflection disappeared, replaced with the other room with stone walls.

The room was lit now by several candles, and there was a fire going in the fireplace. She could hear movement in the room but couldn't see the person. She remembered Agatha's disembodied voice in the cottage.

"Hello? Is Xersal there?" she called.

The rustling, happening just out of view, stopped.

"Hello? I know someone's there. I'd like to speak to Xersal."

"What do you want him for?" asked a ridiculous falsetto voice.

"I just want to talk."

"He doesn't owe you money, does he? Because he's not here."

Naomi was beginning to understand why her grandfather may have cut off all relations with his brother. "I don't know. Did you owe your brother money?"

The voice dropped the grating falsetto. "My brother?"

There was a clatter, and a man with a white chin beard that reached his belly button came into view. "What do you know about my brother?" he demanded.

"Plenty, since I'm his granddaughter," Naomi replied.

"Granddaughter?"

Her grandfather had said his brother had gotten the talent, but he may have intentionally not mentioned brains. "Hi, I'm Naomi, your grandniece."

Xersal stared at her from the other side of the mirror. Naomi waited for him to say something like maybe hello, but he didn't. She waited, and waited, but her great-uncle continued merely to stare.

Hoping to get him talking, Naomi clasped her hands together and lied as convincingly as possible. "I just thought I'd contact you since you were family. I know Grandpa cut all ties with you, but I thought I might reach out anyway."

Xersal continued not to respond. She wondered if she should clap her hands loudly to snap him out of his shock. "Xersal, are you all right? Are you upset I contacted you? Would you like me to call back later?" She waved her hands. His eyes didn't track her movements.

"Xersal?" she asked again. She did finally snap her fingers to get his attention. He didn't react. Was he drugged? His pupils were a bit dilated, but she would have figured that was due to the dim light. Naomi finally blew out a frustrated breath.

"Listen, if you don't want to talk to me, you can just tell me. I won't take it personally."

Xersal shook his head.

"I think there's been a mistake," he said.

"Fine. Bye. I won't bother you again." She wiped her fingers over the glyph. Her reflection reappeared. She was frowning, and her eyebrows were scrunched together. Her eyes began to sting, but she wasn't going to cry. She stalked to the bathroom. She avoided looking at her reflection in the medicine cabinet mirror.

She brushed her teeth aggressively. That had been a complete bust. Her only connection to Terratu was brain-damaged and didn't want to talk to her. Perfect. She swished and spat. She turned on the faucet to wash her face. She wasn't going to allow herself to be saddened by this. She wasn't going to cry. She scrubbed her face and splashed it with water to remove the soap. She stalked back to her bedroom. She glanced at the mirror as she came in. It still only showed her room. She took it off the wall and put it in the closet, taking the framed poster back out. She placed the poster back where it had been and finished getting ready for bed. She shut off the lights and crawled between the sheets and proceeded to stare at the dim glow-in-the-dark plastic stars for the next two hours.

Naomi was cold. She reached out and found a ready warmth. She snuggled up to Tavik's back and put her arms around his waist. He murmured something and rolled over to face her. She shifted against him and sighed.

"Naomi?" he rumbled.

She sighed and kissed his chest and laid her face against it.

"Naomi?" he asked again.

"What?" she murmured, though she didn't really want to talk. She just wanted to sleep.

Tavik's hands found her face and stroked down her cheeks. "Who are you?" he asked.

Naomi groaned and tried to burrow under the

covers. He stopped her and pulled her back up. "Tavik, can't we just sleep? I'm tired after a truly crappy day."

"Who are you?" he repeated.

"I guess I'm having a truly crappy night, too," she muttered. She sat up and looked around her room. Dawn was just breaking. She didn't want to get up but knew going back to sleep would be difficult. She couldn't help glancing at the other side of the bed, but of course, it was empty. There wasn't any ghost of warmth there or an indent indicating anyone else had been in the bed.

She got out of her lonely bed and consoled herself by fixing a pot of coffee. When her mother joined her, Naomi offered to help her with chores. They did laundry, vacuumed, dusted, washed rugs—it was a whole spring-cleaning day. It felt good. Her mother and she worked together and joked around. They went grocery shopping in the afternoon and started supper. Her father came home, and Bobby came over, and they had a nice home-cooked dinner all together.

After dinner, they ended up in the living room watching a movie. Around ten o'clock, the gathering broke up. Bobby went home. Barbara and Phil went to bed, and Naomi went up to her room. She sat down on her bed and looked around. She needed to start reading or something to occupy herself when she was alone. Her eyes fell on the closet, but she made herself turn away.

She got up and began poking around the room,

slowly circling to the closet. The room was still decked out with her childhood belongings. She stumbled onto her high school yearbooks and took them to her bed to flip through them. She cringed at her younger self's sense of fashion and smiled at pictures of old friends and teachers. She willfully ignored the closet door.

She began to grow sleepy as she pored over the pictorial history. Preferring not to end up drooling all over the varsity basketball team (they weren't that cute), she closed the yearbook and put all of them back on the shelf. She began getting ready for bed.

As she shrugged out of her clothes, she realized she needed to go into the closet to get clean pajamas. She shook her head. She'd been so willfully ignoring the closet, and the mirror inside it, she'd forgotten all the other stuff in the closet that she would need. She'd have to reach past it all the time if she intended to keep it there.

She considered stashing it somewhere else in her room, and the only other option was under her bed, and that idea didn't bear considering. There was no way she was putting that mirror and whoever was on the other side of it under her bed. It was just too creepy.

She still needed her pajamas. Her reluctance to open the closet made her angry. The whole evening she'd been holding herself back from opening the closet, and the moment she gave herself permission, she was balking. Naomi didn't know if she could be any more stupid. Yeah, she could be if she insisted on using the magic mirror as a regular mirror. That would be pretty stupid.

Growing frustrated with all her mental seesawing, Naomi acted. She marched around her bed and threw open the closet door. She shoved all of the clothes aside on the rod to reveal the mirror leaning against the back wall.

And found her great-uncle Xersal peering out from the other side. "Hello?" he said and gave her a little finger wave.

"Oh, so now you can talk to me?" Naomi growled. It just figured. When she'd finally decided she didn't give a damn that he didn't want to speak to her, of course he'd try to contact her.

"Yes," Xersal's eyes darted around. He seemed incapable of looking at her.

"So what do you have to say?" Naomi demanded. The hell she was carrying this conversation.

"Um, are we really related?"

"Yeah, I think so. Why? You don't believe me?" Naomi's tone was becoming more and more belligerent.

Xersal shook his head. "No, you actually look a bit like Harrid."

"He went by Harry here," Naomi said, a brush of sadness passing over her at the thought of her grandfather. Why hadn't he told any of them about Terratu?

Xersal flashed her a grin. "He did that here, too. But I have to say, I really don't think this is appropriate. I mean I don't know what the customs are in your world, but I would be more comfortable if you were clothed."

Naomi blinked a second and then looked down at herself in dawning horror. She'd undressed to change into her pajamas. She'd gone to the closet to get her pajamas. She was only wearing a pair of bikini panties and plain cross-your-heart bra. She shrieked and slammed shut the closet.

"We'll talk again in the morning?" Xersal called through the closet.

"Yeah, sure," Naomi said.

Rapid footsteps sounded in the hall. "Naomi, everything all right in there?" her father called. The doorknob began to turn.

"Don't come in!" Naomi shouted and dived for her bed. She quickly wrapped the comforter around her.

The door didn't open. "Is everything all right?" her father asked again.

"Yeah, Dad. A spider fell on me while I was changing. Sorry for screaming."

"Did you hurt yourself?" he persisted.

Naomi rolled her eyes. "Nothing but my pride. I'm going to bed now."

"Okay, good night, honey."

"Night, Dad."

She listened to her father retreat back to his

bedroom. She cautiously got out from under the comforter and put on a T-shirt and a pair of shorts. She could've gone back into the closet to retrieve her pajamas, but even looking at the closet door made her flame red. She couldn't believe she'd let her great-uncle see her in her underwear. She wrapped the comforter tightly around herself and firmly closed her eyes.

"No dreaming about Tavik, either," she told herself. "Especially no dreaming about him where he kicks me out of bed for not being his wife."

As she drifted off to sleep, she wondered what was left to dream about.

"I told my mother about you."

Naomi opened her eyes, but the room was dark, and she couldn't see anything. "And what does Agatha have to say?" she asked. She didn't even bother to get frustrated that her subconscious hadn't listened to her very explicit instructions.

"She thinks you're a succubus trying to steal my soul." He didn't say it like he believed it, though. He sounded amused actually by the idea.

Naomi stretched and rolled over onto her back. The room was dark, but a little silver moonlight came through to show the silhouette of things. Tavik lay propped up on one elbow, looking down at her.

"And what do you think?" she asked, her voice going husky. She wanted to reach out and touch him but was afraid he'd draw away.

"I don't think."

Naomi's eyebrows came together. "Don't think? What does that mean?"

"Are you really here? Or am I asleep dreaming you?"

Naomi propped herself up on an elbow, too, so she could fully face him. She didn't know how best to answer. Did she really want to have a debate with imaginary Tavik about which one was a dream?

Tavik sighed and lay back. "See, it's better not to think."

She moved closer to lean over him. "So you're not going to call the guards and have me thrown into the dungeon?"

"It didn't do any good before, except now all the servants think I'm haunted by some vengeful spirit. They keep doing sacred hand motions around me to ward off evil ghosts."

"Hmm, so we're just going to lie here?" she said, hoping he'd have the correct answer, which was for his arm to slide around her waist.

"I could be persuaded to stay up a little longer."

Naomi smiled. She slid up flush against him and kissed him. "I've missed you," she breathed.

Tavik rolled her over and blanketed her with his body. He slid her T-shirt over her head and cast it to the floor. His mouth peppered kisses down her chest as he made his way to her breasts.

"Oh, God, please don't let me wake up," Naomi

breathed as she arched up.

Tavik didn't release her, but made a questioning noise in the back of his throat.

Naomi didn't verbally reply, just kneaded his shoulders and swept her hands down his back. His fingers snagged the top of her shorts and panties and pushed them down. She kicked them off for him. She lifted her legs and began dragging down his sleep pants as well.

His hands slid up her legs and dipped between them. She gasped when he touched her.

"Tavik," she murmured. She didn't think she could handle drawn-out foreplay. She needed him inside her. She needed the consummation more than anything.

He pulled himself up and dropped his mouth to her neck. She reached down for him and stroked him as she opened her legs to draw him in.

"Why do you feel so right?" he breathed across her cheek as he moved his mouth to hers.

She led him inside of her and sighed when he penetrated. "I'm your wife; this always feels right." She gasped as her legs widened to accommodate him.

As he began to move inside her, Naomi held on to his arms, arching up to drag her mouth against any available skin, letting herself go with the sensations.

"I wish it were like this with my wife. I truly wish it were," Tavik said through clenched teeth as he picked up his pace.

Naomi didn't have the will or truly the desire to argue with him over who was married to whom. The only words she could form were his name.

Tavik didn't say her name. She wished he would say it at least once. Wished he'd call out to her. But he only referred to her in the second person, while all she could do was call out his name.

"You feel so perfect."

"Tavik, don't stop. Don't stop."

"Who are you?"

"Tavik, please."

"Dear Calax, I need you."

"Yes, Tavik. Yes."

Too quickly, Naomi could feel the crest approaching. The crash was imminent. Her breathing quickened, and she called out his name louder. He moaned, and all rhythm was lost as his hips snapped wildly into her. She held on as tightly as she could.

When he lost all words, and she could feel the surge within her, she let herself go. She'd been holding back but now let it happen. Naomi was always amused by how razor-thin the climax seemed. One moment they were gritting their teeth and burning up and then there was a few seconds of quaking disbelief, a feeling of heaven, and then they were both limp and gasping.

Tavik collapsed beside her and put an arm

across his eyes. Naomi turned her head and gazed at the fuzzy profile she could just make out in the darkness.

"I love you," she whispered.

She waited for his reply. None came.

His silence hurt. Suddenly feeling cold and clammy, she turned over and tried to find her shirt. She saw it on the floor over the edge of the bed.

Tavik's hand reached out and landed on her hip. "Don't go. We need to talk. We have to figure this out."

"Figure what out?" she snapped. She felt used and sticky. Even her dream Tavik didn't want her. She reached down for the shirt.

"You can't keep appearing in my bed. It isn't right. I'm married."

Naomi growled to herself in frustration. It'd be better if dream-Tavik just didn't speak. Better total silence if he wasn't going to call her by name, insist he was a married man, and peg her as the other woman. Dream-Tavik should be a *mute*.

"Fine, if you never want to see me again, I'll stop. I just won't sleep ever again."

"What are you talking about?" Tavik sat up and grabbed her arm.

"I'm the one dreaming, idiot. Why does my subconscious hate me so much? I had to give you up once. Why can't we pretend that didn't happen?"

"What?"

Naomi pulled away and reached for her shirt again, but she overshot and slid off the bed.

She got minor carpet burns from her tumble from her bed to her bedroom floor. She shook her head and looked around her dark bedroom, except not everything was dark. There was a fading light coming from underneath her mattress. She lifted the mattress and watched the alicorn's light fade.

"What the hell?" she asked.

She dropped the mattress and scrambled up. She rushed to the light switch and slapped it on. She winced at the sudden light, but she looked around the room. She was naked. Where were her shorts and T-shirt? She threw the comforter and blankets back on her bed and searched for the clothes she'd gone to sleep in. They had to be here. She did find her shorts and panties bunched up at the end of the bed, and when she went back around her bed to where she'd fallen, she found her T-shirt like she'd been reaching for in the dream.

Except now she wasn't sure if she'd been dreaming. She reached between her legs and jerked her fingers back at the sticky wetness that they encountered. She looked at her messy fingers.

"What the hell?" she asked again.

She lifted the mattress again, and with her T-shirt wrapped around her hand, she grabbed the alicorn. She could feel its warmth through the shirt. What had it been doing?

"Tavik?" she said to the empty room.

How could she have been with him? Hadn't she been dreaming? Since she'd been back, she'd had the dreams. The alicorn had been under the mattress since she'd been back. Had the alicorn been responsible for all of them?

She contemplated sticking the alicorn back under the mattress and going back to sleep. It was so very tempting, but she couldn't do it. What about the spell? Obviously her encounters with Tavik hadn't broken it. He still didn't know her, but it had always been dark. He'd never gotten a clear look at her. If he did see her face, the unicorns would be on the verge of war with the dragons again, and she'd have a dragon's mark upon her. And Snowflake's sacrifice would have been for naught. No, she wouldn't knowingly risk that.

She got redressed and took the alicorn to the closet. She laid it down and shut the door. Her closet was becoming quite full of magical things. And she wasn't sure what to do about it.

She climbed back into bed and closed her eyes. A tear leaked out against her will. She knew that she wouldn't dream of Tavik.

CHAPTER THIRTEEN

Dragons once roamed Earth. They left. They can come back.

Naomi was home alone again the next day. It was perfect for her. She didn't know what to say to anyone. She'd had a dreamless sleep after the alicorn was put away and felt rested. Except, she hoped a particular someone would have something to say to her. Something, anything at all really. She needed distraction. She needed to not think about the pros and cons of sleeping with an alicorn tucked under her mattress. She dragged the magic mirror out and hung it on her wall.

She said a brief prayer that Xersal would be around and looked down at herself to confirm that she was fully dressed. She still slipped on a cardigan for good measure.

She wiped her fingers over the glyph and watched her reflection fade out and an image of Xersal's room appear. She let out a sigh of relief when she saw he was hunched over the table grinding something with mortar and pestle.

"Uncle Xersal?" she called.

He fumbled the pestle and almost tipped over

the mortar at her call. He wiped off whatever had spilled from the mortar and came around the table to fully face her.

"Hello!" he said. He waved to her. His palm was streaked with grime. He noticed it and quickly wiped his hands on his long red robe.

"Hi, do you have time to talk?" she asked.

He glanced around the room and bobbed his head when he turned back. "Yes, I have time. How are you? Thank you for wearing clothes. I hope that isn't too much of a hardship."

Naomi gritted her teeth at the reminder. "Yeah, sorry about that. I didn't mean for you to see me in my underwear."

"Oh, well, that's good. I was afraid that was some sort of local custom," Xersal said.

"No, just embarrassing as hell."

Silence fell between them. Naomi waited for him to say something else. He seemed to think it was her turn. The silence grew longer and more uncomfortable. "You know, I've been to Terratu," she finally offered.

"You have? How did you get here?"

"I accidentally used the alicorn that you left with Grandpa."

"Grandpa," Xersal said, tasting the word. "It's amazing to me that he did it. He went and had a family, especially when I remember how he used to cry when he wet his bed."

"Well, he grew out of that," Naomi said, feeling a little defensive on her grandfather's behalf.

"Yes, of course." Xersal seemed to be falling back into memories.

Naomi didn't want to lose him to silent nostalgia. "So how are you doing? I read in Grandfather's journal that you had to flee some warlord."

Xersal snorted. "Yes, Lord Tavik came knocking with his battering rams. I fled with the rest of the castle staff. We found refuge in my lord's cousin's castle. Luckily, they had no wizard in residence so I've slipped into that role here."

"Oh, that's good. What about everyone else?"

"Well, the Lady Naomi didn't make it out, which we feared meant the death of her, but it's become quite the epic romance. Lord Tavik and she fell in love. He, a worshipper of Errilol, forsook his god and put down his sword. But the vile demon god struck him with a wasting disease, and Lady Naomi had to fight the god to save him. Amazingly, she defeated him. They've been living together like a fairytale couple ever since."

Naomi nodded as she took all this in. The unicorns had told her this was what would happen. That Lady Naomi would take her place in everyone's memories. History would be rewritten to erase her. But Lady Naomi now had the dragon's mark. She wondered how they were dealing with that. Xersal's account indicated everything was rosy. Either they'd taken care of it, or his information wasn't up to date.

Not trusting herself to ask further about Tavik

and Lady Naomi, she turned the conversation back to Xersal. "It must be awful, though, for Lady Naomi's husband."

Xersal nodded. "Yes, he's quite heartbroken. He was absolutely in love with her. Plucked her from a tavern and made her nobility. That was very fairytale-like, too, come to think of it."

Yeah, Lady Naomi lived an enchanted life, Naomi thought. One might wonder if she had magical assistance, she thought sourly, recalling the love potion. "So what do you do with yourself? What does a wizard in a castle do?"

"Oh, well, this and that. If the farmers' crops aren't doing well, I take some soil samples and see what I can do to assist. If there's drought, I do some rain spells, and if there's too much rain, I do a drying spell. It depends on what's needed."

"Are you working on anything now?"

Xersal dropped his eyes. "I really shouldn't say."

"Who am I going to tell? My parents don't even know about Grandpa and you. Nobody here believes in magic."

A shudder passed over Xersal. "Not believing in magic. I've never heard of a more foolhardy thing."

Naomi had to silently agree with that.

"Um, there is something I really should ask," Xersal said.

Naomi raised an eyebrow.

A blush started to bloom on his cheeks.

His embarrassment began to worry her. He wasn't about to ask her cup size, was he?

"Well, I can't call you grandniece all the time," he said.

Naomi didn't know what he meant by that. "But I am your grandniece."

"Yes, but I'd like your name," Xersal finally said with a touch of pleading.

"Ooh!" Naomi quickly wondered how she should answer. He'd just been going on and on about the Lady Naomi. She very well couldn't tell him that was her name, too. A normal person would have mentioned the coincidence sooner.

"You can call me Taylor," she said, grinding her teeth at having to go back to that moniker.

"Isn't that the other name Harrid took in your world? He said there were so many people that you needed two or three names."

Naomi cursed herself silently. Of course, Xersal would know their last name. "Yeah, but my parents really liked the name so they made that my first name, too."

"So you're Taylor Taylor?"

"Yep," Naomi said with a nervous laugh. "It's actually kind of unusual here, so it makes me stand out."

"It would here, too," Xersal said.

Naomi chuckled weakly again. "So what are you working on?"

Xersal waved his hand and ducked his head. "I really can't say. It's confidential."

"Oh, come on. I'm family, and like I said, I have no one to tell."

Xersal lifted his head and looked around the room. She watched him go to the door and look outside. He closed it quietly and crept back to the mirror on tiptoe. He motioned Naomi to come closer to the mirror. She got up close to the glass, and he whispered, "I'm actually working on something very important, but it's very hush-hush. It seems the Lady Naomi has somehow contracted a dragon's mark, and no one knows how to lift it. Lady Naomi has requested my help."

She felt guilt begin to well up in her. So the dragon's mark was still a problem. Grisbek was hunting Lady Crazy, and he would most likely kill her. "Have you figured out a way to remove the mark?" Naomi asked.

Xersal shook his head. "I haven't discovered a way yet. We're quite perplexed."

"We?"

"Tavik's mother is also looking into it. But she's not likely to get far. I mean she's only a local hedge witch. Of course, she won't figure it out."

She didn't like Xersal's easy dismissal of Agatha. Naomi knew she was a powerful witch. "I'm sure she's very capable."

"Yes, yes, I suppose. Anyway, I can't figure it out. The only thing saving Lady Naomi at the moment is the baby."

Naomi went cold. "The what?"

"Lady Naomi is with child, and the dragon has

quite honorably decided to hold off eating her until the babe is born."

"Oh." She was pregnant already? Naomi could feel the world tilting around her. She blindly reached for the glyph and pressed it. The mirror went blank instantly. She turned and went to her bed. She sank down onto the edge of it and put her head into her hands. Tavik must be overjoyed. He was going to be a father, and he'd make a good father, too. She was sure of it, and Agatha would be ecstatic about the coming grandbaby.

They were all happy. And there was no chance of going back now. Not with a baby in the picture.

There was a tap on her open door. "Hey, kiddo, I drove home to see if you want go out to lunch?" her father asked.

She raised her head, and her father frowned. "Are you crying?"

She raised a hand to a cheek and found it wet. "Oh, I didn't know I was doing that," she said and wiped her eyes.

Her father's frown deepened and came into the room to sit beside her. He put his arm around her. "What's wrong?"

"I just got some bad news is all," she said and tried to brush it off.

"What was it?"

She sighed and dropped her head. "Tavik's new wife is pregnant."

Her father's face became stormy. "Already? Was he cheating on you?"

She shook her head. "No, I'm sure he wasn't. We split up because I didn't want to get pregnant yet."

"Oh, sweetheart, I'm sorry."

Naomi nodded and wiped her eyes again. "He really wanted kids. I'm sure he's overjoyed."

"All right, I'm going to fix sandwiches downstairs. You clean yourself up and join me, okay?"

"Didn't you want to go out to lunch?"

"Do you want to go?"

Naomi hung her head.

"I want to have lunch with you. I don't care where."

"Thanks, Dad."

Phil patted her back and got up.

Once her father was gone, Naomi glanced at the mirror. She should give a quick apology to Xersal, but didn't know how to explain herself. Should she even keep talking to him?

She got up and went to the bathroom. She splashed some water on her face and looked at herself in the medicine cabinet mirror. If she did nothing, Grisbek would eventually kill Lady Crazy. Once Lady Crazy was dead, she could go back, reunite with Tavik, and they could raise the baby together. It was an awful, evil thought, and it made Naomi feel scummy to contemplate it, but it was an option.

She shook her head and avoided eye contact with her reflection. She couldn't believe herself. She was becoming worse than Lady Crazy. She was venturing into Errilol-level badness. She joined her father at the kitchen table. She looked at the towering sandwich on the plate laid out for her and knew she couldn't eat all of it.

"So how'd you find out about Tavik?" her father asked.

Luckily he was looking at his sandwich when he asked and missed her wince. She needed to learn to keep her fat mouth shut if she didn't want to have to lie with every other breath.

"A mutual acquaintance let it slip."

"I thought it might have been his mother. It sounded like you grew pretty close with her. You were working for her, weren't you?"

Damn, she really hated having to lie. "Yeah, Agatha and I were really close, but she has to support her son. And with a child on the way, she'll be focused on that."

Her dad shook his head. "You deserve better. Wanting to wait to have kids isn't unusual. You weren't even married a year. I'm glad he lives in another country. If he were in this town, I'd have to go yell at him. A lot."

"Dad," Naomi scolded.

He shook his head again. "No, it's not right. You left everything for him, and when you failed to do one thing he wanted, he leaves you. It's not right."

"He didn't leave me. I left him," Naomi said, and realized it was true. Tavik and she'd been having problems, but ultimately, she was the one

246

who'd ended it. He hadn't had any say in the matter.

Her father stilled at her declaration, and he looked carefully at her. "You left him?"

"There were other problems. I can't really explain them, but if I hadn't left, bad stuff was going to happen. Everyone was in danger."

Phil's eyebrows came together. "What in the world could be so dangerous?"

Naomi dropped her eyes. Nothing in their world was that dangerous, but Terratu was another matter, and again, she couldn't explain.

Her father ate the rest of his sandwich quietly. Naomi got the feeling he was disappointed in her. The thought made her miserable. She wanted to open up to him and tell him everything, explain it all, but how could she?

Once they were both done, Phil picked up the plates and took them to the sink. "Feel better?" he asked.

She nodded. "Yeah, Dad. Thanks for coming home. I just wish I knew what to do now."

Phil nodded as he dried the plates. "I think you need to figure out what you want."

She wanted Tavik back, but she couldn't tell her father that. And that was impossible anyway. What else was there? Lady Crazy had the dragon's mark. Naomi knew she'd never be able to live with the guilt if Grisbek succeed in killing the other woman. She had to help her. It was the only thing that felt right. And while helping Lady

Crazy might not make her happy, knowing that Tavik was would be enough.

"I think I know, Dad."

The corner of her father's mouth lifted. "Good. I've got to get back to the office. But think it over. And remember, no matter what, your mother and I will be there for you. Understand?"

Naomi nodded and rose to give her father a hug. "I know, thanks. Love you, too."

Her father gave her a quick squeeze and left. Naomi sat back down at the empty table. She'd been so intent on saving the unicorns and everyone that she hadn't really considered the idea of going back. But if she didn't try to help Tavik, she'd never be happy.

But she couldn't just throw the unicorns under the bus. She couldn't endanger everyone. So she just had to figure out a way to protect the unicorns and deal with the dragon's mark. It didn't have to be either or. But how?

She stared at the table and thought. Agatha and Xersal were working on the dragon's-mark problem. It was the key to everything. If they somehow got Grisbek to remove the mark or destroyed it or even if they possibly slew the dragon, everything would be okay. The unicorns would be all right, and she could work on breaking the love spell on Tavik. Simple. Easy-peasy. Piece of cake. Nothing to it.

Naomi groaned and banged her head on the kitchen table. She couldn't even lie convincingly to herself. She wandered upstairs to her bedroom and sank onto her bed. When she raised her eyes, she was startled by the image of Xersal in the mirror. He gave her a little wave.

"Is this a bad time?" he asked a little tentatively.

"Sorry, Xersal. My father came home unexpectedly to have lunch with me. I couldn't let him see or hear you."

Xersal bobbed his head. Naomi's earlier thoughts about the dragon's mark came back to her. "So what headway have you made with the dragon's mark?"

"Headway?"

"Progress. Have you figured anything out?"

Xersal looked a bit abashed. "Well, yes. We've figured out quite a bit. The dragon's mark protects the bearer from all other dangers and allows the dragon to track his prey anywhere he or she might go. It can't be scrubbed off or washed away. It's resistant to any alteration. Truly, it seems quite impossible."

"So what else are you trying?"

"What do you mean?"

"Have you tried negotiating with the dragon to see if he'd accept something else—or, worst-case scenario, you could kill him?"

"If killing him were simple, I believe Lord Tavik would have already accomplished it, but dragons are nearly impossible to kill. It would take strong magic or a horde of men willing to sacrifice their lives, and there's the danger that if we take any sort of offensive stance with the dragon and don't succeed, he will simply begin rampaging through the land, destroying villages and farms."

Naomi nodded. "But what about talking to him?"

Xersal shook his head. "There's no negotiating with dragons."

She believed him. She didn't think Grisbek would stop just because someone asked nicely. It all seemed pretty hopeless. "And the unicorns?" She knew she was grasping at straws, but there had to be a way.

"What about the unicorns?"

"They won't help?"

"Why would they?"

Naomi realized her misstep. Lady Crazy never had an alicorn. She'd had no reason to seek the unicorns. The unicorns were effectively no longer a part of the story. "Because they might know something and wish to help?" Naomi asked.

Xersal shook his head. "No, they've shown no interest, and I don't know why they would. But it is an interesting idea. Do you still have the alicorn?"

Naomi stilled and stared at her great-uncle. She could sense what was coming. "Yes, I do."

"I wonder how the dragon's mark would react to the touch of an alicorn."

Naomi knew it would do nothing. If all they'd

needed to do was touch the mark with an alicorn, Snowflake would've simply removed it five seconds after Grisbek had given it to her, but it could be her ticket to winning back Tavik. She didn't know exactly, but this was her chance. She could go with Xersal to the castle and figure out how to fix everything, but she didn't want to give Xersal false hope about the alicorn. "Why do you think it would help her? The alicorn heals sickness and wounds. The mark is neither of those."

"How are you so sure?"

Naomi knew she was on dangerous ground. She'd said too much. "I just figure that's how it works."

"Well, I would still like to try it. How would you feel about visiting your great-uncle?"

CHAPTER FOURTEEN

*Green dragons are the most persistent hunters
of all the dragons.*

Naomi stared at Xersal in the mirror and wondered what she should say. She didn't want to appear too eager. She had to make sure not to raise
her great-uncle's suspicions.

"I don't know if that's a good idea," she
hedged.

Xersal nodded and shrugged his shoulders.
"You're probably right."

Naomi waited for him to say something more,
to argue his case, but he seemed content to leave
it at that. She became frustrated. Did he really
want to help Lady Crazy or not? Actually, why
would he help her? Wouldn't Gerry be against the
idea? Where was Gerry? "How does Lady Naomi's
former husband feel about this?"

"I haven't kept him fully apprised. It's a touchy
subject obviously. He is concerned for her and
does not wish her harmed, but he would prefer
her home."

"Of course." Naomi fell quiet a moment. She
wanted to get back to the idea of her coming back

to Terratu with the alicorn, but she needed to tread carefully. "Do you really think the alicorn could help?"

"It might. Alicorns are very powerful magical artifacts."

"What would I need to do?" she asked, though she knew exactly what to do.

Naomi stood at the magic mirror, but it wasn't engaged. She was using it as a simple mirror for once. She was holding a scarf up over the bottom half of her face. She was trying to decide if it was enough to disguise herself. The unicorns had said Tavik and the others could never see her again. She was going to take them literally on that. Sure, they'd also said she was exiled forever from Terratu, but since no one, not even the unicorns, remembered her, there was no one to stop her from going back. Anyway, the alicorn had put her back in bed with Tavik on a number of occasions. She figured he hadn't really seen her face, so she believed that was all she had to do. She'd wear the scarf. She turned her head from side to side. She couldn't decide if she looked more like a belly dancer or a Wild West bandit.

The alicorn lay waiting on the bed. She wasn't planning to bring anything else. She was ready to go, but she was debating over saying anything to her parents. She wasn't sure if she needed to. With the alicorn, she could zip back and forth. She could sleep in her bed every night. It didn't have to be a big deal. She nodded to herself. She would go to Xersal, but she'd be back in a few hours. She still left a note anyway. It said simply she'd gone out to see some friends and not to wait up. She stuck it to the fridge. She hefted the alicorn and couldn't help thinking about it being Snowflake's alicorn. Knowing it had been a part of him made her feel strange about using it. She wondered where her family had gotten the first alicorn. She could ask Xersal.

She placed her finger against the tip. She closed her eyes and filled her mind with a picture of Xersal's room. Her finger pressed down on the tip. There was a sting. When she opened her eyes, Xersal stared back at her, only it wasn't through a small wooden frame. She was in his workroom. She was back in Terratu.

"You're here!" Xersal exclaimed.

Naomi nodded and smiled from behind the scarf. Xersal raised his hand to his chin. "Why are you covering your face?"

She'd thought up a good lie already. She was sort of proud of it. "It's a curse. I have to wear it around anyone who isn't related to me. If they see my face, very bad things will happen."

"That must make courting very difficult," Xersal observed.

Naomi laughed self-consciously. "Yeah, not

many guys are interested in a woman they can't see."

"Well, if it's any consolation, I think you're very pretty."

Naomi ducked her head to hide her blush. "Thanks, Uncle Xersal."

"Is there anything I can do about the curse?"

She shook her head. "No, it's something I'll just have to deal with. Don't worry about it."

Xersal clapped his hands. "All right. In any case, your alicorn will be very useful indeed. Tavik's castle is a week's ride away, but your alicorn should get us there in a blink."

Naomi suddenly felt nervous. Coming back to Terratu had been a big step. She knew she was flirting with disaster. She was putting everyone in jeopardy. "When do you want to go?" She sort of hoped he'd say next week.

"I need to finish gathering a few things. Maybe in an hour or so. How does that sound?"

She nodded, of course he wanted to go immediately. "Anything I can do?"

Xersal waved off her offer. "No, I'm fine. Look around. Just don't touch, taste, or smell anything without asking me first."

Naomi smiled. She'd gotten similar instructions from Agatha when she'd started going to her cottage for training. She looked around and saw something sitting on a shelf. She had to bite her lip from shouting in surprise. Sitting on the shelf, was a pot of blooming fool-me-not. She reached up and touched the leaves reverently. It wasn't like she needed it anymore, but here it was growing nicely.

"Oh, you can smell that if you want. It shouldn't do anything to you," Xersal said as he attempted to close a trunk by sitting on it.

Naomi picked up the clay pot and carefully brought the plant to her face.

"Why do you have this?" she asked.

Xersal was still distracted by the trunk. "It's always good to have the antidote to any spell you make."

Naomi's hands began to shake. She set down the pot in fear of dropping it.

"Antidote?" she asked, her throat catching on the word.

"Yes, it's the antidote for a powerful love potion. Smelling it will counteract it."

"You made this potion?" She already knew the answer.

"Yes, for someone who was in grave danger."

"Grave danger?"

Xersal sighed. "I shouldn't say, but the woman I made it for was in danger of death. She needed the man holding the sword to put it down and never point it at her again."

And there was the missing piece. Xersal had given the potion to Lady Crazy. And it sounded like he'd done it when Tavik was attacking Harold's Pass. He'd given her the potion as a failsafe. If Tavik had captured her, Lady Crazy was meant to give him the potion to make him fall in love with her and not kill her. But instead of that happening, Agatha had rescued Lady Crazy and gotten her to safety, then Naomi had shown up and Agatha had put her in Lady Crazy's place. Then for whatever reason, Lady Crazy had decided to find Tavik and give him the potion anyway, starting the whole mess. In a way, this was all Xersal's fault. If he hadn't given the love potion to Lady Crazy, she would have never been able to steal Tavik from her. But wait, he was also the reason Naomi ended up in Terratu in the first. If he hadn't left the alicorn with her grandfather, she'd have never met Tavik. None of this would have happened at all. Did she want to blame him for that? Did she wish she'd never met Tavik? Her body went cold at the thought. No, she couldn't imagine never having met Tavik. Though, she'd managed to make it so he'd never met her. That was all her doing. She knew now how all of the pieces had lined up now, but that didn't mean anyone could have known how they would fall. In the end, things happened. She couldn't blame Xersal or herself. She just had to do what she could to clean up the fallen pieces now: primarily, free Lady Crazy of her dragon's mark so Tavik and she could have their baby and live a happy life.

"Um, Taylor, could you get this clasp? I can't reach it, and I'm afraid if I move, the whole thing will spring open."

Naomi looked over and had to laugh at the image of her uncle sprawled over the massive trunk. He didn't appear to know his beard was caught in it. She shook her head. Together they managed to get the trunk closed without Xersal's beard in it this time.

"Are we ready?" she asked finally.

Xersal patted down his robe and took one last look around the room. "Yes, I believe I have everything. So how does this work?"

"Hold my hand, and it would probably be best if you close your eyes." They linked hands and for simplicity sat on the trunk to connect them to it. She maneuvered the horn and got it to prick her while imagining Tavik's courtyard.

When she opened her eyes and saw guards scrambling to reach them, Naomi thought maybe she should've picked a spot outside the castle.

Xersal looked around with a grin. He turned to her. "You are very marvelous with that alicorn."

A group of guards with pointing swords surrounded them. "What is the meaning of this?" Boris demanded as he pushed through and came to stand before them.

"Hello! I am the Great Wizard Xersal. The Lady Naomi requested I come remove a dragon's mark from her."

"And who's he?" Boris asked, indicating Naomi.

"*She* is my assistant, Taylor."

"Why does he need an assistant tailor?" one

guard muttered to another. The other shrugged his shoulders.

Xersal appeared not to hear him, and Naomi didn't know if she should correct them or not. She slid off the trunk and kept the alicorn close.

Boris did not appear to know they were expected and wouldn't have been happy even if they were. He seemed even grumpier than when Naomi had first come to the castle. Boris dispatched a boy to ask Lady Naomi if she'd requested a wizard. They all waited tensely for the boy to return.

"You have a very nice castle," Naomi said to Boris, hoping to soften him a bit.

She didn't make a dent. The steward harrumphed and looked away from her. Naomi decided not to say anymore. She missed the friendlier Boris. She hoped his wife and children were well.

The boy came back with Mrs. Boon. Naomi would rather not have crossed paths with the dour housekeeper again, but Lady Crazy must not have sent her packing like Naomi had done.

"Lady Naomi will see the Wizard Xersal. If you will follow me."

"Excellent," Xersal said. He glanced at his trunk. "Um, will someone?"

"Your servant can't carry it for you?" Boris asked.

"Taylor isn't my servant. She's my grandniece, and even if she were my servant, she obviously wouldn't be able to carry this monstrosity. Surely you have a couple of able-bodied men you could set on the task?"

Boris did not seem inclined to offer a few able-bodied men, but he turned and called for a couple to come take the trunk. As the men took hold of it, Xersal moved to follow Mrs. Boon. Naomi said a quick thank-you to the men and Boris. She had to hurry to catch up. She needn't have bothered. She would've known the way. They were headed to her old chambers.

When she had come back for good, she'd stopped sleeping in her old chambers. She'd kept them as a daytime retreat and a place to dress and bathe. Tavik's room was where she had slept. Maybe if she'd gotten pregnant, she would've started sleeping in these chambers again.

She followed Mrs. Boon and Xersal and was glad for her mask because even with it covering her nose and mouth, her eyes watered from the strong perfumes wafting in the air. Xersal had a sneezing jag as soon as he set foot in the room.

"Dear Calax, can someone open a window?" he exclaimed as his eyes streamed, and he mopped at his running nose with his beard.

"I didn't know you were allergic to flowers, Xersal," said Lady Crazy.

She was propped up in the bed by mounds of pillows. Flowers of every color and scent were arrayed around her. Something ran into Naomi's leg. She looked down and found a small gray kitten. She realized with a chill that this was what she'd imagined so long ago when she'd first claimed these rooms. She'd imagined a pink bomb going off and all of this. But she hadn't been crazy enough to go through with any of it. She went over to the windows and opened them with the kitten chasing her feet. She saw various sweets were heaped on a platter at the table. Lady Crazy had certainly been living it up.

"Lady Naomi, you look very well considering all of your current hardships," Xersal said.

"Oh, I look awful. The stress is about to kill me," she said, leaning back with the back of her hand against her forehead. She'd gained a few pounds, and not just from the pregnancy, Naomi observed. But she had on makeup and her hair was perfectly coiffed. Naomi wondered if she got up to let the servants fix it or if she made them fix it with her still in bed.

The elephant in the room that she wasn't acknowledging was the bump under the bedding at Lady Naomi's abdomen. She refused to stare at it, but her eyes seemed to be in revolt because her eyes kept drifting back to it. Tavik's child was underneath there. Tavik's child. She felt her stomach churn at the thought. How far along was she? The bedding made it difficult to judge.

"You look wonderful. You're absolutely glowing," Xersal said. He took a seat by the bed and reached out for her hand. "Now tell Uncle Xersal all about it."

It startled Naomi to hear Xersal tell Lady Crazy to call him that. It made her want to hurl something. Was there nothing in her life Lady Crazy wouldn't lay claim to?

Just then a servant slipped into the room carrying a heavy pail.

"Not now, Yula," Mrs. Boon ordered.

Naomi did a double take. She hadn't recognized her dear friend. Yula's hair was barely contained under her kerchief, and her dress was in disrepair and stained. She'd always taken care with her appearance. Seeing her in such bad shape brought tears to Naomi's eyes. She went over and took the heavy metal pail from Yula. "Here let me," she said. The bucket had to weigh twenty pounds. It was full of ash. She was cleaning the fireplaces. It was the messiest job in the castle. No one liked doing it. When Yula had been the housekeeper, she'd rotated the task among the younger servants. Sometimes she assigned it as a punishment for poor behavior. Seeing her relegated to it showed how far she had fallen.

Yula reached to take it back. "Oh no, I can manage, miss. Please don't trouble yourself."

"No, let me help you. Where do you need to go next?" Naomi insisted.

"Taylor, I need you to stay here," Xersal called.

Yula took the pail, and her back bowed under the heavy weight. "Best get back to your master, miss," she said. She turned and left the room. Naomi wanted to call her back but knew it would be pointless and would only raise questions she couldn't answer.

"Taylor, could you join us?" Xersal called.

She went over to her great-uncle's side. "Who in the world is he?" Lady Naomi asked, raising her bedding up to her chin.

Gritting her teeth, Naomi sketched a light curtsy. "My name is Taylor, milady. I am Xersal's grandniece."

Lady Crazy stared at her shrewdly. "You once told me you didn't have any family," she said to Xersal.

"I had no family in the kingdom. My brother resettled far, far away. I've only recently met my grandniece. She has an alicorn that I believe may be of some help to us."

"Why do you cover your face?" Lady Crazy asked.

"I've been cursed. Anyone who sees my face will die," Naomi said then bit her tongue to stop herself from adding that she'd be happy show it to her.

Lady Crazy's eyes widened. "And you brought this abomination here?" she asked Xersal.

Maybe she'd gone a little overboard with the curse. "I promise not to put you or anyone in your castle in any danger," Naomi swore.

Lady Crazy seemed to only be half-mollified. She sat up a little straighter. "Hmm, and what about this alicorn?"

Naomi raised it for her to see. "It can heal any

wound. Xersal thought maybe it would remove the dragon's mark."

"Will it hurt?"

"I don't know," Naomi said, and she truly didn't know. She was sure it wouldn't work because Snowflake would've removed the mark if that had been possible, but he hadn't tried to remove it, so she didn't know if the alicorn's touch would hurt. She remembered how the horn had glowed brightly when trying to cure Tavik when he'd been made sick by Errilol. The alicorn had burned so bright its glow had blinded her, but Tavik had been unconscious during it, so she had no idea if it'd hurt him. Even if it didn't hurt, Naomi was sure it wouldn't work. What would happen when everyone knew that?

Lady Naomi stared at her for a long moment. Naomi didn't know what she was thinking. Surely, she wanted to try everything.

"My love, do you feel up to trying?"

Naomi had to stop herself from whirling around. She slowly turned toward the voice. There he was. He'd come into the room silently. How could she not have known he was there?

"Oh, my beloved, I don't know. I'm scared," Lady Naomi said in a shuddering voice. Naomi had to stop herself from rolling her eyes.

Tavik came over to the bed. He sat down on the edge and took her hand. "Has anyone tested the alicorn?" he asked. He looked to Naomi when he asked.

She felt her face flush, but luckily the scarf hid it from view. He looked good. Maybe a little thinner, but he looked good to her. She'd asked him if he wanted to grow back his hair, but he'd been against it, saying he'd been shaving his head so long that having hair again would be strange. He'd tried to grow a beard though, which she had complained about profusely. She found it scratchy, and it hid his strong jaw and nice lips. She wondered if Lady Crazy had said the same. She really wished she knew everything that Snowflake's spell had done. Things were really different. She'd assumed people would still be the same and in the same places, but Mrs. Boon was the housekeeper, and Yula was only a maid. What else was different? Naomi realized she was staring, and everyone was waiting for her to speak. "I don't think it will hurt her. If it doesn't work, she won't suffer any ill effects," Naomi said.

"You're sure?" Tavik asked, not sounding convinced.

"I've used the horn on myself."

"Of course. You used it to try to lift the curse," Xersal said.

Xersal's comment threw her for a moment. "Yeah, it didn't work, but it didn't have any ill effects."

"I'd like Agatha's opinion before we try this," Tavik said.

"I don't know if we need to bother your mother," Lady Naomi interjected. Naomi wondered what the story was there. Lady Naomi appeared all too eager to leave Agatha out of this.

"Yes, I don't see how a simple hedge witch will have anything to add," Xersal agreed.

"I want her opinion," Tavik said, and his tone brooked no argument.

Lady Naomi quickly backtracked. "Of course, dear. We will send for her, and she can have her say."

Tavik rose. "She's still in the Darkon Forest. It will take her a day to return. Mrs. Boon, would you show the wizard and—" He stopped and turned to Naomi.

"Taylor, his apprentice," she said.

"Miss Taylor to their rooms?"

"Of course, milord," the housekeeper said.

They were shown to a pair of rooms in another part of the castle. Mrs. Boon didn't offer them any welcome or instructions if they should need anything. Xersal's trunk was at least in his room.

Naomi checked out her room for curiosity's sake. She had no intention of sleeping there. She was going back to her parent's house in the evening, but she still poked around. There wasn't much to poke around. It was very basic. A bed, a chair, and a chamber pot.

She went over to Xersal's room and tapped at the door. "Come in," he called.

She opened the door and found her great-uncle deep into his trunk. His head and shoulders were completely inside it. Naomi began to wonder if it was enchanted. "Do you need some help, Great-uncle?"

"Taylor, is that you? Come hold my feet. I don't want to fall in."

Definitely enchanted, then. She went over and grabbed his ankles. "So, do you have any other ideas in case the alicorn doesn't work?" she asked.

"One or two. Why? Do you think it won't work?"

"Like you said, it didn't work on my curse. Maybe it won't work on the dragon's mark?"

"Well, if I'd put all my faith in your alicorn, I wouldn't have brought this very large trunk full of all sorts of wizardly items, would I? Now I'm coming out; keep a tight hold of my feet."

Naomi did as instructed, and after a few moments of huffing and muttering, Xersal was upright once again. He closed the trunk and leaned against it. "Now why don't you take a walk around the castle, and I'll work on those other possibilities?"

"Can't I help?" Naomi asked, not wanting to be left on her own.

Xersal shooed her away. "No, it's better if I do this alone. That way only one of us will catch on fire. Go explore."

Naomi didn't want to catch fire, but she didn't want to go. "Are you sure I can't help?" She had to snap her jaw shut as she felt herself almost add that she used to help Agatha with her spells occasionally.

"Thank you, grandniece, but I'll be fine."

Naomi nodded and slipped out of the room. She went down to the main hall.

The main hall was empty except for a lone scrubbing woman at work with bucket and brush. It was Yula. Naomi went over to her old friend. "May I help?" she asked. The task was too big for just one woman. Usually three or four servants scrubbed the floor. Mrs. Boon must still despise Yula even in this rewritten history. Tavik should've done better by the camp cook than this. He'd held her in some regard. Why relegate her to this?

Yula wiped her brow and looked up at her. "Oh no, miss. I'm fine."

"But this is too big a job for just you. I can scrub a floor."

"I'm sure you can do a right many things being a wizard's apprentice. I don't suppose you could magic all the grime away?"

Naomi shook her head. "I'm afraid we haven't gotten that far in my lessons. But I can get another bucket and brush."

"No, miss. Go find something nice to do."

Naomi wasn't going to be dissuaded. She knew where to find the buckets and brushes. She set up on the other half of the floor and went to work. Yula didn't protest further. Servants came and went through the main hall. She saw Boris stop and speak briefly to Yula and pointed at Naomi.

The serving woman shrugged and said something in the negative to him. He looked at her again and shrugged his shoulders and continued on to wherever he'd been going. She'd been working a couple hours when footsteps approached.

"What are you doing?" Tavik asked.

Naomi dunked her brush into her bucket and didn't look at him. She really should avoid him. She'd just have to make him not want to talk to her. "I think that's self-evident."

"You are a guest."

"It's not a big deal. Xersal didn't need me, and I was bored."

"So you decided to pass the time by scrubbing floors?"

"Why not? Surely I'm a better choice for it than Yula there. She's the same age as my mother. I couldn't imagine making my mother do this."

"Yula is a servant."

"And is she your youngest servant? Is she the only one who could be spared for this?"

"Are you questioning how I run my castle?"

Naomi's eyes narrowed. "I'm questioning if you run your castle."

Tavik scowled down at her. She waited for him to kick her bucket and storm off. Instead, he crouched and snatched her scrub brush from her.

He straightened, and with a roar, shouted, "Mrs. Boon!"

"Oh shit," Naomi murmured. She hopped up.

"There's no need to yell for her. We're almost done." She tried to take the brush back. Tavik held it out of her reach.

"No, you're right. Yula should not be doing this herself."

Yula had left her own bucket and had come over to them. "Oh no, milord. I can manage. I appreciate the young miss's help, but I can finish this up."

"No, our guest is correct. This should be handled by the younger servants."

"But, milord, I do the scrubbing and the fireplaces. It's how I earn my keep."

Tavik blinked and stared at her a moment. Maybe he hadn't realized how badly Yula was being treated. "Xersal and I could use some help. If we're staying in your castle for a few days, we'll need someone who can fetch things for us."

"Hasn't someone been assigned to you?" he asked.

"I don't think Mrs. Boon had gotten around to that yet," Naomi hedged. The fact was she doubted any servants would've been spared for Xersal and her.

Mrs. Boon appeared at the top of the stairs. "My lord, how may I be of assistance?"

"Find a few of the younger servants to finish scrubbing this floor. I thought Yula was Lady Naomi's maid?"

"Lady Naomi requested one of the younger girls take over her dressing and toiletries. I've been endeavoring to find tasks for Yula to keep her on. If she can no longer manage the scrubbing, I really don't know if we can keep her."

Tavik's brow lowered into a mean glower. "I'll decide if we no longer need Yula or not. She is an excellent servant. Why haven't you been utilizing her appropriately?"

Mrs. Boon did not appear to like her decisions questioned, but she very well couldn't go against Tavik. "I apologize, milord. I did not realize what a diamond in the rough Yula truly was."

Naomi did roll her eyes at this.

"Yula will tend to our guests while they are here. When they depart, we'll discuss more appropriate tasks for her."

Mrs. Boon dropped a small curtsy. "As my lord wishes."

He cast one last look at Naomi that made her want to duck behind a column. He turned sharply and swept out. Yula came to stand beside her. "We should probably go elsewhere," the older woman murmured.

Seeing the scowl that settled on Mrs. Boon's face once Tavik was out of the room, Naomi agreed. "Let's go hide in my room," she said and led the way back.

CHAPTER FIFTEEN

A dragon's roar is deafening, but its whisper is more frightening.

Yula shut the door to Naomi's room with a sigh. "Miss, I appreciate you speaking up for me, but I'm afraid that Mrs. Boon will have her revenge."

"You should be the one running this place, not her," Naomi said, sitting down on the bed. She indicated Yula could have the chair. Yula sat down and looked around the sparsely furnished room.

"I don't know why you would say that, but thank you."

"I'll make sure nothing else happens to you."

"You are a guest, miss. You will leave after a time, and then Mrs. Boon will have complete control again."

"How did this happen?" Naomi wondered aloud as she tried to resolve the changes of the spell.

Misinterpreting the question for her, Yula tried to answer her. "I was the camp cook for Tavik. He favored me on the field. When he put down his sword and dispersed his army, he brought me back here to serve in his castle. He could have left me on the field like all the soldiers. I had no home or family to go back to. If he hadn't brought me back, I would've become a beggar woman and most likely died my first winter."

Naomi straightened to look at Yula. She knew Yula had two sons. Two sons who were alive. One was even married now. "You don't have anyone?" she asked, wondering how she could let her dear friend know her family was alive and well and bigger than before.

Yula sighed. "I had two boys, but they were swept up in the army. I think they're dead."

Naomi couldn't let her continue thinking that. "I'm only an apprentice, but I know how to find things out sometimes." She didn't know how to replicate the spell Agatha had used to find Yula's sons, but she didn't have to. She just had to make Yula think she was using magic to discover them. "Get me a bowl of water, and I may be able to discover their fates for you."

"Truly, miss?" Yula said with her eyes round.

"I can certainly try."

Yula left to get the bowl of water. Naomi tried to remember everything Yula had once told her about her sons. Naomi had met them a couple of times when they came to the castle to see Yula. They'd been nice, strong, young men, who obviously adored their mother. Naomi had even met

Yula's daughter-in-law, a sweet-faced woman who blushed and was quite shy.

Yula soon came back with a bowl and a jug of water. "Will this do?" she asked, setting down the bowl.

"Yes, it's perfect. I just need to stare into the bowl, and hopefully something will come to me."

Yula stood by anxiously as Naomi sat at the table staring into the bowl. She was quiet for a minute before beginning to speak. "You have two sons. One is a blacksmith. His name is Warrick."

"That's right, except Warrick's an apprentice," Yula corrected.

Naomi shook her head. "No, he has advanced from that. He's a journeyman now. I see him in a town set up with a senior blacksmith. Someone whom he likes and respects. He's gotten married to a nice girl named Hannah."

"Really? Are you sure? Where are they?"

Naomi pretended to concentrate harder. She wished she could just spill this all out to her friend and not use this charade. "The town is called Luck's Hollow."

"I know where that is! It's not far from here. He's there? Really?"

Naomi nodded her head. "Your other son Uther is there as well. He has signed on with a woodworker as an apprentice. He is doing well. The war has left him with a scar across his chest, but it does not bother him much. The brothers see each other often. They fear you're dead. They don't know what has happened to you."

"Oh my, oh my," Yula paced around the room, wringing her hands. "Are you sure? Are they truly so close and together?"

Naomi straightened and turned to Yula. "They're both fine. You should go to them."

Yula came and crouched at Naomi's feet. "I don't know what to say. You've given me the happiest news in my life. Both my sons are alive! Thank you, thank you." Yula grabbed both of Naomi's hands and kissed them.

"It was a simple enough spell. I'm glad I could help you."

"Truly you will make a great wizard one day."

"Thank you," Naomi said, feeling uncomfortable with the praise. After all, she hadn't done any magic.

"I don't know what to do. I can't just leave the castle."

"I'm sure if you asked Tavik, he would allow it."

"But Mrs. Boon—" Yula began.

"Don't worry about that old battle-ax. You need to go see your sons."

"But what about you and the wizard Xersal? I've been assigned to you. If I go, I don't think they'll assign another servant."

Naomi shook her head for Yula not to worry. "We can look after ourselves. Or I can look after Xersal, at least."

Yula rose and wrung her hands once more. "I'll

go speak to Lord Tavik. Thank you so much."

Naomi rose and gave her dear friend a hug. "Good luck," she said.

Yula hugged her back fiercely and left.

Naomi sat back down and sighed. She was glad she could help her friend. But she realized that maybe she shouldn't have sent her off so hastily. She really could've used someone else on her side, and with Agatha still out in the forest, she had only Xersal, for what that was worth. No, she'd had to tell Yula about her sons. There was no way she could've kept that information knowingly from her. She then wondered if she'd ever see her friend again. Naomi could be gone by the time Yula returned. She wished she'd hugged her more tightly.

They were to have dinner with Tavik that evening. Lady Naomi wasn't going to join them, being still bedridden, which Naomi still found suspicious. She wasn't sure about having dinner with Tavik. Thankfully, she wouldn't be alone with him.

She went to Xersal's room to go down to eat. She found the room full of thick noxious smoke that made her cough. She hoped it didn't do anything else.

"Uncle, are you in here? And more importantly, are you on fire?" she called as she opened the windows to let fresh air in.

"Taylor, what are you doing here?" He emerged from the smoke and looked stoned. The smoke was only giving her a headache, but Xersal's pupils were completely blown out, and his jaw was slack.

"I've come to get you for dinner. You look like you got the munchies."

"The munchies?"

"Are you hungry?"

Xersal rubbed his stomach. "You know, I think I am."

She gave him a critical once-over. Except for his eyes and general demeanor, he looked presentable enough. There may have been a new stain on his robe, but the dark red hid it mainly. He did reek of the smoke, but hopefully that would fade quickly, and hopefully, no one got a contact high.

They went down together and found the large table in the great hall set for five. Naomi wondered who else was invited. Xersal and she sat down at the table and waited for the rest to arrive.

She soon had the answer to her earlier question of who else was dining with them. Boris and his wife, Gilga, came in. Gilga gave them each a friendly smile as Boris pulled her seat out for her. Boris nodded politely enough at them.

Now they were just waiting on Tavik. She wondered what he was doing. He was probably with Lady Crazy. It made sense. They were married, but it still wrenched her heart. The door opened, and Tavik strode in. Everyone rose.

"Please, sit," he said, taking his own seat. Everyone sat back down. Naomi didn't catch the signal, but servants immediately came and put soup before each of them. Naomi was surprised by how formal the dining was, considering the guests, but she very well couldn't question the pomp without raising suspicion.

She had a different worry as well. How was she going to eat? She stirred the soup dubiously. She could maybe bring her spoon up under her scarf, but she didn't think she could manage it without soiling the scarf completely. She could appreciate Tavik's troubles when he wore the helm. But she very well couldn't ask everyone to put on a blindfold for her.

"Lord Tavik, may I extend my heartfelt thanks for the hospitality you have shown my grandniece and me," Xersal said.

Tavik inclined his head. "You are most welcome. I am eager for whatever help you can offer my wife."

Gilga leaned forward. "How is Lady Naomi, milord?"

Tavik sighed and toyed with his soup spoon before he answered. "Her spirits are a bit down. She's fearful that she won't be able to raise our child."

Gilga made a sympathetic sound. Naomi had to look down at her soup. She kept forgetting the situation she'd placed Lady Crazy in. She remembered far too easily the crimes Lady Crazy had committed against her, but she was no longer innocent herself. They'd each threatened the other's life in one way or another, and Lady Crazy's life was still threatened.

"Have you had any word from Agatha?" Gilga asked.

"She should return by tomorrow afternoon," he said.

She nodded.

The servants cleared away the soup and brought out the main course next. Naomi hadn't tried the soup, and her stomach was quite bitter about that. She hoped to be able to manage a few bits of the entrée. Tavik stood at the head of the table and carved pieces of ham for them. Naomi was still uncomfortable with the formal setting. They'd only done formal when some visiting lord had stopped by, and even then it had been a relaxed affair, though Boris had later informed her that those dinners had been very tense affairs. After all, Tavik had threatened many of these lords' lands. She'd had no clue and had felt mortified by the way she'd chatted and joked. Boris had shaken his head. No, she'd helped Tavik more than anyone else to convince the visitors that Tavik wasn't a power-hungry threat any longer. She hadn't understood, and Boris had shrugged his shoulders. The way she treated the servants and guests with equal warmth and goodwill made a good impression. She still couldn't believe her smiling and good humor had helped make trade agreements.

"Miss Taylor, I do hope you won't be convincing any more of my servants to leave while you are a guest in my home."

Naomi froze as she navigated her fork up under her scarf. She withdrew the fork carefully, ham still on the tines. "Beg your pardon?" she asked.

"Mistress Yula requested permission to leave the castle today because you scried the location of her sons."

Xersal turned with great interest to her at this news. She could see the questions he had in his eyes. "So you gave her permission?"

"Of course. A mother should see her sons. But please don't put ideas into anyone else's head."

"Yes, I understand. I just felt compelled to let Yula know the happy news. She'd thought them dead, after all." And Naomi bit her tongue to keep from saying any more on that subject. She didn't feel it prudent to bring up Tavik's conscription of the men.

Gilga sighed. "I think it's lovely. Yula must be beside herself with joy. I know I'd be devastated if I thought my children were dead and then told out of the blue that they were alive."

Boris coughed nervously and put his hand over his wife's with a minute shake of his head. Gilga blushed slightly and wilted a little in her seat.

"No, it is excellent. I am happy for her, though I do feel a touch of shame that I didn't supply the information myself," Tavik said.

"Well, you've had greater concerns," Xersal offered.

Tavik shook his head. "Recently maybe, but before this, I should have been paying better attention."

Naomi didn't think Tavik should feel guilty. Who knew what was in his made-up past, but when Naomi had been here, Yula had found out about her sons. Sure, it had been thanks to Agatha, but it had happened. She still wasn't sure how events were remembered now. Snowflake's spell had changed things and made them a bit wonky, and she was to blame for that, not Tavik or anyone else. "She knows now; that's all that matters," Naomi offered. Tavik inclined his head to her. They continued eating with light conversation. The weather was discussed, which Xersal was very interested in seeing, as he could directly affect it, but his skills were currently unneeded by the farmers. The reason for Gilga's inclusion became obvious, as she was quick to fill the silence with a happy remark or a polite inquiry. When everyone was full, and even Gilga's chatter was winding down, Tavik rose from his seat.

"Thank you all for a pleasant evening. Hopefully we will be able to do this again soon with the Lady Naomi joining us."

Naomi ducked her head to hide her wince. They'd avoided any further discussion of the woman since the very beginning of the meal.

They all rose from the table and said their good-nights. A servant led Xersal and Naomi back to their rooms. For safekeeping, Naomi had discovered Xersal's trunk was theftproof. She'd stowed the alicorn in it, though she feared it might get lost in its cavernous depths. When she looked inside, all she'd seen was darkness. She'd surreptitiously dropped a pebble in it, but didn't hear it land. Xersal assured her that the alicorn would be safe and retrievable. She'd taken his word but was a bit leery. When they reached their rooms, Naomi asked him for the alicorn back. He disappeared into his room but was soon back with it. He did know his trunk then. He handed it to her with a little bow that made her smile, the gesture reminding her of Grandpa Harry and his tea parties with her. She wished him good-night and pricked herself. She opened her eyes back in her bedroom. Xersal was still with her, though he was peering out of the magic mirror.

"Good night, dear. Hopefully tomorrow we'll finally get a chance to try the alicorn."

"Yeah, Uncle Xersal. I hope so, too. Good night."

When the mirror went dark, she swiftly changed into her pajamas and sneaked out of her room to see who else was home. She could hear the television and found her parents on the couch watching a movie.

"Naomi, I didn't hear you come in! How was your day?"

She joined her parents on the couch and watched the movie idly as she answered, "It was weird. Saw a lot of familiar faces, but they weren't the same."

Her mother nodded. "Well, you've been through a lot recently. It would change your perspective."

Naomi nodded. "I'm going out again tomorrow. I got a line on a job. Can't just mooch off you guys for the rest of my life."

"What's the job?" her father asked.

"Well, remember when I said I'd helped my ex-mother-in-law, the herbalist? Well, I found another one who needs help and is willing to teach me."

Her mother turned to her interested. "Really? I've never heard of any local shops like that. Where is it?"

Naomi really needed to think up her cover stories before opening her big mouth. "It's not a shop. It's just this old guy who offers his services to people. He reminds me a bit of Grandpa."

Her mother smiled softly. "He sounds nice."

"Does it come with any benefits?" her father asked.

Naomi wanted to roll her eyes. "No medical, but it's a good start."

Her father didn't look impressed.

She knew she'd flounder on any more questions. She rose from the couch. "Well, um, I'm pretty tired. I think I'll go to bed."

Both her parents wished her good-night, and she retreated to her bedroom. Naomi began to doubt how well this would work in the long term. She couldn't keep coming and going for weeks without them growing suspicious. But then she didn't know what the situation would be from day to day. Tomorrow, Lady Crazy could be free of the dragon's mark, and then Xersal would be going back to the other castle. Did she want to go with him and make a real go of being his apprentice? Realistically, she should reestablish her life on Earth. She could find a new apartment and job or go back to school like she'd suggested. She could still visit Terratu and see Xersal. Her life would be a lot simpler, but the thought made her feel traitorous.

She stowed the alicorn in her closet. She didn't even play with the idea of putting it under her mattress. Having seen Lady Crazy's baby bump made the thought of visiting Tavik in her dreams unbearable.

Naomi had breakfast with her parents the next morning and waited for them both to be safely gone before going back up to her room to get dressed and ready to go. She took the alicorn and pictured the room she had at the castle. She opened her eyes and looked around. It was still early there. She went to Xersal's door and tapped on it to see if he were awake. There was no answer. She tried going in but found the door barred. She went back to her room to wait.

There were refreshments in the room. Mrs. Boon must have deigned to assign another servant to them, but whoever it was, was being very discreet. She wondered what the servant had made of her unslept-in bed, or rather, what Mrs. Boon would make of it when the servant reported it back to her.

She left the food untouched and went to the window. She looked out at a familiar courtyard, but the familiarity was slightly askew since she'd never seen the courtyard from that window. Things were similar but not the same. Her husband was married to Naomi, who had a dragon's mark. Her mother-in-law was trying to cure her. And there was a blind umbrek nosing in the trash. Naomi leaned out to see Hip Hop better. The umbrek looked thinner, and her coat was filthy. She watched as the blind umbrek picked up some rotted cabbage and put it into her pouch.

This wasn't right. She didn't know what Hip Hop's story was now, but she had the feeling it was similar to Yula's. The people and creatures most cared for by Naomi appeared to have been treated very poorly by Lady Crazy.

Her breakfast had come with a bowl of fruit. She picked it up and carried it downstairs to the courtyard. Hip Hop was still rummaging in the refuse cart. The servants that had to go by gave the umbrek a wide berth. Surely, anyone could see that she was harmless. Naomi walked up to the umbrek and stopped a yard away because the creature hadn't indicated she'd heard her.

"Hip Hop?" she called.

The umbrek flinched and began creeping away. "Hip Hop, come here," she said. The umbrek didn't pay any attention to her. Naomi sighed and crept up to her side and touched her shoulder. Hip Hop snarled and made a swipe at her with one of her claws. Naomi gasped and jumped back. An apple that had been sitting on the top of her bowl fell out and rolled to Hip Hop's feet. The umbrek's nose twitched, and she reached down to investigate. She picked up the apple and brought it to her mouth. She ate it in several large bites. Core and all.

"No one's been looking after you, have they?" Naomi asked.

The umbrek's nose turned to her as she sniffed. Naomi held out a pear. Hip Hop crept closer to her. Naomi placed the fruit gently under her nose to show her. Hip Hop took the fruit and ate it just a fraction more slowly than the apple.

Getting a closer look at the umbrek, Naomi saw just how filthy she truly was. Her hind legs and tail were caked with mud and a truly repugnant smell wafted from her pouch. She needed a bath desperately. Naomi shook her head and set the bowl of fruit down. Hip Hop cautiously crept to it.

"It's all right. Eat all of it," Naomi said in a

calm, gentle tone. Hip Hop put her nose into the bowl and began eating. Naomi worried she'd eat too fast and make herself sick but couldn't bring herself to scold the beast. Instead, she went to the kitchen. The entrance was just off the courtyard. It was midmorning and not a lot of activity at the moment. A kitchen girl blinked at Naomi in surprise from where she stood on a bucket washing dishes.

"Don't mind me," Naomi said as she retrieved two buckets, dipped them into one of the water barrels, and then from a sack took some soap flakes to put into one of the buckets. She left again and then went to the stables to grab a brush and stack of clean rags. Everyone stopped to stare at her, but she just kept going. No one told her to stop or even asked what she thought she was doing.

She came back to Hip Hop. She was still with the bowl. She was nibbling on a strawberry, making it last as long as possible. It made Naomi smile.

She set the bucket down and dunked the brush into it. She stirred up the water to make it sudsy and straightened. Hip Hop had finally nibbled the strawberry to nothing and was rooting in the bowl, but it was empty.

"Hip Hop, you need a bath, and I don't want any arguments. Understand?"

The umbrek's ears twitched in her direction, and she turned toward her. She sniffed the air, obviously hoping for more food.

Naomi brought the soapy bucket over to her and raised the brush. Hip Hop obviously still had no idea what Naomi was going to do. She held the brush out for the umbrek to inspect then brought it up to the beast's shoulder gently and began to scrub. The umbrek didn't seem to quite understand but let Naomi work. Once she really began scrubbing on the umbrek's back and legs, Hip Hop seemed to get the idea and would move to give her better access.

Naomi could see servants coming out to stare at her, but she stayed focused on the task at hand. Soon her bucket of soapy water was empty. She looked at Hip Hop's coat and decided she was pretty clean, though she'd probably need another bath in less than a week. She picked up the bucket of clean water and began rinsing her off.

"What are you doing?"

Naomi glanced over her shoulder at Tavik. "Cleaning your umbrek. You've let her get into a terrible state." Hip Hop pawed at her and raised her chin, wanting Naomi to scrub her there. She seemed to like to be scratched there as well as her chest. Naomi indulged her for a few moments, but then moved to rinsing off her back and tail.

"Umbreks are very dangerous."

Hip Hop was twisting around and raising her chin again for more scratching. Naomi gave in and indulged her some more. "Oh yeah, she's a killer," she said wryly as she petted the umbrek.

She turned and picked up the clean rags and began drying her off.

"You certainly have a way with her."

Naomi rolled her eyes. "I gave her some fresh fruit and a bit of attention. That's nothing special. How'd she come to be here?"

"Agatha's familiar brought her back from the Darkon Forest. Agatha told him to get rid of her."

Naomi didn't know what to make of that. She would've figured Agatha would've shown Hip Hop a little more care, but then again, before the spell, Agatha hadn't even met the umbrek. Maybe she had no interest in keeping pets.

"What's in the Darkon Forest?"

"It's where the dragon Grisbek lives. I believe she's looking for possible ways to remove the dragon's mark."

Naomi nodded. She'd slowly stopped paying attention to Hip Hop as she spoke to Tavik. Hip Hop obviously wanted her attention back. She put her forepaws on Naomi's shoulders and began rubbing her cheek against hers. This made Naomi giggle. "All right, all right. I'll get back to drying you, you silly thing."

"She really does like you," Tavik observed in surprise.

"Yeah, I guess," Naomi turned back toward Hip Hop and began brushing the beast's chest. She already looked ten times better than before, now she just needed to get regular meals, and she'd look one hundred percent again.

Hip Hop was obviously grateful for the food and the bath. She reached out and began patting Naomi. This made Naomi smile. "Oh, so it's my turn for petting? Thank you very much, Hip Hop."

Hip Hop seemed very curious about her scarf and began nibbling at it. Naomi tried to shake her off. "No, Hip Hop. Bad," she said, but her words held little heat, and the umbrek paid her no attention.

Tavik came up to the umbrek and held out his hand. "Oh please pet her, she likes her chin scratched," Naomi said, still trying to keep Hip Hop from eating her scarf. Tavik's hand landed on Hip Hop's shoulder, but she barely paid him any attention. She appeared to very much like the taste of Naomi's scarf.

Naomi dropped the brush and was trying to push her away, but the umbrek was bigger and determined. "What's wrong?" Tavik asked with a touch of alarm.

"Hip Hop, stop," Naomi said with some heat in her voice this time, but still the beast didn't listen to her.

The umbrek let out a frustrated snort and reached out with one of her forepaws and dragged the scarf down. Naomi tried to stop her, but one of her claws had snagged on the cloth. Naomi threw her arm across her face.

"Don't look!" she cried. Her scarf was around her neck now. Her face was exposed. She threw her arm across her face and ducked her head. She needed to get away. She cast her eyes around the courtyard, but she'd gathered an audience of servants while tending Hip Hop. She couldn't let any of them see. She ran to the closest building, which was the stables. No one was there. She quickly ducked into Stomper's stall. The horse placidly looked at her. She paid him no mind. She went to the back corner of the stall and struggled to untie the scarf to get it back over her face.

"Are you all right? Did the beast hurt you?" Tavik asked from the stall entrance.

"Don't come in here!" Naomi said desperately. Stomper didn't like her tone of voice and stamped the ground.

"Taylor, did the beast hurt you? I'll have it killed if it did. I should've killed it as soon as Agatha brought the damned creature here."

"Don't you dare!" Naomi's frantic struggle with the scarf was causing her to fumble with the knot. She was going to rip it if she didn't take care.

Tavik sighed from behind her. It was such a familiar sound. It made her stomach tighten. "Then what happened?"

"She pulled down my scarf. None of you can see my face. It would be bad. There's a curse," she explained and felt a brief moment of triumph when she got the knot undone. She quickly wrapped the cloth back over her face and pulled the hood back over her head. She patted her face for a few moments to be sure everything was covered.

"What's the curse?"

"Hmm?" Naomi asked. She wished she had a mirror to check the scarf. It felt like everything was covered, but she wanted to be absolutely sure.

"What happens when people see your face?"

"Bad things. Trust me, you don't want to find out."

"I used to cover my face," he said.

Naomi turned around to face him. He stood at the entrance of the stall. "I know. It was to hide your allegiance to Errilol."

Tavik nodded. "So what are you hiding?"

Naomi was silent a moment, then shook her head, holding on to the lie. "I've been cursed. My face will cause misfortune for anyone who sees it."

Tavik tilted his head and looked at her. Why was he questioning her? She moved around Stomper to exit the stall, but Tavik continued to stand in her way. She grew nervous and paused. His questions worried her. She turned and began scratching Stomper as though it was what she'd intended to do. The horse was happy for the attention. He appeared not to have been as well cared for as when she'd been around as well. It appeared everyone and everything she'd held dear was being neglected. She wondered if it was somehow willful, but if so, whose will? Snowflake wouldn't have done this, and Lady Crazy shouldn't have any inkling about who and what Naomi had loved.

"He's a very good horse," she commented.

"He's a draft horse. Nothing special."

"He's very calm and steady," Naomi argued.

"You seem to have very definite ideas about things that you should have no ideas about."

Naomi averted her eyes. He had a point there. "You just know things sometimes," she said and silently called herself a fool. She needed to get away from Tavik. He was acting far too suspicious.

There was a scraping noise outside the stall. Tavik looked down and jerked. "Dammit, you're not allowed in here. Get out!"

"What's wrong?" Naomi asked, unable to see what he was looking at.

"The damn umbrek followed us in. If the horses catch wind of her—" As if on cue, Stomper let out a fierce snort and started whinnying. The horses in the surrounding stalls began to panic as well.

Naomi tried to reach out to calm Stomper, but he wasn't having any of it. "Taylor!" Tavik shouted. Naomi backed away. Stomper was beginning to rear up. Tavik reached in and grabbed her. He'd barely pulled her out before Stomper reared up and crashed down. Tavik slammed the door shut as Stomper continued to panic. In her peripheral vision, she saw Hip Hop scurry out.

S.A. HUNTER

The poor thing. She hoped the umbrek didn't run off. Tavik had pushed her against a post and pinned her when he pulled her out. She waited for him to step back from her, but he didn't. His chest heaved against hers, and his thighs interlocked with hers.

His breath was warm and moist on her face. "Are you all right? Did his hooves get you?"

Naomi shook her head. "I'm fine. Thank you." She tried to ease out from under him, but he was still breathing harshly and staring at her hard.

"What's the curse?" he asked again.

"It's not to upset horses. I didn't mean for that—"

Tavik let out an impatient breath. "I know. It was the damn umbrek. She scares the horses, naturally. Need to tie her up."

"I'll take care of her," Naomi said, hating the idea of Hip Hop being tethered to some tree somewhere.

Tavik shook his head.

"I swear I'll look after her. It'll be fine. She really is completely harmless."

"Why do you care?"

"I told you she's harmless! If you'd just let her be, maybe—"

"You can keep the damn umbrek. I don't care."

Naomi's mouth snapped shut. She tried again to ease out from under him, but he stopped her and leaned in even closer to the point their foreheads touched. "Who are you?" he asked.

294

"We told you. I'm Taylor, Xersal's grandniece."

"But that's not all," Tavik said. He was overwhelming her.

Naomi put her hands on his chest and pushed at him. "I'm no one special. Pay no attention to me."

Tavik wasn't budging. A smirk crept onto his face. "What's the curse?" he asked again. In alarm, Naomi felt his thigh move in higher between hers. He was bracing one hand on the post behind her, but the other had crept around to the small of her back to pull them even closer. They were so close now that she was going cross-eyed trying to look him in the eye.

While her heart pounded and her knees were melting, an alarming thought occurred to Naomi: he was married with a baby on the way, and here he was putting the moves on her. Had he done anything like this while married to *her*? If she'd gotten pregnant, would he have been chasing after the chambermaids? The thought made her sick and brought tears to her eyes. "Get off me." She tried to make it an order, but her voice cracked.

Immediately Tavik eased up. "What's wrong? Did I hurt you? Please, forgive me. I didn't—"

"You're married! You have a pregnant wife, and you're doing this?" Naomi demanded, motioning to him and her.

He blanched and turned his eyes away. "I—I love my wife. I wouldn't do anything to hurt her," he stammered.

Naomi shoved him off her. She turned and walked out of the stable. "Keep repeating that to yourself," she said.

Hip Hop was waiting outside, looking forlorn. Naomi went up to the umbrek and held her hand under her nose. Hip Hop nuzzled it. "Come on, Hip Hop. You're staying with me." Naomi's voice was only a touch watery.

She led Hip Hop back to her room. She knew Mrs. Boon wouldn't approve of the animal being inside, but frankly she didn't give a damn. The fact was, she hoped the housekeeper did show up to express her displeasure. Naomi really wanted to yell at someone.

There was a tap at the door. Hip Hop had been exploring the space and turned at the sound. Naomi marched to the door, expecting a servant or Mrs. Boon standing at the other side. She swung the door open to find Xersal.

"Good morning, grandniece. Shall we head to..." He peered past her at Hip Hop.

He paused and rubbed his eyes. He looked again. Hip Hop wandered up behind Naomi and put her paws on Naomi's shoulders to sniff in Xersal's direction.

"Taylor, um, I hope I am seeing things because there appears to be an umbrek behind you."

Naomi reached up and scratched Hip Hop's chin. She was enjoying Xersal's discomfort, which she should be ashamed of, but she couldn't help herself. "Yep, this is Hip Hop. She'll be staying with me."

"Hip? Hop?"

"Yep."

Xersal still looked discombobulated. Naomi took pity on him. "She's harmless. Put out your hand and let her sniff it."

Xersal didn't look convinced. He extended his hand to Hip Hop, but he kept it clenched in a fist as though afraid he'd lose a finger. Hip Hop sniffed the hand and gave it a little lick before turning back into the room and lying down on the rug in front of the fireplace.

"Now where did you want to go?" Naomi asked.

Xersal was still watching Hip Hop. Naomi had to snap her fingers under his nose to get his attention. "Oh, um, I believe the witch has returned. We should go to Lady Naomi's room to convince them to try the alicorn cure."

"Sounds good. Lead the way."

Xersal pointed over her shoulder at Hip Hop. "Are you sure you want to leave that in your room?"

"I don't see why not."

"Well, at least warn the poor chambermaids."

They paused outside Lady Crazy's room. They

could hear several raised voices in argument beyond the closed door.

"I wonder what this is all about?" Xersal whispered. Naomi shrugged her shoulders. He knocked to announce their presence, and the voices quieted. The door was opened by Tavik. Naomi peered past him and saw Agatha standing by Lady Crazy's bed. She had her arms crossed and looked mad that they'd interrupted whatever argument had been in progress.

"If now isn't a good time, we can come back," Naomi offered.

"No, please come in," Tavik said, holding the door open for them. Xersal and Naomi entered and stopped midway in the room.

Agatha was clearly taking their measure and wasn't impressed by them. Her eyes narrowed as she took in Naomi's scarf-covered face. Nervously, Naomi raised a hand to make sure it was securely in place. "Tavik tells me that you possess a unicorn horn."

Naomi raised the alicorn. "It has curative powers. We thought it might dispel the dragon's mark."

"So if you would let us try, we'll finally find out," Xersal said.

Agatha frowned at him for a moment, but her eyes came back to Naomi. She seemed to be scrutinizing her very closely. "They tell me that you've been cursed."

"Yes, but covering my face nullifies it."

"Is it true that anyone who sees it dies?" Mr. Squibbles asked.

Naomi looked around the room for the familiar. Xersal seemed curious, too, as to where the new voice had come from.

"Over here," the mouse said.

They found him sitting on the table with several pieces of cheese stacked beside him. Xersal peered more closely at him. "Your familiar, I presume? Never seen a mouse used. Would think a larger animal would be more suitable."

"Size is overrated," Mr. Squibbles said.

"But what could you fetch or do?"

"Not a stinking dog," the mouse said.

"He could go unnoticed to many places," Naomi offered.

"Hmm, like a spy? Now what type of witch would choose a familiar for that purpose?" Xersal said, giving Agatha a look.

Agatha's back stiffened. "At least, I can keep a familiar. You've had several, yes? None of them stayed long."

Seeing the conversation deteriorating rapidly, Naomi stepped up to the bed. "Why don't we try the alicorn? No reason to keep Lady Naomi in suspense."

Lady Crazy, who hadn't seemed to be paying attention to their conversation, sat up straighter and put her box of chocolates aside. "Are we sure that this is safe?" she asked, looking to Agatha.

"May I see the alicorn?" Agatha held out her

hand.

Naomi gave it to her.

Xersal raised his hand. "Wait, Taylor. I don't think that—"

Agatha took the alicorn from Naomi and looked at it. She looked over at Tavik and gave him a nod. Naomi didn't understand what that was about until Tavik opened the door and a group of guards came in with swords drawn.

"What is the meaning of this?" Xersal demanded.

Agatha placed the tip of the alicorn against Lady Crazy. It began to glow. Everyone held their breath, but the glow soon faded.

"Did it work?" Tavik asked.

"Lean forward, dear," Agatha asked.

Lady Naomi leaned forward so that the witch could peer down her back. She shook her head. Tavik's shoulders slumped. Lady Naomi's eyes dropped, and she covered her mouth.

"I knew it was too good to be true," she murmured as her eyes watered.

Naomi felt bad that she'd let them believe the alicorn might work when she'd known it wouldn't.

"Take them to the dungeon," Agatha said.

The guards stepped forward and surrounded Naomi and Xersal. "Oh, this is a fine thank-you for trying to help! Because one possible cure didn't work, you're going to punish us?" Xersal spat.

"No, Xersal. We're not going to punish you. You're going to help us with another possible cure," Agatha said.

"What's that?" Naomi asked.

Agatha turned to her. "Your curse," she said.

Naomi again raised her hand to her scarf-covered face. "What do you mean?"

"They tell me that anyone who sees your face will die. I wish to test that theory."

"How?" Naomi said. She turned to look at Tavik, but his eyes were firmly aimed at the floor.

"We're going to see if it's strong enough to kill a dragon."

Xersal sputtered and struggled against the guards holding him. "And if it doesn't? She'll be killed! How dare you put my grandniece's life in jeopardy for your own gain. I won't allow it. You won't get away with this!"

"Xersal, stop. Don't get yourself hurt," Naomi said. She turned to Agatha. "I'll help you. Just let my great-uncle go."

Agatha shook her head. "No, I will not have that fool popping up to ruin everything. Take them both to the dungeon."

Naomi looked to Tavik one last time as the guards took her arms. He'd turned away completely now. She stared at his back as the guards pulled her from the room. She knew he was the one who must have told Agatha about the curse. Maybe he'd even been the one to come up with the plan to give her to the dragon.

CHAPTER SIXTEEN

Not many know this, but a dragon's talons are poisoned, though the talons generally rip the prey apart before the poison can affect them.

After ranting for an hour about the injustice of it all, Xersal appeared to have worn himself out. He sat slumped over asleep. Naomi was thinking. During all of Xersal's ranting, he hadn't put forth any alternative solutions for Lady Naomi's dragon's mark. Naomi had to assume he had no ideas. Agatha didn't appear to have any other solution than sacrificing Naomi, so that left Naomi to think of a proper solution. As she sat in the dungeon, listening to the Xersal's soft snores, an idea came to her. It hit her like lightning and was just as dangerous. She had it: a solution to get rid of the dragon's mark. It was risky. Insane even. But she'd thought up a loophole to the dragon's mark. She just needed the alicorn to pull it off.

"Hello?"

Naomi looked down at her feet and saw Mr. Squibbles. He stood on his hind legs, looking up at her.

"Hello," she said, unable to keep from smiling

at the familiar familiar.

The mouse's whiskers twitched a moment. "Do we know each other?" he asked.

Naomi raised an eyebrow. She hadn't said his name. She didn't know why he would ask that. "I'm wearing a mask. How would you recognize me?"

"You smell familiar," he said.

Naomi's eyes widened a fraction. Of course, animals recognized others by more than sight. Scent and sound were also traits they would recognize. She remembered, then, how friendly Hip Hop had been. She'd put it down as simple gratitude for being kind to her, but the blind umbrek had never seen Naomi, so obviously she'd learned her by sound and smell, and she'd disguised neither when she'd met the umbrek again. Could the same have happened with Stomper? Had they both recognized her? Neither creature could tell anyone what they knew though. Mr. Squibbles, on the other hand, could blab her secret to the entire castle.

"I don't think we've met before. I think I would remember meeting a talking mouse," she said, hoping he wouldn't be able to tell she was lying.

"Hmm." She needed to figure out a way to alleviate his suspicions of her.

"What brings you to our cell? If you're looking for food, I'm afraid we don't have any to spare."

"Hip Hop sent me."

Chill bumps rose on Naomi's arms. She'd also

forgotten that while Mr. Squibbles could speak to humans, he was also capable of speaking to any creature in the animal kingdom. What had Hip Hop told him?

"She wants you back. She keeps asking for the nice woman. I heard Tavik mention how you'd taken her in. Thank you, by the way. I appreciate the kindness you've shown her."

"She's very sweet. Why doesn't Agatha like her?" She'd wondered about this. It hadn't seemed like the witch to cast off the poor creature.

"Oh, she just doesn't have time for her. She's completely focused on saving Lady Naomi and the unborn baby."

Naomi nodded. "Well, tell Hip Hop that I'm fine, and I'm sorry that I can't bring her any food or scratch her chin."

The mouse nodded. "I think maybe what Agatha and Naomi have planned isn't very kind to you."

"Agatha and Naomi?" Naomi's eyes widened, and her breath caught.

"Yes, Lady Naomi told Agatha about your curse and how they could use it to her advantage. She can be quite clever when it suits her."

Naomi blinked and let out a long breath. She had told Lady Crazy of the curse but hadn't made much of it. She'd been wrong then. Tavik hadn't been the one to suggest the plan. Wait, the argument right before they entered, had that been about their plan? "Lord Tavik did not seem very keen on the idea," Naomi hedged, hoping to draw more information from the mouse.

"He is quite against it, but we must do all we can to save Naomi and the baby."

"I understand, but I wonder if I may suggest an alternative idea?"

"They won't release you from the dungeon."

"That's fine. That's not what I'm going to ask for."

"Go ahead."

Naomi liked that the familiar seemed willing to help her, but she was scared that he'd figure out who she was. She needed help, though. She sighed and glanced over at Xersal. He was no longer snoring. His eyes were closed, but she suspected he was awake.

"I need my alicorn," she said.

"Lady Naomi has it."

Naomi bristled at the news. It was one more thing Lady Crazy had taken of hers. "Well, I need it. I think I know a way to fix all of this, but I need the alicorn to do it."

Mr. Squibbles sighed and looked away.

"What's your plan, Taylor?" Xersal asked.

She glanced at him again. His eyes were open now. "It's better if I don't say. I need to go somewhere, and then I'll come right back." She paused and thought about her plan more. It was very risky and might not work. "Timing will be everything. I'll need the alicorn when I'm given to

Grisbek. I'll leave and come straight back. I'll show my face to him, and Lady Naomi will lose the dragon's mark. I swear it."

"Obviously they won't trust you to keep your word," Mr. Squibbles said.

"That's true, but I promise you I will. When Grisbek sees my face, this will all be over."

Mr. Squibbles sighed. "Agatha won't go for it."

She knew she shouldn't say it, but she did anyway. She should avoid him as much as possible. He was off limits, but she knew he'd help. "Ask Tavik."

The mouse's eyes narrowed as he peered up at her. "And why would he be amendable?" he asked.

Because he seemed to be attracted to her. Because he'd turned away as she was led out of Lady Crazy's bedroom. Because he seemed to care. She couldn't give any of those reasons, though.

"Because he wants his wife to be cured and his unborn child saved," Xersal said.

Naomi's shoulders slumped. Yeah, there was that, too.

"I'll talk to Tavik. You'll just have to wait here."

"Like we have a choice," Naomi said ruefully.

"I'll come back as soon as I can," the mouse said and ran back into the hole in the wall.

"Thank you," she called.

In the silence that followed, Xersal sat up and began picking bits of hay from his beard. "That's one powerful curse if it can kill a dragon," he commented.

"It is."

"How did you acquire it?"

Naomi glanced nervously at her great-uncle. He was still cleaning his long beard, acting nonchalant, but she'd begun to catch on to his act. Half the time he only acted bumbling and absentminded to gauge other people and to trick them, but he'd shown with his knowing questions that he had a sharp mind. She'd have to be careful with him. "I pissed off the wrong person," she said.

"What did you do?" he asked.

Crap, she didn't know what to tell him. "I'd rather not say. It's shameful."

"You know you don't strike me as the type of woman who would do something so awful that would require such a terrible curse, especially on a planet that supposedly has no magic."

Naomi tried to laugh off his suspicions. "We all do stupid things for love."

"You must have loved him very much to take on such a terrible burden."

"I didn't have much choice. It was either the curse or all-out war."

"War?"

"Yeah, and I couldn't accept the thought that any more would have to die because of me."

Xersal nodded. "That sounds more like it."

Naomi turned to say something to her great-uncle because she felt like he was getting too close to the truth, but the cell door opened. She turned in dread. Tavik came through the door.

Naomi held onto the bench to stop herself from rising and approaching the bars. She had to keep her distance because Tavik did not seem inclined to keep his. Tavik came to stand on the other side of the bars. He wrapped a hand around a bar and peered in at them. Naomi stared back. Xersal kept grooming himself.

"Agatha's familiar said you wanted to speak to me."

Naomi nodded. Mr. Squibbles had worked fast. She appreciated that.

"I need you to get me something."

"Are you well?" Tavik asked. She frowned slightly at his question. This wasn't the time for pleasantries.

"Fair." She had to keep this short. She knew she shouldn't be talking to him. She should have avoided him from the moment she came back. Stupidly, she'd thought covering her face would be enough, but as Hip Hop proved, she could be recognized by more than her face.

"I'm sorry we put you in here, but we think your curse may be our salvation, and we fear you'll flee." Naomi noticed that he was referring to everything as we, even though Mr. Squibbles had said the plan was Lady Naomi's and that he'd been against it. Maybe he'd been brought around. Maybe he wouldn't help her. Naomi couldn't look at him.

"I came here to help." And she was beginning to feel like an idiot for doing that. Sure, giving the dragon's mark to Lady Naomi had been evil, but she'd also given her everything else, as well. Did she really need to fix everything for her? Make her life perfect?

Tavik sighed. "I know. Your alicorn is a powerful magical item. Once this is over, I will give it back to you."

"That's assuming I'm alive to accept it."

Tavik's grip tightened on the metal bar. "I'll do everything I can to protect you."

Naomi looked at him and considered his words. "If you mean that, then give me the alicorn when you leave me for the dragon."

"The alicorn can't kill Grisbek."

"No, but it will help me fix all of this."

"What will you do?"

Naomi shook her head. "You'll just have to trust me. I'll take care of everything. Lady Naomi will be saved, and you and she can have your baby and live happily ever after."

"How can you be so sure?"

"My plan will work. I know how to remove the dragon's mark. My face will stop him, but if you really want to give me a chance of surviving this, you'll let me have my alicorn."

"That wasn't my question."

Naomi peered at him. "What do you mean?"

"How can you be sure Lady Naomi and I will

live happily ever after?"

She didn't know why he was asking that. "Because you love each other. And the baby will make you happy."

Tavik continued to stare at her. She didn't know what his look meant. It was far too serious. Maybe he didn't believe her. "I swear I'll fix everything," she said.

"What about you?"

"What?"

"What happens to you once this is over?"

She looked over at Xersal. It looked like he'd nodded off again, or he was faking and trying to give them a semblance of privacy. "I'll go back with Xersal and be his apprentice."

"And that's it?"

"What more do you want?" Naomi was tired and unhappy about his questions. Couldn't he leave her alone? He'd live happily ever after with Lady Crazy and Junior, and she'd learn how to make it rain. If it required tears, she'd be well stocked.

"What about the curse?"

Naomi rolled her eyes. "What about it?"

"We could break it for you or find a way to do it."

She shook her head. "Don't worry about the curse." Why'd she tell them it was a curse? She should've said it was a severe disfiguration or maybe due to religious belief.

She jumped when Tavik violently rattled the

bar he held. "I know who you are. Just admit it!"

"And I think you should walk away, young man. You have no right to talk to my grandniece like that." Xersal wasn't pretending to be asleep or picking at his beard anymore. His brown eyes were focused on Tavik. Naomi was frozen in shock. Tavik knew? This ruined everything.

"Tavik—" Naomi began, not really knowing how to explain.

"What do you know?" Xersal asked, cutting her off.

Tavik let go of the cell bar. "It was her. She's the one who's been appearing in my bed. Is it some plot you hatched with Lord Gerald? Send a temptress to me in the hopes I'll abandon Lady Naomi?"

Naomi's eyes grew round. Oh, he didn't know. Boy, did he not know.

Xersal said something that Naomi couldn't follow. It was gibberish that made her ears ring. Tavik stiffened and crumpled to the floor.

"Xersal, what did you do?" Naomi leapt from the bench and rushed to the bars. She reached out to Tavik's prone body, but he was out of reach. She couldn't see any blood, and she saw his chest rise as he breathed.

"I did warn him."

"Warn him of what? What did you do?" she begged.

She looked to the exit of the dungeon. The door was closed, but surely there was a guard stationed still outside. "Help! We need help in here! Something's wrong with Tavik!"

The door cracked open, and a cautious guard stuck his head in. "Lord Tavik, do you require assistance?" He jumped when he saw Tavik lying on the ground. He rushed to his side.

"Is he okay? Get Agatha. She'll be able to help him," Naomi said.

The guard gave her a wide-eyed unsure look.

"Get Agatha!" she ordered.

He nodded and ran out. Xersal had risen from the bench. He went to the cell door and rapped it with his knuckles. It swung open. Naomi stared at him in disbelief.

He held out his hand to her. "Time to go, my dear. We've humored these idiots long enough."

Instead, Naomi rushed past him and knelt by Tavik. She turned him over and looked at his face. He was still unconscious. "What did you do to him?" she asked. She patted Tavik's cheek in the hopes of rousing him.

"It won't kill him or even really harm him. Now we need to go before more guards show up."

Naomi sighed in relief as Tavik's eyes fluttered open. "Hey, don't try to move. I don't know what Xersal did to you, but you should stay still until Agatha gets here."

Tavik stared up at her and a small, high-pitched whine came from him. Naomi covered her mouth in shock. She scanned his body again. She didn't see anything traumatic. He didn't appear to have any broken bones, and he wasn't bleeding.

"Xersal, what did you do?" she begged.

The wizard shrugged. "Made his voice reflect his nature."

"What does that mean?"

From outside, they could hear the approach of a group of people. Xersal grabbed her arm. "There's no time. We must leave now."

Tavik grabbed her other arm and made another high-pitched whine. Naomi pulled her arm out of Xersal's grasp. "No, I'm not leaving. I know how to deal with Grisbek. What did you do to Tavik?"

"Taylor, we have to go! Now!"

"No, I'm not leaving Tavik!"

Xersal grabbed for her hand again. "Grand-niece, I think we need to have a long, serious talk about your curse and desire to help these ungrateful people, but for now, leave the stupid warlord and let's go!"

He tried to pull her to her feet, but Tavik had other ideas. With Xersal pulling on one arm and Tavik holding onto the other, Naomi found herself the rope in a tug-of-war.

"Tavik, you let her go this instant, or I'll hex you even worse that I already have."

Tavik snarled. Literally snarled. He sat up and pulled Naomi from Xersal with such force she found herself toppling into him. Naomi was sprawled on top of Tavik when the dungeon door opened to reveal Agatha.

"What is going on here?" the witch demanded.

Before Naomi could get her bearings, Tavik had both of them up on their feet, and he'd pushed Naomi behind him, very much like he was shielding her. Her heart melted at the chivalry, but then froze when the barking began.

She peeked around Tavik to find the dog but couldn't see the dog. The dog should be right there by her. The barking was right next to her.

"You've cursed my son?"

Naomi looked at Agatha. "I what now?"

There were a few more barks, and then a doggy snort. She turned around and looked for the dog. Still no dog. "What in the world possessed you to make Tavik sound like a dog?" Mr. Squibbles asked.

"What?" She pulled Tavik around to face her. He looked down at her, and whined softly. Her eyes widened.

"No. No way. I did not do that." Tavik turned and barked something. Seeing his lips move and canine barks issue from his mouth was doing bad things to Naomi's head. It was making her feel ill. She did not like it.

"Can I go back into my cell, please?" she asked. She wanted to sit down.

"And what are you doing free? Where's Xersal?"

Naomi realized then that her great-uncle had disappeared. Tavik again put himself between her and his mother. He growled at them.

"He says Taylor is innocent. Xersal cast the curse and opened the cell."

Agatha let out her own growl. "I knew that bumbling buffoonery was just an act. We should have shackled him and cut out his tongue."

Naomi's eyes widened.

Tavik made some sort of soft doggy sound at her. She looked at him blankly.

"He says she would've reattached it, eventually," Mr. Squibbles explained.

"What?"

"Xersal's tongue. Agatha would've reattached it."

"Oh." Somehow that wasn't very comforting, and Naomi thought maybe she shouldn't say much around Agatha in case she decided Naomi shouldn't have her tongue either, after all she could always reattach it later. Things sort of started going gray then. Tavik's arm slid around her waist to keep her steady. She turned toward him to thank him, and he made a little snuffling sound that had her swallowing her words.

Seeing her distress, Tavik guided her back into the cell. She sat down gratefully on the bench. Tavik didn't leave, though. He got down on bended knee in front of her. She'd always found that position so romantic. She smiled at him, and he smiled back. He smoothed her hair back from her face and made a friendly growly sound.

She shook her head and let out a rueful sigh. "I

didn't think things could get any weirder, but my great-uncle certainly proved me wrong."

Tavik didn't try to reply, which she was grateful for.

"Tavik, get out of there. We need to post more guards. Xersal will most likely come back for her," Agatha said.

He turned and barked something to his mother.

Mr. Squibbles translated. "He says Taylor won't go with the wizard. It's why she's still here. She wants to help us, and we should let her out of the dungeon."

"Tavik, really? That's preposterous. Now get out of there."

Tavik let out a frustrated growl and sat down on the bench beside Naomi. She looked at him in surprise. "It's okay," she whispered. "I need that alicorn, though. If you're in here, who's going to get it for me?"

Tavik picked up one of her hands. He turned it over and peered at her palm. Something rumbled up in his throat. She figured he was saying something about not liking her being kept in there. Her hand closed around his and gave it a squeeze. "It's not so bad, and it won't be for long. And I have to have that alicorn."

Tavik let out a heavy sigh. He stood up from the bench and looked back at her. He reached out to touch her cheek, but Naomi shied away. Tavik's hand hung in the air a moment before dropping back to his side. He growled something. She waited for Mr. Squibbles to translate, but he didn't speak up. Agatha was at the cell door.

"I'm sure Lady Naomi is distressed and could use some comforting," the witch said.

He growled again and exited. Agatha closed the cell door and stayed a moment, watching her. Naomi dropped her eyes, unwilling to meet her stare.

"He is married with a child on the way," the witch said.

Naomi sighed and hugged herself. "I know. That's why I'm trying to help."

"Why?"

Naomi did look at Agatha now. "What do you mean?"

"Why help my son and his wife? You don't know them, do you?"

"Xersal knows Lady Naomi, and her plight is quite tragic. Who wouldn't want to help?"

"Plenty of people would gladly turn their heads away from us. Who are you?"

Naomi sighed. "Just a cursed woman trying to make her way in the world."

"Well, you've certainly picked a bold course," the witch said. When she left, Naomi was alone in the dungeon. She went over her plan again. It was all she had.

CHAPTER SEVENTEEN

Dragons hate being wrong.

The next morning, a pair of guards escorted Naomi from the dungeon. Her hands were tied in front of her. She stared at her bonds dolefully. Her spirits briefly lifted when the guards led her to Stomper, who was bridled and saddled for her. She stroked his forehead. He stamped a hoof in friendly greeting and head-butted her gently. Receiving such a friendly greeting brought tears to Naomi's eyes. She wanted to throw her arms around the big horse and hug him, but with her wrists tied, there was no chance of that. She moved to get on the horse. Tavik appeared on bended knee to help her mount. She paused, nervous about accepting his help to mount. He had to be the one who picked Stomper for her to ride. His consideration and care for her was going to get her in trouble.

"We need to be going, Taylor," he said to get her moving.

At least Agatha had been able to lift Xersal's curse. She tentatively stepped up and put her foot on his knee. He lifted her smoothly, and she was soon mounted. He rose and put a hand on her knee. "Don't try to do anything. If you try to escape, we will stop you." Naomi barely heard his words due to the pressure of his hand on her knee. Her eyes were glued to it. He gave her knee a squeeze. She nodded dumbly, afraid to lift her eyes to his face.

"Taylor?" he asked softly.

"Make sure to get the alicorn," she said, still refusing to meet his eyes.

"Tavik, we're ready," Agatha called out.

Both turned to look at the witch. She was looking at them grimly. Tavik's hand fell away from Naomi's knee. He moved to mount his black charger Victor. Naomi still stared at Agatha. The witch lifted her chin at her. She appeared to have noticed Tavik's attraction to Naomi, and she didn't approve. If the witch decided to act, Naomi hoped the worst that happened to her was yowling like a cat.

By horse, the trip to the Darkon Forest would take more than a day, unlike with a flying cottage. When they stopped to camp for the night, Naomi dismounted and stretched her legs. Guards were constantly with her. She'd had the unenviable opportunity of peeing with them in earshot. She could handle everything else, but that had really irked her.

Soon enough they all bedded down to sleep. Naomi stared at the stars, thinking about the plastic ones back home, she hoped her parents weren't worried about her. She hadn't told them she was staying out late, and she had no way to call them. Maybe Bobby could reassure them somehow. She prayed her plan would come together the next day, though she didn't know what god might listen to her.

She was fast asleep when someone shook her shoulder to rouse her. It was still night. Dawn was hours away. She opened her eyes to peer up at a dark silhouette. "Who—" A hand covered her mouth.

"Be quiet," Tavik whispered.

She nodded and sat up quietly. He was crouched beside her. She looked around and took in all the slumbering forms around them. "What's going on?" she whispered.

"Now's your chance to go," he said. He put a knife between her wrists and cut the rope.

Naomi frowned. "Go where?" she asked, rubbing her eyes.

"Run away from here. I'll lead them in the opposite direction."

"Tavik, what are you talking about?"

He grabbed her by the arms and dragged her up. He turned her toward the road and pushed. "Head toward the forest. I'll lead them away. Hide for a few days and then take the east road to Harold's Pass and then keep going to Ravant. Take these supplies." He slipped a satchel onto her shoulder.

Naomi grabbed the strap and shook her head. "Tavik, I can't just go. What about Grisbek?"

"I'll deal with him. I'm sure I have enough men to slay him."

"But you don't need to. I can take care of him. I have a plan."

Tavik kept pushing her toward the road. "I'm not letting you risk your life for me."

Naomi balked. "I'm not risking my life for you. I'm doing it for Lady Naomi. She doesn't deserve the dragon's mark."

Tavik let out a frustrated growl. It was reminiscent of his recent curse. "Why do you care about my wife?"

Naomi didn't answer. She took the satchel off her shoulder and held it out to him. "I'm not leaving."

Tavik took the bag and threw it on the ground. Naomi nervously glanced at the sleepers around them to see if they'd been disturbed. No one stirred. Tavik grabbed her by the arms. "Do you want to die?" he whispered harshly.

"No, but I don't think I will. At least, I think there's a possibility that I won't."

"A possibility?"

"Yeah, I think so."

Tavik shook her. "You think you might survive?"

Naomi raised her arms to get him to stop. "I have a better chance than Lady Naomi!"

Tavik let her go. They were both panting now.

"Why do you have a better chance?" he asked.

Naomi shook her head. "Just trust me, Tavik. I know what I'm doing."

"I don't like this," he said.

She shrugged her shoulders and crossed her arms. "It's just how it is."

He stepped up to her, and before she could dodge him, he took her face in his hands. She grabbed his wrists and tried to pull his hands away. "Tavik, don't!"

"Shhh. I can't see anything right now."

"Doesn't matter."

Tavik chuckled, and she trembled as his thumbs dragged the scarf down her face. It was true: Both moons were absent, and the starlight was so dim, it just made the outlines of things visible. She couldn't make out Tavik's features at all, so he couldn't possibly see hers, but this was a very dangerous game. If there was a spark of light and he caught a glimpse of her face, everything would be ruined. His fingers fluttered over her face, touching her nose, lips, cheeks, brows.

"Why do you seem so familiar?" he asked.

Naomi closed her eyes. Why'd he have to say that? What did it matter? Her eyes flew open again when his lips touched hers. She tried to protest, but his mouth muffled hers. His arms wrapped around her and pulled her close. She closed her eyes again and told herself that this was bad, that she shouldn't be kissing him, that she should push him away and pull her scarf back up, but she couldn't do it. She kissed him back.

His tongue swept through her mouth while his hands roamed her back. She sighed and put her arms around his neck. Their lips slid apart, and his mouth moved to her neck. She pressed her face to his shoulder. "Tavik, we need to stop before someone sees us," she whispered.

He didn't respond, and she realized what his mouth was doing to her neck. "Tavik, stop," she said, trying to push him away. She blew out a breath in frustration. "Tavik, I'm too old for a hickey," she whispered. She could feel his shoulders shake in mirth, but he didn't let go of her neck.

Naomi countered with a tickle attack. Of course, she knew all of his sensitive spots. His mouth let go of her neck so he could drag in air, but he had to clamp his jaw to keep from laughing. He managed to grab both of her hands. She tried to step away to break them apart, but Tavik had other ideas. Still holding her hands, he put them behind her back and pulled her back to his body. He began kissing her again, but there was a desperation to it that had Naomi's heart pounding and head spinning.

"Tavik, you can't be doing this," she said.

He paid no attention to her words. He pressed kisses to her jaw, cheeks, and forehead.

"Tavik, if you don't stop, I'll scream and wake the entire camp."

The threat didn't faze him.

"Dammit, don't you love your wife?"

Tavik finally lifted his head. "I do. But what I feel with you is so different. It's like my heart is cleaved in two. One half still adores my Naomi, but the other half pounds when I look at you. My muscles clench, and my breath quickens. I don't know why, but my hands itch to reach out to you."

Naomi stood mute at this revelation. It was not the reply she'd expected. She'd thought he'd have a flash of guilt and back off. This was something else entirely.

"Tavik, let her go."

Naomi froze at Agatha's voice. Oh no, she was about to be hexed to kingdom come. Tavik's arms tightened around her, and a single ragged sob escaped him. It broke Naomi's heart. She squeezed his arms. "Tavik, it's okay. Everything will be okay," she said.

He wasn't letting her go. Naomi tried to pull his arms off her, but couldn't. "You have to let me go," she whispered.

Tavik's shoulders shook. She didn't know where Agatha was until she felt another hand land on Tavik's arm to help pull it away. "Think about Naomi," Agatha said.

Tavik finally let her go. Naomi hugged herself, feeling empty and alone. She turned her back and listened to Tavik and Agatha move away. Once she was sure they were gone, she carefully found her way back to her borrowed bedroll. She tied her scarf securely across her face again and closed her eyes. She didn't bother drying them.

They'd pounded a large stake into the ground. There was a single manacle on a long chain attached to it. Tavik led her to it. No one else came with them. Naomi almost wished there were guards because being alone with Tavik was torture. During breakfast, he'd been silent across the fire. Everyone had been subdued, but he'd been stony. His heavy stare had ruined her appetite. "I don't like this," he said as they walked.

"If you don't have the alicorn, then I don't like this either," Naomi said.

"I have it, but what are you going to do? I've heard of dragons and unicorns fighting, but not of a unicorn slaying a dragon, just the other way around."

"Yeah, and the bad press generated by that usually makes it not worth the trouble."

"What?"

"Unicorns make terrible meals."

"How do you know that?"

"A dragon told me."

"You are a very curious woman, Taylor."

Naomi couldn't help smiling ruefully at Tavik from behind her scarf. "You don't know the half of it."

S.A. HUNTER

He picked up the manacle and stared at it as if unsure what to do with it.

Naomi held out her arm. Instead of putting the manacle around her wrist, he gave her the alicorn. "What do you plan to do?" he asked.

"Wait for Grisbek. Once he appears, I'll put my plan in motion. Put the manacle on me. It's okay."

Tavik sighed and snapped the manacle in place. "I'll be watching on the hill. I don't know if I'll be able to reach you in time if things go badly."

"Oh, don't come down here at all, no matter what. Don't even watch. Promise me."

"I won't let you face your fate alone."

"And I don't want you seeing my face. Promise me you'll withdraw."

Tavik stared at her.

She could see he was going to argue. "Think about your unborn baby. He's the most important thing in the world to you. I know it. You know it. Think about him and how happy he'll make you."

Tavik sighed. "You're right, but for the first time in my life, I wish it weren't true."

Naomi didn't know what to say to that. "Go. I'll be fine. Once this is over, I'll give you a sign. Okay?"

Tavik still didn't leave. Branches began to snap from within the forest.

"You have to go! If you aren't gone by the time Grisbek gets here, I won't follow through with my plan. I'll just let him eat me."

"You wouldn't."

"You have no idea how irrational I can be. Now get the hell out of here!"

Tavik finally turned, but as he climbed the hill, he kept looking back at her. She kept her eyes on him, making sure he went over the hill even as there was more rustling came from the forest. She only hoped it wasn't a herd of umbreks.

"Hello, aren't you a curious gift?" Grisbek said from behind her.

She turned around and held up a finger. "One moment, please. I'll be right back."

Before Grisbek could reply, she raised the alicorn to her held-up finger and pricked it. She had to catch her balance when she opened her eyes.

"Who are you, and what are you doing here?" Torreng demanded.

Naomi quickly looked down and saw a gold coin at her feet. She picked it up and held it high for the dragon king to see. "I'm the thief stealing from you," she said. Torreng opened his mouth, and she could see the fire gathering to gush out at her. She quickly pricked herself and went back to the meadow. She took a deep breath and closed her eyes for a moment. Now was the moment of truth.

"You're back," Grisbek said.

There was a whoosh of air, and Torreng appeared.

"Stand aside, Grisbek."

Naomi let out a silent sigh of relief. Grisbek

turned to the dragon king and immediately bowed his head.

"So you have marked me, dragon king?" Naomi said.

"Of course, stupid human. Prepare to die."

"Not yet. Grisbek, guess what?"

The green dragon turned and peered at her. "What, human?"

"I win!" She reached up and jerked the scarf down from her face.

Grisbek's eyes widened, and a shudder rippled through him. "What— What trickery is this?" he demanded.

Torreng shook his head as well. "What is happening?" he demanded.

Naomi swayed on her feet. She didn't feel so good.

"I believe I just created a paradox," she said.

Both dragons stared at her.

"Here. You can have your gold coin back," Naomi said, holding it out to Torreng.

Grisbek growled, and his head dipped toward her, his jaws opening. Torreng, though, moved in to block him.

"Is she still marked?" he asked.

"Let's find out," Naomi said and pricked herself. She sat down heavily on her bed in her parent's home. Her head was spinning. She stared at the floor and waited in silence for a dragon to crash through the windows to gobble her up. Nothing happened. She got up woozily and grabbed the magic mirror from the wall and went into the bathroom. She took off her shirt and held the magic mirror up and angled it to get a look at her back. The only mark on it was the branding scar. No dragon's mark. She let out a sigh of relief. It had worked. The two marks had cancelled each other out. But were the others safe?

"Taylor, are you there?" The reflection in the mirror changed to Xersal's face.

He peered out and gasped.

"Grandniece, put a shirt on!"

She turned the mirror away, almost fumbling it in her embarrassment. "Xersal, why are you calling me?"

"Why? Because you just confronted two dragons and disappeared."

"You saw? What's happening now? What are Grisbek and Torreng doing?" Naomi laid the mirror face down on the bed to free her hands to redress.

"They're still down by the forest. They appear to be arguing."

That didn't sound good. "What are they arguing about?"

"I don't know, and I'm not about to move closer to find out. What is the legendary gold dragon doing here?"

"I lured him there. I hope he's not too upset. I did give him back his gold coin."

"You took a gold coin from the Dragon King? Grandniece, have you gone insane?"

"Maybe a little bit. Lady Naomi should be free of the dragon's mark, though."

"I don't give a rat's ass about Lady Naomi. What's going on with you? What's that strange scar on your back? Why were you looking at your back?"

Naomi only answered the last question. "I was checking to see if I had a dragon's mark."

"And why would you have a dragon's mark?"

"Because I stole a coin from the Dragon King, like I said."

"But why would you do that? Grandniece, explain yourself!"

Naomi had put her shirt back on. She picked up the mirror and hung it back the wall. "I'm sorry, Xersal. But I can't explain."

Xersal looked away from the mirror. "Oh, dear gods, Tavik's charging the dragons with his men."

"What?" Naomi pressed her nose to the glass and tried to see as well, but couldn't.

"This is going to be a bloodbath," Xersal said.

"Oh, no, no, no," Naomi said. She retied her scarf around her face and grabbed the alicorn.

"Taylor, stay there! You don't owe these people anything!"

Naomi prepared to prick herself. "No, great-uncle. I do."

When she pricked herself, she looked up to find herself between Torreng and Grisbek. "Hi, guys, I'm back."

Grisbek growled. "What? No more dragons to

drag into this mess?"

"Can you really fault me for doing everything in my power to get rid of your mark?"

Tavik rode up with his men and stopped short. He stared at Naomi. "You're alive?" he cried out.

"I told you to not look over the hill."

"I must give you credit, Tavik. Your mate is very resourceful," Torreng said.

Oh no, she needed to get rid of the dragons ASAP. "Yeah, that Lady Naomi sure is great. Well, I'm sure you dragons have more important things to do now. Sorry about this. Happy hunting!"

Grisbek lowered his head and peered closely at Naomi. He began to chuckle. "Oh, is that how it is?"

Naomi laughed nervously. "I'm sure I have no idea what you mean. I'm really sorry about all of this. Better luck next time, right?"

Smoke curled from Grisbek's nostrils. Naomi started feeling dizzy again.

"Grisbek, stop," Torreng commanded.

"Stop what?" Naomi asked as the dizziness faded.

"He's trying to re-mark you, but is failing. It appears neither of us can."

"You tried re-marking me, too?" Naomi asked, feeling a little hurt.

"You did steal from me."

"But I gave it back."

"What's going on?" Tavik demanded.

Torreng cast a curious look from Tavik to

Naomi. "It appears we have been bested. This woman has managed to remove Grisbek's mark. Such a thing has never been done before."

"She removed your mark, too," Grisbek groused.

Torreng shot the green dragon a dangerous look. Grisbek had the presence of mind to look sheepish.

"It was dumb luck. I didn't know if it would work. And I think it's safe to say, no one will ever be able to replicate what I did," Naomi said.

"That is true. But I could ask one of my brothers to mark you. You won't be able to escape them using this trick."

Torreng sighed. "Do not bother, Grisbek. You know they would have to delay the hunt the same as you did."

Naomi didn't know what Torreng meant by that, but she was happy to hear him tell Grisbek not to sic another dragon on her.

"Delay the hunt?" Tavik asked.

"Of course, we don't hunt those heavy with young."

"Wait. What?" Naomi shouted.

"You're pregnant?" Tavik said. His voice was a touch strangled.

"Yes. I wonder who the father is?" Grisbek asked slyly.

Tavik stared at her with wide eyes. She didn't know what he was thinking. Honestly, she didn't know what she was thinking. Her pregnant?

Now?

"Oh, you didn't know," Torreng said. He sounded a touch apologetic.

"Taylor?" Tavik asked.

"Taylor?" Grisbek repeated, clearly enjoying nettling her. He was a petty dragon.

"I think I need to sit down." She looked around for a place to sit and didn't see anything except the ground. She raised the alicorn and prepared to prick herself. She wanted her bed. Hiding under the covers and freaking out seemed like a very reasonable course of action.

"Taylor, wait!" Tavik lunged for her and grabbed her arm as she pricked herself.

She opened her eyes and stared at Tavik.

In her room.

She swooned. Tavik grabbed her and guided her to the bed. She sat down and stared up at him. "You can't be here," she said.

"And where is here?" he asked. He picked up a framed photograph of Naomi with her family from when she was ten.

Naomi swallowed thickly. She felt sick. Could it be morning sickness? The thought made her feel sicker. "Come on. I have to take you back." She reached out to take his arm, but he moved out of her reach.

"What is this place, Taylor?"

"It's my home, and you weren't invited. Let's go."

"I've never seen a room like this before. In

what land are we?"

"Nowhere you need to worry about. The only way here is by alicorn. The same as the only way back. Come on," Naomi stood up to herd him away from her dresser, but found her knees buckling. She sank onto the bed again.

She put her head in her hands. "I can't believe this is happening."

Tavik came to sit beside her. "Who is the baby's father?"

"It doesn't matter," Naomi muttered.

"It matters to me."

"Why? You're married with a baby on the way."

"You showed your face to Grisbek, but it didn't kill the dragon."

"He's tougher than he looks. The dragon's mark's gone, though."

"Let me see your face."

"No, Tavik. Just stop it. This is the way it has to be."

Tavik frowned. "Why haven't we shared a dream since that night?"

She knew what he meant and shook her head. "The alicorn did it. I didn't know what was happening. It won't happen again."

Tavik smoothed the comforter. "This is where you were sleeping?"

Naomi sighed and straightened. "Yeah."

She stiffened as Tavik stretched out on the bed.

"What are you doing?" she asked.

"Getting some perspective."

Naomi got up and took a step away from the bed. "What are you talking about? We need to go."

"Come back," Tavik said.

She turned and stared at him. She found herself taking a mental picture because she would most likely never see the sight again, and honestly, she'd never thought she'd ever see the sight of Tavik lying in her old bed.

He turned onto his side and bent his arm to prop his head on. He crooked a finger at her. She couldn't help the little bubble of laughter that escaped her at the sight. "You look ridiculous," she said.

He smoothed the comforter with his hand and dropped his eyelids. "Do I? I bet if I weren't alone it wouldn't seem so silly."

Naomi swallowed nervously. She felt trapped but in a good way. Her heart was racing, and her palms were sweaty. What was she going to do?

There was a tap at the door. "Hey, kiddo, are you in there?"

Naomi threw herself at the door to keep it closed. "Busy, Dad! Did you need something?"

"Nope. When did you get home?"

Naomi had no idea when it was. It was dark outside. It'd been afternoon on Terratu. "I got home just a little while ago. I hope I didn't worry you."

"No worries. Are you feeling better?"

Naomi braced herself against the door. "I'm doing good. Thanks for checking."

Tavik sat up. "Have you been unwell?" he asked.

Naomi's eyes widened, and she held a finger up to her lips to shush him.

"Is someone in there with you?" her father asked.

"I'm on the phone. I'll talk to you later. Okay, Dad?"

"All right. Yell if you need anything."

"Thanks, Dad."

Naomi held her breath as she listened to her father walk away. She slumped when she was sure he was gone.

"That was your father?"

Naomi rolled her eyes. "Yeah, and he can't know you're here."

Tavik crossed his ankles and leaned back in her bed. "Is that so?"

She quirked an eyebrow at him, not sure what he was getting at. She picked up the alicorn and moved back to the bed. "We need to go," she said.

"I don't want to leave yet."

Naomi huffed and shook her outstretched hand. "Why am I the one who's concerned about your pregnant wife?"

Tavik's eyes dropped to her stomach. "Maybe because you share a lot in common?"

Naomi took a deep breath to calm herself because he had no idea just how much Lady Crazy and she had in common, and who the hell was he to bring that up? Her hand dropped, and instinctively, she touched her stomach. Was she really pregnant? What was she going to do? She had no insurance, no money, no job. How was she going to raise a baby? Sure, her parents would help, but having to rely on them made her feel like such a failure.

"Am I the father?" he asked.

She looked at him silently while touching her stomach. This couldn't be happening. She had somehow become the other woman carrying the illegitimate child. She breathed in and let loose the lie. "No."

Tavik's jaw tightened, and his eyes narrowed. "Who is the father, then?"

"You don't need to know."

"I don't?"

"No, you don't! Now let's go! You don't belong here."

Tavik's eyes widened. He snatched the alicorn from her hand. "You're absolutely right. I don't belong here." He took the alicorn and stabbed himself in the thigh and disappeared.

Naomi stood there in shock. "Oh God. Tavik?"

She stared at where he had been in disbelief.

CHAPTER EIGHTEEN

*If you trick a dragon, it's best not to tell them
that you did.*

Naomi looked at the two blue lines in dismay. She was pregnant, single, unemployed, and living with her parents. She'd never thought she'd be in this situation. She'd always been so careful and avoided risk. She looked at the second test still in its wrapper and wondered if she should double-check the results. No, she couldn't bring herself to open it. She knew it would show the same. She'd just torture herself by waiting for two blue lines to appear again. She threw the used test and the unused one in the trash. She'd only taken the test to confirm what the dragons had said. She was double-checking them. She'd be double-checking the double-checking, and where would it end?

She exited her bathroom and sank onto the bed again. After Tavik had disappeared with the alicorn, she'd curled up in bed until her mother had come home. She'd had a quiet dinner with her parents and afterward had asked her mother to drive her to the drugstore. She'd had to borrow money from her mother to buy the pregnancy test. She'd claimed to want some toiletries and had hidden the test among her purchases. Could her life get anymore pathetic?

"Grandniece, are you there?"

Naomi contemplated ignoring Xersal, but he could probably see the lump that was her on the bed. She dragged herself out from under the covers and went to the mirror.

"What have you been up to?" Naomi asked. She could make out his old room from behind him.

"I was researching ways to get rid of dragons because I assume at least two are now after you."

"No, no dragons are after me. Torreng said not to hunt me."

"Truly? And I've had confirmation that Lady Naomi is dragon's-mark free. How did you get rid of it?"

"I used a loophole that won't work for anyone else ever."

"Tell me at least," Xersal asked.

Naomi shook her head. "It wouldn't make sense if I tried. Let's just say there were some special circumstances related to my curse."

Xersal looked disappointed that Naomi wouldn't share, but didn't press further. "So are you coming back? I'd been looking forward to working with you. The idea of having an apprentice was beginning to appeal to me."

Now it was Naomi's turn to look disappointed.

"I can't. Tavik latched onto me when I came home and then took the alicorn when he left. He has it now in Terratu."

Xersal's eyes widened. "Why that great big bastard! How dare he! You save his wife, and he steals your alicorn? I'll have to do something about this. Barking like a dog will seem sweet once I'm done with him."

"No, don't. It's fine. Maybe it's for the best."

"How can you say that? That alicorn belongs to our family. He had no right to take it from you."

Naomi didn't know what to say to convince him. She bowed her head and let her shoulders slump.

Xersal sighed. "Taylor? What happened? What was that scar on your back?"

Naomi looked at her great-uncle in silence for a moment. She was pregnant, back on Earth sans alicorn, and dragon's-mark free. The curse didn't matter anymore. It was over. What did it matter anymore?

"Xersal, my name's actually Naomi, and I was married to Tavik once upon a time."

The wizard looked at her a moment. He didn't seem completely shocked. He nodded his head and sat back in his chair. "Begin at the beginning."

So she did. She told him everything. She told him how she'd met Tavik, killed Errilol, worked with the unicorns, got kidnapped by the real Lady Naomi, Tavik's love spell, the quest to get some fool-me-not, the dragon's mark, Snowflake's solution, and finally how she'd come back to clean up the mess she'd left behind.

"And now everything's okay. Tavik and Lady Naomi don't have anything to worry about anymore. They can have their baby and be happy."

"And what about you?"

Naomi shrugged her shoulders. "I'll figure something out."

"But will you be happy?"

She forced herself to smile. "Yeah, I'll be fine."

Her answer didn't appear to convince Xersal. "I think I need to have a chat with Lord Tavik."

Naomi was tired. All she wanted to do was curl up and sleep. She let out a weary sigh. "It won't matter. He's in love with Lady Naomi. They're going to have a child. In their minds, they've been happily married since the beginning. I'm no one to them. If I come back, it'll just complicate things even more."

"We'll see. You deserve better, grandniece."

"I'm fine," she said again, even though they both knew it was a lie.

Xersal turned off the magic mirror, and Naomi stared at herself a moment. She looked worn out. There was no happy glow about her that pregnant women supposedly had. But a happy glow wouldn't suit her anyway. She shook her head. She should rest. She was in her bedroom. She could go to bed. It was as simple as that. She placed a cloth over the mirror. She really didn't want to make it a habit of flashing her great-uncle. Twice was quite enough.

She changed into pajamas and climbed into bed. She turned off the lights and stared at the dim glow-in-the-dark stars on her ceiling. Tomorrow would be a new day, and she'd start figuring out her life then. She fell asleep quickly as she refused to think about anything.

Almost immediately, dream Tavik's arms slid around her. She groaned and tried to push him away. "No, this isn't happening," she muttered as she struggled to free herself.

"Taylor," he pleaded.

"Oh, for crap's sake," Naomi muttered. She turned away from Tavik and buried her face in the pillow. It was dark, but all it took was him lighting a candle to break the spell.

He placed a hand on her hip and urged her to roll over toward him, but she didn't budge. "Wake up and put the alicorn in your wardrobe," she said with her face still pressed into the pillow.

"No."

Naomi sighed in frustration. She moved to get up from the bed to break the spell or whatever it was that the alicorn did. Tavik wrapped an arm around her waist and pulled her back. From behind, he pressed his face to the crook of her neck. "Why did you say you were my wife in the first dream? Why did the king of dragons call you my mate?" he asked.

Naomi didn't have an answer. She was tired of

lying. She was tired of all of it. "Please let me go."

"No."

"You have to."

"No."

She lay back in frustration and stared at the ceiling. It was stone with plastic glowing stars, an amalgamation of their two rooms. Tavik's arm slackened, and he settled down beside her. His hand drifted to her abdomen and rested there. He didn't speak, but the weight of his hand said everything. Her own hand itched to cover his. But there was another abdomen out there, rounder than hers that blocked her hand.

"What do we do now?" he asked.

"I am the wrong person to ask. This wasn't supposed to happen. You weren't supposed to notice me."

"How could I not?" he asked.

"Because you're in love with another woman."

Tavik sighed. His hand rubbed over her stomach, smoothing out her pajama top. "Don't judge me, but I think I'm falling in love with you."

Naomi's breath froze. "What?" she breathed.

"I still love Naomi and will have this child with her, but since I've met you, I think of you, not her. Even when I'm standing by her bed, I wonder what you're doing, where you are."

"But you're by her side," Naomi said. And really that trumped thinking about her. He was with Lady Naomi. Not her.

There was a distant crash. Tavik sat up and

looked across the room. Naomi couldn't see any-thing. The room beyond the bed was a hazy blur to her. "Who's there?" he demanded.

As if from a very long hallway, she heard a voice. "Tavik, you will give us back what is ours."

"Xersal? What are you doing here?" Tavik asked.

"Xersal? What's going on?" Naomi tried to see, but everything was so murky. She couldn't make out her great-uncle. He'd sounded far away when he spoke, but Tavik appeared to see him just fine.

"You will undo whatever you did to my grand-niece, and she'll have her alicorn back now."

"Wait, Xersal!" Naomi yelled, but she couldn't tell if he could hear her. If she couldn't see him, he probably couldn't see her. Tavik was becoming difficult to see as well, and he was right beside her. She grabbed his arm. "Tavik, tell Xersal to stop and call me. I told him not to do anything. Tell him—" Words failed her as she tried to think of something for Tavik to repeat to stop her great-uncle. "Tell him I'm fine. Tell him that."

Tavik turned to say something to her but winked away. Her hand fell to the mattress, and she found herself wholly back in her room. "Dammit," she said. She waited a few minutes for Tavik to reappear, but she remained alone in her room. She tried to go back to sleep, thinking to remake the connection, but she was too wired to rest. She was afraid to leave the bed in case Tavik did show back up, though. She lay rigid, waiting.

Nothing continued to happen.

"Xersal, what in blazes do you think you're doing?" she muttered in frustration.

She lay for a few more minutes and finally got up. It was two in the morning. Too late and too early to do anything. She went to the magic mirror and turned it on. She could dimly see Xersal's workshop in the moonlight that filtered in. She stared at the empty room and waited.

"Taylor?"

Naomi jumped and fumbled with her T-shirt to pull it over her face. She held it over her nose and turned around to find Tavik sitting on her bed.

"What the hell are you doing here?" she demanded.

Her eyes roamed over his body looking for any injuries. He looked fine. That didn't mean Xersal hadn't cursed him again.

"Your great-uncle is very upset with me."

"Yeah, I know. Did he do anything to you?"

"He yelled a lot. I told him I would come to you, and he let me leave."

"Fine, you came. Now you need to go."

"He wants me to give this back to you." He held the alicorn out to her. She reached out with her free hand and took it. It felt natural to take it back. It had become something she relied upon and accepted as hers.

"Fine, now let's go."

"Xersal did something else. It has opened my eyes."

Naomi's head tilted to the side in puzzlement. "What did he do?"

"Have you ever heard of a flower called fool-me-not?"

Naomi stared at him. Why was the flower coming up now? Tavik loved Lady Crazy. She'd killed Errilol and gotten a dragon's mark for him. She was pregnant with his child. Of course, he loved her. Like he'd once loved her. "I know what flower you mean," she said.

"Have you ever smelled one?"

She nodded.

"It has a pretty smell," Tavik murmured. He looked down at his hands.

"What happened, Tavik?"

He dropped his head.

"Tavik?" She went over to him and placed her hand on the back of his head. Her palm molded to the curve of his skull.

"Xersal showed me the truth. He gave me some fool-me-not. I don't love her. I never did."

"Oh God. Tavik, are you sure? Think about it. You both went through a lot recently. Maybe you both just need a breather to calm down." She couldn't believe she was encouraging him to go back to Lady Crazy, but he looked so dejected and unhappy. He pulled her closer and pressed his face into her stomach. The action gave her goose bumps. He'd done this before when he needed comfort. She wondered if he'd ever done this with Lady Crazy. She knew she shouldn't think about it, that it would drive her crazy, but the thought still happened.

"She slipped a love potion into my wine to make me love her. Considering the circumstances, it's understandable. She was in fear for her life. I could have killed her. I wouldn't have, but I could have. I can't fault her. But now I know. I never loved her." He pressed his face into her stomach, hiding his eyes.

Naomi stroked his back and let him find what comfort he could from her. She felt awful for him.

"And her child isn't mine."

Naomi's hands stilled.

"What?" she breathed.

"The baby is her first husband's."

"How do you know?"

"After Xersal gave me the fool-me-not, I confronted her. She told me then."

"Oh God, Tavik. I'm so sorry."

He moved his hands to Naomi's stomach and laid them flat against it. "And this little one isn't mine either."

Naomi didn't know what to say. Her hand covered his on her stomach. "Tavik, I..." He deserved to know the truth, and it would restore his spirits, but it felt skeevy to tell him the baby was his. "Oh, sorry your wife lied to you. I did, too. The baby's yours. Congratulations! Never mind the entire I erased your memory and left you so I could go home and hide from a dragon."

He raised his eyes from her stomach and finally looked at her. "Show me your face," he asked.

"Tavik, I..." Why couldn't she say something else? Finish a sentence at least?

He reached to take her hand away to let the shirt collar drop.

"Tavik, I'm sorry," she blurted.

His hand paused. "Sorry for what?"

"For everything. Oh God, you're going to hate me, and I'm sorry. I didn't mean to hurt you. What I did was selfish, and I know I'll never be able to make it up to you."

He blinked and stared at her. His hands dropped back to her hips. "Show me your face," he asked again.

It was time, wasn't it? There weren't any more reasons not to reveal herself. The dragon's mark was gone. Tavik no longer thought he was in love with Lady Crazy. Naomi was pregnant. She'd never really thought she'd reach this point, but she'd hoped. Oh, how she'd hoped! The funny thing was that she'd imagined this being a happier occasion, but anguished tears were sliding down her face.

She took a deep breath, wiped the tears from her cheeks, and let the shirt drop away. Tavik stared up at her, and she stared back. As they held each other's gazes, she watched closely for his reaction. Grisbek had shuddered when he'd seen her face. Tavik didn't move a muscle. He didn't even blink. Her eyes watered again. She lifted her hands to wipe them, but Tavik's hands shot up to do the job. He gently wiped the tears away with his thumbs then stroked her cheeks while cradling her face.

"Why did you call yourself Taylor?" he asked.

"I couldn't call myself Naomi, obviously. It's my family name. I knew I'd answer to it more easily than if I chose a completely random name."

Suddenly Tavik's face darkened. "And who is the father of the baby?"

Oh, she'd assumed he'd know once her face was revealed, but obviously not. "It's yours, of course. I'm sorry I lied."

He sighed and a great tension left his body. He blinked rapidly and looked away. "Thank Calax," he murmured. His hands slid around her waist and pulled her in. She placed her hands on his shoulders and looked down to the top of his head.

"Tavik?"

"Then Xersal isn't your great-uncle?"

"No, he is. My grandfather was his brother. Grandpa left Terratu with the alicorn and settled here. I found out by reading his journals when I came back. Xersal had given him a magic mirror to stay in touch, and I used it to contact him. It's amazing that he worked for Lord Gerald."

He nodded against her stomach.

The way he kept his face turned from her was beginning to hurt. "Tavik, please look at me. I didn't mean to hurt you. Snowflake said it was the only way to deal with the dragon's mark, and you were be-spelled by Lady Naomi; it seemed like the only way."

Tavik squeezed her. "Stop saying you're sorry. How can you assume any of the blame for this? I put you in the dungeon, twice! I put a price on your head! You wouldn't have gotten the dragon's mark if it weren't for me."

Naomi sighed and hugged him tighter. "Things sure got messed up. You were under a spell. I knew that. It was awful, but it wasn't your fault."

"But the things I said to you." He trailed off and shook his head.

Naomi swallowed as she remembered some of them. The dark side of their love. "Tavik, I didn't want to get pregnant. I'll love this baby, but I didn't exactly like how everyone was pressuring me into getting pregnant. Like everyone was disappointed with me for taking so long, but it's my body, and it's a big step. If I'd known I'd get pregnant now, I would have tried to stop it."

Tavik pulled away from her and looked up at her face. "You're not happy about the baby?"

She sighed and backed away from him. "I'm not upset, but it wasn't something I was looking for. I'm still getting used to the whole idea."

Tavik's shoulders slumped. "Oh."

She stared at him a moment and wished she could jump for joy over the pregnancy, but it just wasn't true. She wasn't ready to have a baby, but honestly, she didn't know if she ever would be. She'd always thought she'd have kids, but that had always been in the hazy distant future. Being pregnant made it much more immediate.

"I will have this baby, but just understand, I'm not having it to make you happy or to fulfill my role as your wife or something. I'm still trying to find my purpose, and getting pregnant is not going to stop me. Like I said, I'll love this child and be the best mother I can be for him or her, but I'm not going to reduce myself to just being a mother."

Tavik's brows had come together as she gave her speech, and she tensely waited for his reply. She didn't know how well he'd take it, but if he couldn't accept it, they were still going to have problems. But better to be aware of them now than when the baby was born.

He reached out and took one of her hands. "I can accept that. But I am very happy that you're pregnant. I wish you were as happy as me."

She squeezed his hand. "I know you're happy and that you're excited to become a dad. It's okay. You're going to be a great dad. I'll get used to the idea. I've got some time, after all."

Tavik sighed. He got up and lay down on the floor at the foot of her bed.

Naomi watched this in confusion. "What are you doing?"

"Please don't make me leave."

She stared at him. "Tavik, get up."

His face fell as he sat up.

She pulled back the covers and got in. She

made a space for him. "You're not sleeping on the floor," she told him.

He looked at her a moment. She could see some of the weight lift from his shoulders. "Are you sure about this, Naomi?"

"I'm sure I don't want you sleeping on the floor. We're both exhausted. Anything else can wait till morning."

He nodded and climbed into bed with her.

Having him beside her again felt strange. And being in her childhood bed added to the strangeness. They shifted around a bit and fidgeted to get comfortable, but when his arm went around her, and she slotted into his side, all of the strangeness fell away.

CHAPTER NINETEEN

"Humans are troublesome prey and should only be eaten if tied to a tree as a proper offering." — Torreng, King of the Dragons

Naomi could feel the sun. It was time to wake up, but she didn't want to. Tavik's body was molded to hers. She'd missed that. *Just a few more minutes then I'll face the day,* she thought.

"WHO THE HELL ARE YOU, AND WHAT ARE YOU DOING IN MY DAUGHTER'S BED?"

Naomi jackknifed upright. She must not have been as awake as she thought if she hadn't heard her father come into her room. "Dad! What are you doing in here?" Her mother was there, too. She was trying to pull Phil out of her room.

"I'm sorry, Naomi. He was walking by when I opened the door to wake you. I was startled by your male friend."

"A male friend you have NOT introduced to us, and I don't recall giving permission to stay over-night," Phil added, shaking off his wife's hands to stand at the foot of the bed with clenched fists.

"Dad, I'm a grown woman."

"If you're sleeping under my roof, I say who gets to spend the night."

Tavik had sat up now, too. "Sir, you have my sincerest apologies. I meant no disrespect to you. I arrived very late last night. We did not wish to disturb you. But it is an honor to finally meet you and your wife. Naomi means the world to me and being reunited with her blinded me to everything else."

"Reunited?" Barbara murmured. Her hand crept up to cover her mouth.

"You're Tavik?" Phil demanded. To Naomi's chagrin, her father's face grew redder.

"Dad, it's okay. We've reconciled."

"What about the other woman with the baby?" he demanded.

Now both hands covered Barbara's mouth. "Other woman? Baby?" Obviously, her father hadn't shared that little tidbit with her mother.

"The other woman lied. It wasn't his baby."

"But you two separated because of her. You can't trick a man into thinking you're pregnant with his child without doing the act."

"Uh," Naomi didn't know what to tell them in regard to that.

Luckily, Tavik stepped in. "Sir, I know I do not deserve your daughter's forgiveness, but I can't live without her. What happened was due to a lot of lies and deceit. It was awful for Naomi, and I don't know how I'll ever make it up to her."

"Out!" her father said.

"Dad!"

"No, he needs to get out right now. He can't be

here in your goddamn childhood bed and tell me that this was all one big misunderstanding! And if you believe him for one second, I'm ashamed of you."

"Phil!" her mother exclaimed.

Tavik got up.

Naomi stayed in bed frozen. This was terrible and surreal, and she had no idea how to salvage it.

Luckily, her mother spoke up. "Maybe we should all go to the living room to talk."

Her father's jaw was still clenched as he gave a clipped nod, did a one-eighty, and stomped out of the room. "Don't take too long joining us," her mother said as she shut the door.

After her parents were gone, Naomi still sat in shock.

Tavik sat back down on the bed. His shoulders were slumped, and his hands hung limply between his knees. "I had once hoped to make a good impression on your father. I had thought I would show him how much I loved you and prove to him that your life was the most important thing to me. Now I believe the only way he'll accept me is if I give him a dagger, spread my arms wide, and say, 'Have at me.'"

She turned to Tavik and blinked. "I really don't think we should let my dad near sharp objects around you. Not until this is smoothed over. I have no idea though how to explain to them what happened. We can't mention magic because they won't believe it. There aren't any witches, wizards, dragons, or unicorns here. No one believes in them. Without mentioning any of that, I don't know how to explain it to them to make them understand."

Tavik shook his head. "I must apologize to your parents."

"But Tavik, you aren't to blame."

"I need to atone."

"Let's just get dressed and get downstairs."

Tavik had arrived in his sleep clothes. In the light of day and impending family meeting, Naomi gave them a critical look. He was wearing a loose, rough-woven shirt with a collar tie and cloth pants. He had put on knee-high leather boots to see her, so he didn't have to go down barefoot, but he looked medieval. She had an old zippered hoodie of Bobby's. She had him put that on at least to try and soften the medieval look. It helped a little, but he still appeared out of place. She'd just have to hope her parents thought he looked foreign rather than alien. She put on jeans and a T-shirt and led the way to the living room.

Naomi halted in the entryway when she saw only her dad sitting in the recliner with his arms crossed and a scowl on his face. "Where's Mom?" she asked.

Her father jerked his head toward the kitchen. Naomi hoped her mother was coming back and not intending to hide in there the whole time. She led Tavik to the couch and tugged his hand to pull him down to sit with her, but he didn't sit on the sofa. Instead, he got down on his knees before her father with a bowed head. Phil gave Tavik's supplicating position a haughty glare.

"Sir, I know I have done a terrible wrong to your daughter, and I must atone. Whatever punishment you wish to give me, I will accept gladly."

"Tavik!" Naomi said. She tried to pull him up, but he was an immovable object.

Her father seemed to be considering his offer very seriously.

"Dad, you're not going to do anything to Tavik. Whatever happened is between him and me. We'll resolve it."

"She cried every day. I've never seen her so listless. I hurt my hand punching a wall because I couldn't help her. She gave up everything for you, and you abandoned her in less than a year. What sort of man are you?"

"Dad—" Naomi began.

Tavik held up a hand to stop her.

Her father continued, "She had a bright future here. She had a good job, an education, her own place, then poof—She meets you and decides to move to Timbuktu and leave everything behind. I didn't like it, and when she came back, I was upset. You hurt my daughter. I can't forgive you."

Tears sprang to Naomi's eyes. She hated hearing how upset her father had been. She hadn't realized how this had affected him. Her mother chose that moment to come back into the room.

She was focused on the tray of drinks she carried. "I thought we could use some refreshment. What would everyone like for breakfast?"

She stopped and looked at everyone when she received no answer. Tavik was still crouched on the floor in front of Phil. "What's going on?" Barbara asked.

"He's trying to get me to forgive him, and I'm not doing it," Phil said.

Barbara shook her head and set the tray on the coffee table. "If Naomi has taken him back, then we shouldn't interfere. I'm just glad I finally get to meet you. I was so sad I didn't get to before now."

"Yes, why was that?" Phil asked with suspicion in his voice.

Tavik glanced over at Naomi. Shit, she had to come up with another lie. "I told you he lived very far away."

"Yeah, but obviously he was in town at some point," Phil said.

Naomi sighed. "No, he was never in town. I met him on a trip."

"When?" Phil asked. He was like a dog with a bone. He was going to worry at this until he got to the marrow.

"Fine! It was online. We met online. Happy? I didn't want to tell you because I knew how you'd react, but everything's okay now."

"Shouldn't trust the Internet," Phil muttered with a shake of his head. Naomi rolled her eyes.

She took a deep breath. Time to lay it all on the line. "We fell in love, Dad. We got married. We hit a rough patch. We got through it and are committed to each other again. And I'm pregnant."

"What?" Barbara squawked.

Phil's jaw dropped.

"We just found out. It's still really early."

Tavik finally rose from the floor and stood by Naomi. He took her hand in his.

"Oh my God! I'm going to be a grandmother?" Barbara exclaimed. She went to Naomi and pulled her into a hug.

"Yeah, looks like it. And you'll be seeing more of me because I want to come back here for my checkups and whatnot. They don't have the best medical care there. I don't know how we'll pay for it all exactly. I mean I don't have insurance any longer, but I think we have the money."

"You know the coffers are completely open to you," Tavik said.

"Yeah, but there's the matter of converting it to US currency," Naomi said. There was also the matter of it being unrecognized legal tender. She'd have to go to a shop that paid for gold and silver.

Phil shook his head. "We'll help out. If you're having to travel back and forth, don't want you to spend all your money."

"The traveling isn't an issue," Naomi said.

Phil didn't look convinced.

"Oh my gosh, I just can't believe this!" Barbara exclaimed happily. She got up and headed to the kitchen. "We need to celebrate! I'm going to call Bobby with the good news!"

"Mom, wait!"

Naomi got up to follow her but stopped short when she realized she was leaving Tavik alone with her father. She cast a nervous look at them. Tavik's eyes caught hers, and he nodded that it was okay for her to go. Her father's eyes didn't flicker from Tavik. Well, she should be able to hear them from the kitchen if things got heated again. She dashed into the kitchen to stop her mother.

"Mom, don't call Bobby. I don't want—"

Barbara held up a hand for her to be quiet. Her other hand held the phone to her face. "Bobby, come over here as soon as possible. Your sister and Tavik are here. Yes, Tavik! And guess what? You're going to be an uncle!"

Naomi groaned and slumped against the counter. Barbara hung up the phone and turned to her. "Of course we have to tell Bobby. I won't call anyone else, okay? But he's your brother. We have to tell him."

"Well, if it's just Bobby," Naomi said weakly.

Barbara's eyes lit up. "I can't wait to tell your aunt and grandmother."

"Not yet, Mom. Okay?"

Barbara nodded and began opening cabinets. "I know, dear. Does Tavik like eggs? How should I make them?"

"Scrambled's fine." Everything was going too fast.

"Have you told Tavik's mother yet?" Barbara asked.

Naomi jumped at the mention of Agatha. She still thought she was Taylor, and she needed to tell Yula, too. "No, but we're leaving today to give them the good news."

"Today? But Tavik just got here!"

"Sorry, Mom. We really do need to get back."

Barbara appeared unhappy with this news, but Naomi really couldn't handle the thought of an extended stay with her parents and Tavik.

She heard Bobby call out from the front door. Naomi quickly slipped out of the kitchen to escape her mother. She passed by the living room and nervously looked in. Her father still didn't look happy, but he was keeping his displeasure to himself. Tavik, for his part, didn't seem upset. He'd gotten up and was looking at the photographs around them room, safely out of reach of her father. She kept going to greet Bobby. He smiled and surprisingly held his arms open for her when he saw her. They didn't usually hug like that, but she stepped into his arms with a small sense of relief.

"So Mom said I'm going to be an uncle," he said.

She nodded into his shoulder. "Yeah, come on. You need to meet Tavik."

"Can't wait. It's not every day I get to meet the king of Mars."

Naomi groaned.

They went into the living room. Tavik had a picture album in his lap. "Naomi, these portraits are amazing." She smiled nervously, hoping no one noticed his odd praise.

He looked up and saw Bobby. He rose and held out his hand. Bobby took it with a hearty shake. "Hey, man, good to finally meet you," her brother said.

"It is a pleasure to meet you as well."

Phil rose and gave his seat to Bobby. "I'm going to see if your mother needs help," he said. Naomi's head drooped at his departure. She didn't know how she was going to make things right with him.

She sat down again by Tavik and glanced at the photo album in his lap. Her six-year-old self smiled up at her from beside a sand castle on the beach. It didn't look anything like her current home.

"So, Tavik, what exactly do you do?" Bobby asked.

Naomi quickly whipped on a proud smile to lie. "He has a very important position in government. He manages all the local resources and works with the people to best help them."

"Yeah, but what do you do?" Bobby asked again, still looking pointedly at Tavik.

Naomi squeezed Tavik's arm in silent warning.

She really needed to start making moves to the door. The sooner she hustled Tavik out of there and got them back to Terratu the better.

"Maybe it would be easier if I described a problem I helped solve," Tavik said. Naomi stilled and stared at him, afraid of what he might bring up. Dragons? Witches? Fake memories? "There was a band of brigands threatening a popular road to travel. I gathered my men, and we went there to rout them out. We were not successful the first time, but I found them the second time my men were there and han—"

"Handled the situation and handed them over to the local magistrate for a fair trial," Naomi said. She wasn't absolutely sure, but she was pretty sure Tavik was going to say hanged, and while she wasn't sure how her brother felt about the death penalty, he might be shocked by the thought of just hanging a bunch of people.

Tavik had raised his eyebrow and looked at her. She gave his arm another squeeze and laughed nervously when a better lie occurred to her. "He's in law enforcement! Don't tell Mom. I know she'll worry," she said.

Bobby thought about this for a moment and shrugged his shoulders. "Cool. Do you guys carry guns?"

"What—"

Naomi cut Tavik off again. "No, they don't. They have very strict gun laws. The criminals can't get them either."

Bobby gave her a skeptical look. She needed to change the subject.

"Breakfast is ready!"

Naomi sighed. Her mother was a godsend. Everyone filed into the kitchen. Barbara had set everything on the kitchen counter for people to fill their plates. Naomi got behind Tavik and hoped all of the food would seem normal to him. It was just breakfast stuff. None of it seemed to faze him, and he piled his plate with scrambled eggs, bacon, sausage, and toast. Everyone took their plates into the dining room to eat.

Barbara sat down with an ecstatic smile on her face. "This is just wonderful! Everyone's here. We're eating together. I love it!"

Naomi thought her mother might have on blinders. How else could she miss the grumpy expression on Dad's face?

"So, Sis, what are you doing today?"

"Oh, we have to leave soon to get back."

Barbara's happiness wilted a little again.

"But we'll return soon," Tavik offered.

Naomi turned to him in surprise. "Your family will want to see you more often now, and it is not a hardship."

Naomi knew that. It was the "we" part that threw her off. She wasn't sure how to handle Tavik on Earth. She suddenly imagined Agatha coming along, too. She'd surely hex someone or become very upset when she couldn't. It would be a nightmare. No, no one else from Terratu could make the trip.

After breakfast, Naomi took Tavik up to her room to get ready to go. She intended to take the mirror with her. That was all she could really see taking at the moment. Her primary concern was getting Tavik back to Terratu.

He sat on her bed and watched her fidget around the room. "Naomi, what's wrong?"

She'd been in the process of wrapping the mirror in a blanket for transport. She needed some string to tie it up. She turned to look in her dresser. "Nothing's wrong. I mean it's great. You're here. My parents have met you. I told them about the baby. We had breakfast together, and now we're heading back. What could be wrong?"

Tavik didn't respond, but it didn't look like her answer had convinced him. She found a ball of yarn in her closet. Something her mother had overlooked when she'd cleaned her crafting supplies out of it when Naomi had moved back into the house.

"Everything's fine," she reiterated.

He still looked skeptical.

She tossed the string on the bed and put her hands on her hips. "Everything's great. Everything was terrible yesterday, but everything's great today. You remember me now, I'm pregnant, we're going home, my parents are happy. Everything's great. Yesterday, I was almost dragon chow, and you didn't know who the hell I was, but that's all over now. So it's great! Why should I still be worried? It wasn't like I haven't been miserable and scared out of my mind for the past couple of weeks. Everything's fine now!"

Tavik got up and folded her into his arms. She was shaking and panting. Her heart was racing. But everything was all right now. There wasn't anything to worry about. They were back together. She was pregnant. Everyone would be happy. The ragged sob that came out of her didn't really surprise her.

Tavik's arms tightened.

"I'm sorry," Naomi said and tried to push Tavik away. She had to tie the mirror up in the blanket. She didn't really need to tie the mirror up. It wasn't like they were traveling by ship or plane. She'd prick her finger, and boom, they'd be back in Terratu. She could just carry the mirror. Tavik wouldn't let her go.

"I need to finish up," she insisted. Tavik shook his head and pulled her in tighter.

"You need to let it out," he said.

"Let what out? I'm fine! Everything's fine! We've reached the happy ending, and now we'll live happily ever after. Let me go, and we'll get on with it."

"You've had to go through a great deal."

"Yeah, yeah, but it's over now."

Tavik shook his head and rubbed her back. Naomi sniffled and leaned into him, letting herself relax. She felt so tired. The day had just begun. She'd had a nice breakfast. Why was she so tired? She wiped her eyes and gave Tavik a hug. "I'm okay. You can let me go."

"I'm never letting you go."

She smiled and gave him a squeeze. "I know, and I'm not letting you go either."

Tavik smiled. "Yes, obviously." He sighed and stroked her cheek. "I will begin groveling as soon as we're back."

Being reminded of her own words made her laugh. "Yeah, I did say you'd have to do a lot of that once this was over."

He nodded. Her stomach sank a bit. "But is it really over? Can you really get rid of her? What about Harold's Pass? Isn't there still trouble there?"

Tavik shook his head. "I'll deal with it."

"I want to help. I have to help."

"How?" he asked.

She didn't have any idea. She knew next to nothing about medieval politics. "We need to help the people. Make sure the poor are being fed and cared for. We need to find something for those soldiers to do now that you aren't going to war."

He nodded. "Yes, but that won't stop the wealthy from scheming and trying to overthrow me."

She sighed. She didn't know how to solve that. "Yeah, but let's deal with the other stuff first, and maybe a solution will come to us for that."

Tavik smiled. "You're going to make a fine lady."

"Maybe. Is there anything else we should be worried about? Does anyone have it out for us? What about our neighbors?"

Tavik shook his head. "Our neighbors are fine. My spies don't report anything suspicious at the moment."

Naomi was surprised to hear mention of spies. They had spies? She nodded as she absorbed this.

"Let's go home, Naomi."

There really wasn't anything stopping her now. She felt calmer. Tavik tucked the mirror under his arm. She picked up the alicorn, and with Tavik's other arm firmly around her, she raised the alicorn to her fingertip. She paused and looked up at Tavik. She gave him a rueful smile. "Do you think I'll have as rough a time as you had with my parents when I see Agatha?"

"Considering she made you a dragon sacrifice, I think she has no right to yell at you too much."

"Yeah, but still," she said. She was suddenly very nervous. She'd been eager to get away from her parents, but the thought of facing everyone back at Terratu was making her reluctant to lift the alicorn.

"It will be fine, my love," Tavik said.

"Promise?"

He nodded.

"Okay, but if she starts hurling curses, I'm hiding behind you."

"Let's go home, Naomi."

She took a deep breath and pricked her finger. She'd brought them to their castle bedroom. It didn't look the same. Her modesty screen was no longer there. All feminine touches were gone. It was strictly Tavik's room. Seeing that Lady Crazy hadn't invaded this space relieved her, but looking at the bed gave her a lurch. Her mind had always stayed purposefully hazy on the fact that Tavik and Lady Crazy had lived together as husband and wife. Had they slept together?

Tavik had opened the door, obviously ready to greet everyone. She'd remained rooted with her eyes glued to the bed. It was made without a hint of wrinkle in the sheets, but a ghostly image of Lady Crazy flickered upon it.

"Naomi?" Tavik called.

Did she want to ask? Did she need to know? He'd thought he was the father of Lady Crazy's baby. That would indicate the deed was done at some point. Like her father had said, "You can't fake a pregnancy without sex." It could be all implanted memories. But what about before the spell when she was on the run? He'd been under a love spell. Had anything happened?

She felt ice-cold. Like she'd drunk a draught from Rhylim's fountain. Her lips moved stiffly as she asked, "Did you sleep with her?"

"No."

"But what about the baby? You thought it was yours."

He sighed. "It was a fake memory, and not even a very good one. I remember getting drunk and waking up beside her. She made me think I'd slept with her, but I believe we did no such thing. That's all."

"But—"

Tavik came back to her and took her in his arms. "I've only ever made love to you. Even when I couldn't remember you, I could feel something was missing. Something was wrong. When you appeared in my dreams, I couldn't shake the feel of you. Your body, your scent, your voice—it all felt right. You were who was supposed to be in my bed, but I didn't know who you were."

Naomi continued to stare at the bed. Tavik's words comforted her a great deal, but she wasn't sure she could believe him. She knew Lady Crazy had been attracted to him. She wanted to believe him. She wanted every word to be true, but felt it would be foolish to believe him.

"I love you," he said.

"I love you, too," she said. She finally tore her eyes from the bed and looked at him. He stood waiting for her. They still needed to let everyone else know she was back. Let everyone else remember her. She went to her husband and slipped her arm in his. "Let's go," she said.

Their first destination was Lady Crazy's room. Naomi could feel her heart rate increasing as they approached. She was going to have another panic attack. When they reached the door, she stopped.

"Stay out here," she said.

Tavik's brow rose at the request. "Why?"

"I need to talk to her alone. Stay here, please?"

He nodded and let her go. "I'll be right here," he said.

She gave him a kiss on the cheek and turned to the door again. She took a deep breath and went inside. The room was still a girlie disaster area. Naomi stepped in cautiously and shut the door.

"Who's there? I'm thirsty. Bring me some wine."

"Wine isn't good for the baby," Naomi said.

The other Naomi sat up and turned to her. "What are you doing—" Naomi watched as the sight of her face had its effect on her. "What's going on?" she said. She touched her stomach in disbelief.

"The baby's Gerry's," Naomi said.

"I know that," Lady Crazy said, rubbing her stomach reverently.

Things began to click for Naomi. Lady Crazy hadn't been pregnant when she'd first kidnapped her, but if she'd gotten pregnant before Tavik came to Harold's Pass, she should have been. How could she be pregnant now?

Lady Crazy began to weep. Tears streamed down her face and landed on her baby bump, but she was smiling. "How is this possible? I'd lost the baby. Did you do this?"

Naomi walked to the side of the bed to stare at Lady Crazy's belly. "You lost the baby?"

Tears still rolled down her face when she looked up at her. "Yes, it was terrible."

"Snowflake must have done this. He knew putting the dragon's mark on you wasn't right. Maybe he did this as a way to make it up to you."

Lady Crazy laughed and hugged her belly. "Getting a dragon's mark is a small price to pay for having my baby back. When I lost it, I was desolate. I blamed everyone for her death. I couldn't be consoled."

Naomi looked at her in wonder. "Is that why you came after me?"

Lady Crazy nodded. "I thought if Tavik had captured me, I'd still have the baby. I thought if everything had been different then I'd still have her. I hated you. I wanted you to suffer."

Naomi wasn't sure she liked this. She didn't like developing sympathy for Lady Crazy. And she realized she was about to kick a pregnant woman to the curb. "Tavik loves me again," she said.

Lady Crazy waved a hand to indicate she didn't care. "Good. I need to get back to Gerry."

Naomi couldn't help backing up a step in guilt at that. "He's being held by bandits."

"What? But I've received word that he's still at his cousin's castle. Inconsolable with grief."

Did everyone have spies? Naomi wondered when she would get her own spies. Wait, was Yula already her spy? If she was her spy, Naomi should give her a raise. She didn't know what she paid Yula, but she was sure it wasn't enough. And she should really learn the monetary system.

Lady Crazy began getting up. For some reason, this alarmed Naomi. "What are you doing?"

"I need to rejoin Gerry, obviously. Prepare your best carriage."

"Really? That's it?"

Lady Crazy raised an eyebrow. "Do you expect more?"

"You almost ruined my life!" If she weren't so very pregnant, Naomi would have thrown herself at her.

Lady Crazy stepped behind the modesty screen. "And if I understand correctly, you placed a dragon's mark on me."

"Only because I got one while trying to get my husband back. The husband you were intent on stealing."

Lady Crazy looked over the top of the screen at her. "I believe he only married you because he couldn't have me. You should be thanking me for leaving Harold's Pass so that you could have him."

"What? I did not intend to marry Tavik."

"No, but you're happy you did, aren't you?"

Naomi opened her mouth to angrily agree, but snapped it shut. The reason she'd wanted to talk to Lady Crazy alone came back to her. She knew she should trust Tavik, but she couldn't stop wondering.

"Tell me truthfully. I won't do anything to you. Did you sleep with him?"

From over the screen, Lady Crazy's eyes softened. "No."

"For real?"

"He loves you. Even before we forgot you, when I was trying to seduce him, he would not have me. He insisted we wait until we were wed and then kept finding reasons to delay the wedding, like capturing you, finding you, he was always going on about how you had to be dealt with when it was clear to see he just wanted you, even in his be-spelled state, he couldn't stop loving you. And then after everyone forgot you, he had no real interest in me. I gave him the love potion when we first met, which kept him from wanting to kill me, and on our wedding day he drank so much wine, he passed out. The next morning, while he was still hung over, I made him think we'd consummated the wedding, and when the baby began showing, that sealed the subterfuge. He never approached me. He was courteous and thoughtful toward me, but he had no passion for me. For the most part, we lived separate lives, only connected by the baby." Naomi blinked and could feel her knees going weak. She reached out to the wall to steady herself.

Lady Crazy stepped back out from behind the modesty screen, dressed in a long pink gown. "And I'm happy he rebuffed me at every turn. If I had to go back to Gerry with the knowledge I'd soiled our marriage bed, I don't know what I would do. But instead, everything has worked out perfectly. We both got what we wanted. You know, if we ever decided to work together, I bet we could do incredible things."

Naomi's eyes narrowed. "Maybe, except I don't like you very much."

"What sisters do?"

"We are not sisters!"

Lady Crazy breezed past her with a light laugh. "My dear, we're practically twins!"

"I really don't like you."

"Yes, as I said, that's standard for siblings." Lady Crazy opened the chamber door to greet Tavik. "Aw, milord, could you please have a carriage readied for me? I really do need to be getting home to my husband."

Tavik looked cautiously back at Naomi. Naomi waved the hand. "Oh, just get her whatever she wants if that means getting rid of her."

Lady Crazy turned back and smiled. She even batted her thick black lashes at her. "You will come to the naming celebration, won't you?"

Tavik coughed uncomfortably. "I'm not sure that would be appropriate."

Unfazed, Lady Crazy swanned down the hall. "We'll see. Carriage?"

Tavik looked helplessly at Naomi, who said, "Don't look at me; you're the one who married her."

Tavik winced and followed Lady Crazy to the hall.

Naomi looked around the room. Something

grabbed her jean leg. The gray kitten with blue eyes looked up at her with all four claws dug into the material. She carefully pulled him free and brought him up to her nose. "Your mistress is leaving. Don't you want to go with her?"

The kitten growled and swiped her nose.

Naomi lowered the kitten from her face with a soft curse. It was a nasty little demon. It gave her an idea. She ran to catch up with Lady Crazy.

They were already in the courtyard. The servants were bustling to ready a carriage for Lady Crazy. Naomi rushed up and handed over the kitten. Lady Crazy took the small feline in surprise. "I can't let you go empty-handed. I'm sure there are those in the castle who would regret not going with you."

The kitten was hissing and spitting. Lady Crazy was holding it out at arm's length, looking less than thrilled.

"Mrs. Boon!" Naomi shouted.

Several servants stopped and gaped at her, but as they took in the sight of her, they shook their heads in confusion and looked around.

"Mrs. Boon!" Naomi shouted again.

"What is the meaning of this?" Mrs. Boon demanded, coming to the hall doors and looking down at everyone. She spied Naomi and froze. "You!" she gasped.

"Yes, I'm back, and you're going, again. Please travel with this Lady Naomi with my compliments."

Lady Crazy hastily shook her head and protested, "That's really not necessary. I wouldn't dream of robbing you of your housekeeper."

Naomi smiled. "Nonsense. Consider this an early naming gift."

Once carriage was ready, Tavik held out his hand to Lady Crazy. "Lady Naomi, allow me."

Lady Crazy sighed and took Tavik's hand. He escorted her to the carriage and helped her inside. Mrs. Boon scurried in after her. Tavik shut the carriage door. He stepped back, and Naomi joined his side.

Lady Crazy leaned out the carriage window. "We will be seeing each other again."

Naomi opened her mouth to protest, but the carriage started up, and Lady Crazy withdrew. Tavik slipped an arm around Naomi's waist as they watched the carriage exit the castle. It had just made it out when a cozy cottage dropped from the sky into the courtyard with a resounding boom.

Naomi was more startled by Tavik putting her behind him than the sudden arrival of Agatha's cottage. "What are you doing?" Naomi demanded, trying to move around Tavik.

"Agatha has been in a foul mood for weeks. If she's heard the truth about Lady Naomi, her mood will be dire. She may throw a hex at you before she sees you."

The cottage door opened, and Agatha filled the space. Naomi peeked over Tavik's shoulder at her.

Tavik was right. Agatha's mood looked foul. Her face had a powerful frown upon it. She spied Tavik, and her eyes lasered onto him and then on Naomi.

Naomi waited a moment for the witch's memories to return and then slipped cautiously out from behind Tavik. She gave the witch a nervous smile. "Hi, Agatha."

Agatha's eyes traveled up and down Naomi slowly. The witch's jaw tightened. "Well, I guess it's too much to hope that you're pregnant."

Naomi still felt weird about the pregnancy thing. She knew everyone else would be thrilled by it, but she still felt nervous and unsure. She spread her hands across her stomach. "Actually, I am."

Agatha's back stiffened. Her eyes swung to Tavik. "And you accept this?"

Naomi's brow wrinkled. "Why wouldn't he? He's the father." And the fact that Agatha hadn't cracked a single smile upon seeing her was beginning to really upset Naomi. She'd thought the witch would welcome her back. Maybe Agatha had preferred the other Naomi.

Agatha's face brightened. "Oh, so you were the succubus!"

The servants, who had gathered upon Agatha's arrival, twittered. Naomi threw them an embarrassed glance. Agatha finally left the doorway of the cottage and came to Naomi. She placed a hand on Naomi's stomach.

Understanding now Agatha's chilly response, Naomi was hurt. "You thought I cheated on Tavik?" she asked.

Agatha had her head bent as she rubbed Naomi's stomach. She sighed and gave Naomi's tummy a gentle pat before removing her hand and stepping back to look Naomi in the face. "Well. It seems apologies are in order."

Again the crushing guilt of all that she had done laid into Naomi. She dropped her eyes and again covered her stomach. "I'm sorry. I didn't know what to do about Grisbek. Snowflake did the spell without asking me. He sacrificed himself to save me from Grisbek, but if there'd been another way, I would have done it." Remembering the elder's fears of the dragons going to war with the unicorns, a bolt of ice went through her. "Oh God, have I put the unicorns in danger again?"

She'd been so focused on saving Lady Crazy that she hadn't spared any thought for the unicorns. She hadn't initially planned to show anyone her face, and then when that very action became essential to thwart Grisbek and then with the news about the pregnancy, she hadn't spared a thought for the unicorns. Would Torreng declare war on them now?

Agatha scrunched her brow. "Naomi, I don't understand everything you went through, but you don't need to apologize. I'm the one who needs to apologize. I almost had you killed to save that damnable woman. As for the unicorns, I wouldn't worry about them. They can take care of themselves."

"Also, as a concession for interfering with a dragon's hunt, they have withdrawn from Terratu, leaving it to us," Grisbek said.

Naomi gasped and wheeled around. The green dragon peered into the courtyard from just the other side of the castle gates. There wasn't room for him within, unless he crushed Agatha's cottage.

"Naomi, what is it?" Tavik asked.

She pointed to the gates, but when she looked again, Grisbek was gone.

"Naomi?" Tavik asked.

"None of you saw Grisbek?" she asked.

Tavik's eyes widened. He reached for the nonexistent sword at his hip. "Where?"

"I don't know now. He was just outside, but now I can't see him. He may have made himself invisible to me as well."

Tavik's jaw tightened. "I don't like the thought of such a threat being right outside with no way of knowing it's there."

Agatha peered out the castle gates as well. "I'll get to work on a dragon detection spell."

Naomi nodded and then felt lost. She looked around the courtyard at the gathered servants and family. Hip Hop was there, too. She looked relatively clean still.

"Um, Lord Tavik? What should we do about the wizard?" Boris asked.

"Xersal?" Naomi asked.

Boris nodded. He didn't seem able to look at her. She may have destroyed all of the goodwill she'd developed with the steward. That upset her. She liked being on good terms with him. He did so much for the castle, and Tavik trusted him implicitly.

"Where is he?" Tavik asked.

Boris dropped his head and rubbed his hands. "In the dungeon."

"Oh no," Naomi said and headed to the dungeon.

"We didn't know. He was ranting and raving about Lord Tavik and the unicorn horn. And Lord Tavik had disappeared. I feared he'd done something to you, milord. I take full responsibility, sir," Boris said, following them.

"Did you hurt him?" Naomi asked, growing alarmed.

She didn't wait for an answer and ran down the steps. She pulled open the door to the dungeon and rushed in.

"Xersal, are you all right?"

He was sitting in the cell with his arms crossed and a monstrous scowl on his face. His expression cleared, though, at the sight of her.

"Grandniece?"

"Yeah, let's get you out of there." She turned to look for a guard. Tavik and Boris were right behind her. Boris had a heavy ring of keys in his hand. He moved past her to unlock Xersal's cell door.

"Your face is uncovered."

She couldn't help raising her hand to her cheek. "Yeah, I broke the spell. Everyone can remember me now."

Xersal turned to glare at Tavik. Oh no, it seemed like the men of her family were not going to go easy on her husband. At least Bobby had been nice to him. "And what are your intentions now, warlord?"

Tavik moved to Naomi's side and put a hand on her back. "To make her happy and to raise our child the best we can."

"Child?" Xersal asked.

She hadn't told him that part yet. "Yeah, I'm pregnant."

"I'm going to be a great-great-uncle?"

Naomi nodded. "Looks like it."

Xersal's face scrunched up. "This won't do. I'm far too young for that." This made Naomi break into a true smile.

Agatha pushed her way into the room. "You don't have a say in this," she said dangerously, squaring off with the wizard.

"Grandniece, are you still going to be my apprentice?"

"She can't be your apprentice. She's mine," Agatha cut in.

"Oh no, she's not. You tried to feed her to a dragon."

"I didn't know who she was."

"And I'm family. Clearly, she should be my apprentice."

"I'm her mother-in-law!"

Tavik pulled Naomi back from the arguing pair. "I don't think they'll notice if we leave," he murmured.

"Where will we go?" she asked.

"I believe my bedroom needs some attention," he said with a gleam in his eyes.

Naomi could feel her cheeks heating up. "What, now?"

"Would you really rather listen to them argue?"

"I've had proper training!"

"You can't even keep a familiar!"

"Let's go," Naomi whispered to Tavik.

"Let me get the shield out of the armory."

Now Naomi's cheeks really were burning. "You and that shield," she said with a shake of her head.

"No, you and that shield," he corrected with a grin.

They slipped out of the dungeon, leaving Agatha and Xersal to argue over who would mentor Naomi. She hoped they didn't hex each other to kingdom come, but at the moment, with her husband's hand warmly wrapped around hers, she didn't really care. The pair raced up the stairs back to their bedroom.

THE END

ABOUT THE AUTHOR

S.A. Hunter lives in Virginia
and works in a library.

She can be found online at
www.sahunter.net.

She also writes The Scary Mary Series.